Praise for The Forever Year:

"*The Forever Year* is pure pleasure from beginning to end, beautifully written and emotionally rich."
– Susan Elizabeth Phillips, *New York Times* bestselling author

"*The Forever Year* is a wry, tender, beautifully written novel.... Once I started, I couldn't put it down."
– Lisa Kleypas, *New York Times* bestselling author

"Better than Nicholas Sparks's best. There's more wit, more wisdom, and yes, there are tears."
– John R. Maxim, *New York Times* bestselling author

"*The Forever Year* is a warm, engaging story with a valuable contemporary lesson inside – it is well structured and funny and keeps you turning the pages till the very end to find out what happens. It may even make you rethink your own attitude toward love! I really enjoyed it."
– Suzanne Vega, multiplatinum recording artist

"*The Forever Year* is a delightful family relationship drama with a wonderful romantic subplot."
– *Allreaders*

"*The Forever Year* is a true keeper of a book."
– *A Romance Review*

"It feels real, will keep you glued to the pages, and will touch your heart."
– *Bookloons*

The
Forever
Year

The Forever Year

A novel by

Lou Aronica

Studio Digital CT, LLC
PO Box 4331
Stamford, CT 06907

Story Plant paperback ISBN-13: 978-1-61188-100-4
E-book ISBN-13: 978-1-943486-30-4

Visit our website at www.TheStoryPlant.com
Visit the author's website at www.LouAronica.com

Originally published under the name Ronald Anthony

Original Forge Books hardcover publication: May 2003
First Fiction Studio Paperback Printing: January 2013
First Story Plant Paperback Printing: September 2013
Printed in the United States of America

For my father, who taught me different lessons.

And for Kelly, who taught me precisely these.

Acknowledgments

I originally published this book in 2003 under the pseudonym Ronald Anthony. I'd like to thank the people who helped *The Forever Year* see publication then, along with those who have helped in the production of this new edition.

It was because of my wife Kelly and my children Molly, David, Abigail (and Tigist, who wasn't around in 2003) that I chose to write this novel in the first place, and it was their continued presence and support that kept me going even on the days when the words didn't want to come.

My original agent Marilyn Allen deserves my unending gratitude for helping get me started and for being such a staunch advocate for my work. I also want to thank her husband, Bill Liberus, for being an early reader and cheering me on with his encouragement.

My current agent, Danny Baror has been a tremendous champion in the foreign market and a staunch supporter of my work in the years since.

I'd like to thank Peter Miller for his help in pushing this novel in Hollywood and for regularly reminding me how much he loved it.

Linda Quinton at Tor/Forge got on board with this novel when it was little more than a thinly sketched story and for that I am eternally grateful. My original editor, Stephanie Lane, did a truly impressive job of getting inside this novel and showing me where I didn't say what I wanted to say. I know how difficult that is and I'm very glad she was there for me.

Debbie Mercer first suggested that I write this novel and for that I'm grateful. However, I'm even more grateful for her consistent willingness to read whatever I write and for her willingness to risk an embarrassing reaction on the Long Island Railroad.

Keith Ferrell has been much more of an inspiration to me over the years than he will ever know. If this novel is good, it's largely because his dedication to his own craft and his willingness to "talk writing" drove me to work harder.

Thanks too to the Harry Bennett Branch of the Stamford Public Library for providing the occasional place to write where I was free from my numerous self-imposed distractions.

Thanks to Dan Howard for copyediting the revised edition.

Chapter One

In his eighty-third year and the fourth season since his wife of more than half a century had passed, Mickey Sienna opened his eyes early, as he did every day. He listened as commuters hustled to pick up the newspapers at the ends of their driveways, believing they were already falling behind in that day's corporate competition. He heard school buses creaking to a stop to pick up some other generation's children. If this were a Tuesday or Thursday, the garbage men would be coming to visit; if it were a Monday, the recycling men would come instead. Soon, that overexcited little girl next door would be squealing as she played outside, regardless of the day and regardless of the weather.

Each sound would send his thoughts in a new direction. Those bracing early years at the brokerage and the life that accompanied them. Darlene's first day of kindergarten. The piles of boxes left at the curb after the Christmas bounty. Denise's delight at a piggyback ride.

Lying there, as he sometimes did for hours, Mickey would listen and remember. He was incapable of falling back asleep even though he was weary and knew he was going to feel that way the entire day. But while dozing wasn't an available option, rising wasn't a particularly appealing one. There was the pain in both of his knees, the decreasing dexterity in his fingers, and the simple fact that without Dorothy his life didn't seem to have much of an agenda.

After Dorothy's death, the children implored him to move out of the New Jersey colonial they had lived in for the past forty years. Too much space. Too many stairs. *You don't move around as well as you used to.* They told him that no person living by himself needed a house this size. But what they were really telling him was that he was too old to remain independent and surely too old to learn how to do the things that Dorothy had always done for him. As much as he loved his children, this grated on him. His knees might feel like the cartilage had been replaced with steel wool, and his arm would sometimes go numb for a few minutes without warning, but his mind was as sharp as ever. And if he didn't feel like getting out of bed on most days, and if the simple act of descending the stairs and walking to the den made him tired, that was his business and his alone. This was his house. He was keeping it. End of discussion.

As much as he loved to eat, Mickey had never learned to cook. There had always been someone else available to do the job. First there was his mother, a stout woman of Neapolitan descent who embraced the kitchen with nearly as much passion as she embraced her firstborn son. Then, when he was living on his own, there were the endless offerings of the restaurants of New York. And one of the things that had settled his heart after he met Dorothy was how utterly comfortable she seemed making the dishes of their respective heritages. With access to this continuous stream of good meals, Mickey had never found any reason to learn even the rudiments of the craft. It never dawned on him that there might be a time when he would need this skill. Certainly, he never considered the possibility that his wife, eight years his junior, would go before him.

And so it was that ten months after Dorothy died, Mickey made his way tentatively to the kitchen and took two eggs out of the refrigerator. Making hot meals was a point of pride for him. Anyone could fill a bowl with cereal and add milk. A hot meal required a certain level of mastery, mastery that someone like Mickey Sienna could surely attain even at his advanced age. Someday soon, he would invite all of his children over for dinner and give them the surprise of their lives.

He pulled out a frying pan, placed it on a burner, and filled the bottom with oil. He lit the burner, but having never figured out which knob controlled which, he ignited the wrong one. Without turning that burner off, he lit the proper burner and cracked two eggs into the pan. It always took the eggs longer to cook than he thought it was going to take, so while he waited to flip them over, he went down the hall to see what was on TV.

Mickey didn't really like television, especially morning television with its preponderance of vapid talk shows, uninformative self-help programming, and noisy "education" for toddlers. Still, he was never in the mood to read when he first got up, and he preferred to trade stocks in the afternoon. And there was a certain amount of comfort to having some kind of noise in the house. Mickey chose a show nearly at random and settled on the couch. It was an old family drama from the seventies. The poor sound quality and the simplemindedness of the storytelling, combined with the weariness that seemed to be his constant companion these days, made him lethargic. While once he was awake in his bed he could never get back to sleep, the same was not in any way true about the couch. Not long after the first advertising break, Mickey was out.

It was possibly the first time in history that a television commercial saved a man's life.

In the time between Mickey's dropping off and the next promotion that awakened him – its sound a crisp and blaring contrast to the muted melodrama – the eggs had burned and the overabundance of oil in the pan had spattered onto the naked lit burner across from it. Eventually, the entire pan ignited and spread to the Formica countertop where the oil had leapt out. Black billows made their way down the hall to where Mickey was sleeping. The smoke, which might have killed him if enough time had passed, didn't startle him from sleep. But a loudmouthed announcer telling him that he could have "a washboard stomach in only ten minutes a day" did.

Mickey coughed and choked as he picked himself off the couch. He slowly treaded into the kitchen, hindered not only by his degraded joints but also by the heightened sense of fear that comes from awakening to danger. He tried throwing water on the flames, but that just generated more smoke. He tried to smother the pan with a kitchen towel, but the towel caught fire.

A portion of Mickey's mind more willing than his conscious mind to accept his physical limitations told him that if he was going to get out of the house safely, he needed to start moving now. As quickly as his screaming knees would carry him, Mickey struggled through the smoke and out the front door. Once outside, he stood breathing deeply on the lawn. What was he supposed to do now? He thought about everything he had left in the house and considered going back to rescue the most precious items. But he knew that was unrealistic.

He had to do something. He couldn't just let the house burn down. Mickey was only thinking clearly enough to realize that he wasn't thinking clearly. He tried to calm himself down to allow some sense to seep in.

"Hi, Mr. Sienna," came a little girl's voice. Mickey turned toward the sound. It was Maureen, the three-year-old who loved to play outside.

"Hey, Mickey," said her mother, Lisa, waving and walking toward him. "Out early this morning, huh?"

Mickey started to move in their direction. The distress and disorientation must have been apparent on his face, because he had barely taken a few steps when Lisa quickened her own pace to come up to him.

"Is everything okay?" she said.

"The kitchen – the house – is on fire."

Lisa's mouth formed into an O and she glanced back quickly at her daughter. She walked up to Mickey and took him by the arm.

"Come into my house," she said. "Did you call the fire department?"

"No, nothing. I couldn't think of what to do. I just left."

"Let's go call them right now."

They took a few steps. Even in his agitated condition, Mickey could only move so quickly. Lisa let go of his arm.

"You know what, let me run ahead and make the call." She turned to her daughter. "Maureen, could you come with Mr. Sienna into the house?"

"I want to play some more," the little girl said in a voice that made clear her sense of inconvenience.

"We'll play outside again in a little while. Can you show Mr. Sienna your new rocking horse now, please?"

A few minutes later, Mickey was sitting at Lisa's kitchen table. His heart was still pounding, but he was at least somewhat mollified by the knowledge that firemen were on their way. He had more than forty years of his life invested in that house. Much more than that if you considered the memories that he brought there with him. He couldn't begin to imagine how he would feel if the house were destroyed.

Lisa seemed to understand what he was going through. She patted him on the hand. She had been a good neighbor since moving in a few years ago. She baked cookies for him and his wife every now and then, and she came each day to Dorothy's wake.

"The fire department will be here soon," she said.

Mickey gripped her hand and offered her a faint smile.

"I should call my son. Can I borrow your phone?"

Matthew would be in his office by now. It took him a moment to remember the number. Damned speed dial.

"Dad, I was gonna call you in a few minutes," Matthew said when he came to the phone. "What's up?"

"I'm having a little problem here," Mickey said as casually as possible.

"What's wrong?" Matthew's voice was growing tense. Mickey could imagine his agitated face. Matthew was an excellent husband and father, and he had a big, responsible job, but he tended to get riled up way too easily.

"There's a little fire in the kitchen."

"A fire in the kitchen? Dad, where are you? You have to get out of the house right away."

"I *am* out of the house. I'm at Lisa's."

"Good, that's the right thing." Mickey could hear Matthew's voice ease back a bit. His son was going to give himself a heart attack some day if he wasn't careful. "Are you okay? Are you feeling short of breath? How much smoke did you inhale?"

"I'm fine," Mickey said, feeling an increasing need to underplay his own anxiety. "I'm more worried about the house and our things. I should have thought to at least take the photo albums with me."

As he heard the exhalation, Mickey could imagine the exasperated look that Matthew was no doubt wearing, having moved from concern to consternation. Mickey wondered when exactly the point came that your children felt they could start treating you like an infant.

"The photo albums are hardly the thing to be worrying about at the moment, Dad. There's no such thing as a little fire. I'm just glad you got out of there alive."

"Don't be dramatic."

"That's an interesting thing to say after you tell me that the house is burning down."

Mickey gazed up at Lisa, his eyes suggesting he was under siege. She smiled back at him. He wondered if she treated her parents the same way.

"The house isn't burning down," he said. He looked out the side door. Was that smoke coming out of his windows? "I probably just won't be able to use the kitchen for a while."

"Then why did you call me?" Matthew was fully beyond his initial distress about the situation. The lecture about the house being too big for him was likely to start in the next minute.

"I was calling to see what you thought I should do next. This is the kind of thing your mother would have taken care of."

"Dad, I'm in Chicago," Matthew said, his voice rising again. "I can't exactly jump in the car and get there in a half an hour."

"Denise never seems to be in her office."

"Don't get me started on Denise. When was the last time you saw her, by the way? Does she send one of 'her people' to check on you every now and then?"

Mickey shook his head. He should have called Darlene.

"Denise is very good to me, and you know that." He never appreciated it when his children sniped at each other and he thought he had sent that message clearly enough over the years. "She just has that big job that keeps her very busy."

"This is not the time to get into this," Matthew said abruptly. "Look, you have to deal with the insurance company and all of that stuff. Why don't you call Jesse?"

Jesse had never entered Mickey's mind. "Why would I call Jesse?"

"Well, for one thing, he lives ten minutes away from you."

"Jesse doesn't know about these things. He's just a kid."

"Dad, he's thirty-two. He even has his own house."

Mickey looked out the side door again. The fire truck was pulling up to his curb.

"The fire department is here. Let's not worry about this now. I'll see if I can get Denise later."

"Call me when you know what's going on."

"I'll call you tonight."

"Call me as soon as you know."

"Fine. I need to go see the firemen."

Mickey broke the connection and handed the phone back to Lisa.

"The fire trucks are here," he said.

"Maureen's already at the window. She heard the sirens."

Mickey made his way toward the front door.

"My son thinks I'm incapable of doing anything on my own."

Lisa patted him on the shoulder.

"Children get that way sometimes." She took him by the arm. "Come on, I'll walk you out."

Chapter Two

For essentially my entire life, bringing all of my siblings under one roof required an official "get-together." My sister Darlene, who is twenty years older than I am, moved out of the house before I could walk. That fall, my brother Matty went off to college. By the time I could add two numbers, Denise was doing considerably more complex calculations at Dartmouth, where she prepared for her now-storied corporate career.

My mother used to refer to me as her "wonderful surprise," since she became pregnant with me when she was in her early forties. Denise, twelve years my elder, would refer to me as "the accident" whenever she was forced to babysit me in her teens. There was no question that I was completely unplanned. And while my mother, who would have "gone pro" as a parent if such a thing were possible, tended to me with the pleasure of someone who had been offered a free second ride on a roller coaster, it was difficult for me not to feel like a bit of an appendage in the family. This became even truer when Darlene and Matty both got married and had children in close proximity, giving me a niece and a nephew much nearer to my age than any of my brothers or sisters. I was too young for one group and too old for the other. I was a man without a generation.

My most vivid recollection of family gatherings when I was young was the sound. Darlene telling colorful stories about life in "the real world." Matty regaling us with profundities gleaned from whichever class was capturing his imagination at the moment. Denise suggesting that neither of them knew what was really going on, in tones much too cynical for someone her age. My father engaging each in debate with a voice that spoke of both authority and admiration. My mother calling down to the den from the kitchen on a regular basis to make sure that everyone had everything they needed. And all of this taking place at extreme volume.

I found the entire thing both entertaining and daunting. My image of that time always has me looking up at the family as though each member were a towering, pontificating mountain and I were standing at the foothills. I was enormously impressed with their ability to express themselves, to cajole one another, to generate so much spirit. I was envious of the attention my father gave the opinions of his older children, and the obvious joy he took in being able to converse with them in this way. It was easy to fade into the background when everyone was over at the house. I had nothing to say that was nearly as important as what they were all saying, and even if I did, I had no idea how to project my voice over the din. I was the little one. My thoughts came too slowly. By the time anything of even passing value entered my mind, the conversation had moved on. I suppose this is one of the reasons that I became a writer. It was a way for me to state my case without risking interruption.

Over the years, the number of get-togethers declined dramatically. Darlene's husband Earl got a management position with a textile company in Orange County, California. Matty and his wife Laura moved to Pittsburgh for a while, and then to Chicago about ten years ago. Denise moved to various apartments on the Upper East Side before buying a condo overlooking the Hudson River. That put her about fifteen miles away from my parents' house physically and several continents away emotionally. Denise had obviously taken my father's oft-repeated advice that she needed to be her own person to mean that she should stand in virtual isolation from the rest of her family.

I'm not sure why things with Denise bugged me so much. I suppose it had something to do with the fact that we actually spent a fair amount of time together under the same roof and therefore I expected more from her than I did from Darlene or Matty. I knew Denise was brilliant, I knew her accomplishments were genuine, and I had seen their development closely enough to come to a true admiration for them. But when it became clear to me that my admiration not only went unheeded, but in fact unnoticed, my feelings for her became considerably less charitable. I didn't want to acknowledge that she adored my father, only that she couldn't be bothered to visit him when he needed her the most. I didn't want to acknowledge that she had been extremely generous with my parents, only that she had always been stingy with her time. I didn't understand how you could do this with people you genuinely cared for.

The last time all of us had been in one place was after Mom died. I remember sitting at the dinner table with them the night before they all left and feeling an uneasiness beyond anything associated with the funeral that had taken place earlier in the day. Through the haze of my grief, I felt that something else was out of skew. I ate with my eyes cast down toward my plate, but with my senses extended outward, as they almost always were when I was amongst these people. I couldn't get a handle on what was wrong until I finally realized that it was quiet. There was virtually no conversation.

While we had begun to contemplate my father's frailty, we were completely unprepared for my mother's death. She had been hale up until the point when she experienced complications from a minor respiratory procedure. She spent a week in Intensive Care and, even though she ultimately returned home, she was never the same. Within two months, she was dead, and it was enough to shock everyone into silence. Her passing wasn't supposed to happen this quickly. It wasn't supposed to happen at all for at least another twenty years. I'm not sure what everyone else was thinking that night, but I thought that perhaps it was appropriate that this dinner feel and sound different from all others that had come before. Everything in the family would be changed from that point on.

Since then, we'd all made our attempts to convince my father to give up the house. He wasn't moving well any more, he seemed tired and sullen, and we were all concerned that he was going to hurt himself if he tried to keep up with everything he needed to do to live in that space. He wasn't interested in talking about it, though. My own conversations with him had been brief and perfunctory. To say he was dismissive with me would be to suggest that he considered what I was saying in the first place. I tried various techniques of provocation I'd picked up from his interactions with Darlene, Matty, and Denise, but they seemed different coming out of my mouth, sharper, filled more with sarcasm than persuasion. The others were quietly relentless, though, all trying to find a way to treat him gingerly and respectfully while still getting the point across.

After the Fried Egg Crisis, all bets were off. We knew that we simply had to get him out of there. As an indication of how seriously everyone was taking this, Darlene and Matty flew in, and Denise actually hosted the sibling conference in her apartment. Of course, she was a half-hour late and blew into the room crowing about an employee who would "simply not let her get out the door." Still, she proceeded to enter the conversation as though she had been conducting it in her head the entire cab ride home. Even when I found her annoying, which was most of the time, I had to be impressed with the way she could make her presence felt immediately.

"I'm just saying that I think a nursing home might be too drastic a move," Matty said in response to the suggestion Denise entered with. "It's not like he has Alzheimer's or needs a wheelchair or something. He's old and slow, but he's not three feet from his grave."

"Nursing homes aren't only for people who are about to die," Denise said curtly.

Matty smirked. "Actually, I think that's the exact dictionary definition."

Denise shook her head and did that little thing with her teeth. It was like she was grinding them together, except the top level and the bottom never touched. It was code for "I can't believe I'm wasting time trying to communicate with you."

At that moment, Denise's eight-year-old son Marcus entered the room with a book in his hand to ask his mother what she thought the snow symbolized in *White Fang*. Marcus is the kind of kid who gives precociousness a bad name. Without acknowledging the boy, Denise turned to her husband Brad and said, "I'm kinda into this right now." Brad escorted Marcus from the room. I'm sure he made some kind of notation of the task in his Blackberry before returning to the meeting however, so he could receive the proper *quid pro quo* later.

"We could hire him a full-time nurse," Darlene suggested. "A nurse would make sure that Dad was safe and could offer companionship at the same time."

"Feels like we're getting him a substitute for Mom," Matty responded. "And Dad's not going to go for the nurse thing." He altered his voice to my father's rougher tone. "'If I'm not sick, why do I need a nurse?' You know how hung up he gets about any of us suggesting that he can't do everything he used to."

"What Dad needs is an assisted living community," Laura suggested. Of the three siblings-in-law, Laura was the one closest to my father by far. It probably had something to do with my father's being nothing at all like the man who had abandoned Laura, her mother, and her sister when Laura was eleven. "These places are like apartment buildings – some of them are really nice – and the people who live in them still retain a good level of independence. They just don't have to worry about things like laundry or cleaning." She smiled knowingly. "Or cooking."

"Amen to that," Denise said sarcastically.

"They're popping up everywhere in Southern California," Darlene said. "They're like Starbucks. I'll bet it's the same in New Jersey."

There were lots of heads shaking and discussions of procedure. How do we research the different facilities? How do we discuss it with Dad? *Do* we discuss it with Dad, or do we just tell him to start packing?

I got up from the sofa to get more coffee. I hadn't said a word since the conversation had begun, which meant that I was right on my quota as far as sibling meetings were concerned. It certainly wasn't that I didn't have any opinions or that I was intimidated. I had simply fallen into the same pattern that I fell into whenever the group of us got together. I've often wondered what the others thought of my regular silence. Actually, what I've really wondered was whether or not they even noticed it.

Regardless, I had to stand up, because I needed a moment to gather my thoughts. I had something I wanted to say, something that seemed absolutely fitting to me and that none of them could possibly have anticipated. It required my walking a few steps and then returning to the room, as though I had just gotten there.

I hadn't put any advance thought into this. Like everyone else in the room, I had given the evening's agenda serious consideration. But it wasn't until I was there with the rest of them listening to suggestions that ranged from serviceable to frightening – and all more than a little empty – that I realized there was something more to be done with this decision. Something that offered my father more than just a coda to a rich life.

"I want Dad to come to live with me," I said before taking another sip of coffee and doing a quick scan of everyone in the room.

Denise adopted another of her annoyed expressions. Darlene simply appeared confused. Matty turned to face me head on.

"Right, great idea," he said sharply.

"I'm serious." I sipped some more coffee.

"No, you're not, Jesse."

"Yeah, I am. You can't tell me that living with me isn't going to be better for Dad than living in some elder care facility."

He screwed up his face as though my suggestion came dissolved in a quart of lemon juice.

"Jess, it ain't even close," he said.

I could feel myself getting flustered, my frustrations looping between having no idea how to talk back to my siblings and how easily I lost my composure when challenged by them. I finished the coffee and muttered something like, "I really think it would be a good idea."

"Babe," Darlene said, "it's great that you want to be involved and I'm sure Dad would appreciate the gesture. But I think this assisted living thing makes a lot more sense. You could be a huge help to us here if you scouted around for the best facility in Jersey. None of us can really do it long distance."

I had been dismissed. I knew my face was red and I knew I wasn't in any condition to continue the argument. I immediately wished I had thought about this ahead of time and e-mailed my justifications to them before we all gathered. I should have known better than to introduce an idea this provocative without a huge amount of preparation. As a result, I fell back on my traditional role. I simply said, "Sure, whatever," and left it at that.

I spent much of the rest of the time I was there in my own personal funk. The others were moving forward with the plans. My father's fate had been decided, my role as advance scout confirmed. If anyone had given any further thought to my pronouncement, they gave no indication of it. I certainly didn't mention it again.

But I knew there was something right about this, and while I hadn't even considered it before that sibling conference, my conviction grew exponentially in the days that followed.

~~~~~~~~

Marina understood. She usually did. Even before I kissed her for the first time, I valued the fact that she just got me. By the time all the stuff with my father and my siblings was happening, we'd been dating for nearly four months and had known each other for close to six. We spent three or four nights a week together and talked on the phone almost every day. We had stuff at each other's places and we sometimes made plans months ahead. I had a great time with her, I thought she was stimulating company, our sex life was warm and fulfilling, and it felt great to hold her and be held by her. There was little question in my mind that Marina was a woman I should be with for a while.

But that was about as far as I was capable of taking our relationship in my mind. It wasn't anything as simpleminded as an inability to make a commitment. When one is unable to make a commitment, it either means that one values one's independence and individuality (code for the freedom to sleep with any other woman who shows an interest) over any vow of long-term fidelity, or it means that you don't really feel the relationship is as good as what might be available around the corner. Neither scenario had anything to do with me. I had never once dated more than one woman at a time and wasn't sure I would even know how to do it. I also had no need or desire to compare Marina to other women, real or imagined. She was one of the best people I'd ever met and I considered myself deeply fortunate to know her.

There was something far more insidious at play here and something far more intractable. In my mind, among the small handful of Absolute Truths that define humanity was one that specifically related to romance: love always dies.

My heart had developed a fair amount of scar tissue by the time I was twenty-five. I had fallen madly in love with a woman named Georgia in my freshman year of college. We were together nearly every day for two years. I wrote her poetry, I bought her flowers at least once a week, I learned how to cook earnest dishes for her using a skillet and a hot plate in my dorm room. She would leave me little presents in unexpected places, buy me cute little cards, sing to me as we lay in bed. We were always kissing, always expressing our affection for one another, always touching. I thought I'd been in love before – at least a half a dozen times in high school – but the extent of my desire for Georgia made all of these encounters trivial. When she told me that she'd decided to spend her junior year abroad in London because it would make a big difference in her future career opportunities, we both cried about it for hours. I didn't think I could possibly survive that much time away from her. I focused hard on my education that year, writing with unprecedented fervor while I awaited her return. We corresponded three or four times a week and I mistakenly interpreted the distant tone of her letters as nothing more than losing something in the translation of her devotion to me from flesh and spirit to the written page. As the spring semester came to a close, I grew sleepless in anticipation of her return. I sometimes wrote her two or three times in a single day, while her letters became less frequent.

A week before she was due back, I bought her an engagement ring with the money I'd saved from the part-time job I took primarily to fill the hours she was not with me. I picked her up at the airport and planned to present it to her in an elaborate ceremony that very night. But the ring never made it out of the box. A half hour after she touched down, Georgia told me that she would be returning to London in less than a month. She'd decided to finish her education in England. And yes, there was this guy she'd met and, well, she hadn't planned on anything happening, but it just did.

After getting over the initial shock of what Georgia had told me, I was at least equally astonished to realize that I could have been so utterly devoted to her while she was capable of being swayed by another man. It wasn't the first time that a woman had left me. It wasn't even the first time that a woman had left me for someone else. But it was without question the first time that a woman had left me when I was ready to give myself to her. I found it truly scary that I had no inkling that this was coming. Of course I could re-read her letters (as I did often) and find the tiniest of clues. But I couldn't find any warning signals in my own heart. I was fully devoted to Georgia, but a trip to London had allowed her to move on.

I had never before felt as disconnected from my life as I did over the next few months. All of my plans, all of my thinking, revolved around my future with Georgia. It took until well into my senior year before I could adjust to the reality that I wasn't part of a couple anymore. After dating a number of women who seemed very exciting for a short period, I met Karen and began to believe I could fall deeply in love again. Where my romance with Georgia was shot with a soft focus lens, my relationship with Karen was produced for an action movie. It was frenetically paced, filled with hairpin turns and pyrotechnics. I was more impulsive with Karen than I had ever been in my life. We'd get in a car and just drive somewhere, stopping on the side of the road to make love. We drank lustily and sated our lust while drinking. For the first time in my life, I felt like I was flouting convention. I said and did whatever came to my mind and didn't care if others were uncomfortable with it. Georgia turned me into a lover, and Karen turned me into a rebel. It was about as close to Dionysian as my life had ever been.

Within a couple of months, we moved in together and for a while we were on one extended passionate high. This was the antidote. This was what I needed. If innocent love could end up in such a devastating way (and I still thought about Georgia daily and wondered where she was), then the right love for me obviously had a much darker cast. But when the sexual energy started to dissipate and when the partying started to take its toll, we began to notice how often we disagreed and how little we cared for each other's values. At that point, we discovered that we could fight as fervently as we could make love, and for a short while even that had its appeal.

I'm not sure when I would have started wondering about the friends I'd left behind or the fact that I was turning ugly in my own eyes. I had remade myself for love, and I'm sure at some point I would have had to acknowledge how unnatural it felt. But it didn't come down to that. While I was out of town on an assignment, Karen departed for the other coast, leaving behind only a note that read, "I'm gone."

It was after Karen that I realized that there were many kinds of romantic love and each one had a shelf life. You could be soft and giving and sweet. You could be sharp and self-absorbed and salty. But no matter how you dressed yourself, ultimately the costume fell to the ground in tatters. There was no way to maintain the depth of emotion. And if you cared really deeply, it just hurt that much more when the end came.

It wasn't just my own experiences that proved this. All around me, people were having their hearts broken by love affairs gone bad. And I found no hope among those who had managed to stay together. I was surrounded by utilitarian and passionless relationships that had to have had more sparks at some point, though not a flicker was visible now. Darlene married a "solid" man who seemed preconfigured for grandfatherhood. Matty married a woman who could talk about the latest Girl Scout cookie drive with great verve, but fell asleep in front of the television every night at 9:30. Denise married a guy who was so buttoned-down and career-oriented that I imagined they scheduled sex every week only because they'd read that it could lead to quicker professional advancement.

Even my parents' marriage, while it lasted for more than fifty years, seemed more like a partnership than a romance. They made a good team and they complemented each other well. But I don't recall their ever sharing more than a perfunctory kiss, and never saw them join each other in a momentary embrace. There was no doubt in my mind that they cared about each other, and my father had been devastated when my mother died. I surmised from their mutual admiration that they had to have been more romantic at some point before I was born. But there never seemed to be any electricity between them. They simply built a lot together. Like an architectural firm.

Clearly this was the way all relationships went eventually. You fell in love with someone, you believed that you could have a great life together. Maybe it turned out that you did have a great life together, but somewhere along the line you either burnt out or became roommates rather than lovers. To me, it just wasn't worth the bother. I wasn't looking for companionship in my old age. I wasn't looking for grandkids to bounce on my knee. If love couldn't last long term, then what was the point of being in a long-term relationship? My feeling was that you simply let everything play out to its natural life, always aware that the inevitable was coming. You had fun until you weren't having fun anymore and when it was over, you avoided the temptation to stay in bed for a week or create a playlist of all the maudlin ballads on your iPod.

So with Marina, I just let it go where it was going to go, though I spent a lot less time thinking about the inevitability of the end than I had with any woman in a long time. We were on the same page as far as our feelings about romance went. She had been involved for four years in a relationship that split up horrendously, and I was sure that she was as unwilling as I to take any new affair too deep.

I had met Marina when we found ourselves seated next to each other at a lecture at the local library. I liked her instantly, and we wound up going for coffee after the event. We returned to that coffee shop more than a half dozen times before I officially asked her out. I went into the relationship more focused on how much I enjoyed her presence than on whether this could last romantically for any length of time. That in itself was a refreshing change. Before Karen, I started every relationship wondering if this could be the Great Love. After Karen, they all started with me telling myself that I had nothing better to do on Friday night.

I was truly enjoying myself with Marina, but there was still no question in my mind that the chemistry would ultimately combust or fizzle. It had to. It always did. In the meantime, though, we were having a lot of fun. That seemed to be enough for both of us.

And she understood me. Certainly better than any of my siblings did.

"Why is this so inconceivable to them?" I said as we sat on a couch in my den. "It's not like I'm irresponsible. It's not like I'm living in a one-bedroom dive. I work out of my house. I can cook. I know how to dial 9-1-1. That pretty much covers it, doesn't it?"

"I think a lot of people have trouble not thinking of the youngest as the 'baby of the family,' no matter how old he is," Marina said gently. "Your siblings just don't know how competent you've become and how good this would be for both of you."

Yes, how good it would be for both of us. That was the inspiration that flashed in my mind in Denise's apartment that night. Something I hadn't even considered until that very moment. I believed it would be good for my father to live in a house where his son could offer him companionship and take care of his basic needs. But I also believed it would be good for me.

Everyone carries around a lot of unresolved stuff with his or her parents. In my case, the unresolved stuff with my father was that I had virtually no "stuff" with him at all. He was fifty years older than I was and I'm sure that I'd never figured into his plans. He always seemed confused by my being around. It was like he'd revved himself up to be an active parent for only a certain length of time and he wasn't sure how to re-start the motor. He wasn't negligent or insensitive, but he spent a lot of time at work. We pretty much led separate lives under the same roof. As a result, I had a completely different relationship with him than any of my other siblings had. I learned that my father had become seriously engaged in his children's lives only once they were old enough for reasonable conversation and interaction. He wasn't much for changing diapers or getting down on the floor to play, but he was great at going camping or building models or taking long drives – and especially good at deep, probing discussion. I believed that my time would come, that he hadn't been any more involved with Darlene or Matty or Denise when they were six than he was with me, and that he would really show up when I was ten. By the time I was ten, though, he was sixty, and I guess he no longer had the energy required to have an involved relationship with a preteen. Most of our dealings came via my mother, whether it was his giving me twenty dollars to "pick out something nice for your mom's birthday" or her telling me, "Now that you're twelve, your father would really appreciate it if you started cutting the lawn." I had friends with grandparents my father's age, and I essentially thought of him that way. Your grandfather didn't play catch with you or ride bikes with you. He came around fairly regularly, dispensed advice, passed you a few bucks, patted you on the back, and left.

After I moved out, my father and I would talk when I came over to visit or if he answered the phone when I called. But the conversations were always brief, rarely more substantial than a review of the headlines, a comment about the weather, a query about my work, or his observation about the stock market. I never felt neglected, and I never believed that I would have been a better, more well-rounded person if I had received more attention from him. But those stories from Darlene and Matty and Denise nagged at me a little. And seeing my father interact with his three eldest children at family dinners made me a bit jealous. There was a big piece of Mickey Sienna that I never had access to, and because of that, I felt like something was missing.

Now this opportunity was sitting in front of me, a chance for a little substance in our relationship after thirty-two years. If Marina could understand that with only a passing knowledge of the players involved, why couldn't three people who were much closer to the situation?

"What does your father think about the idea?" Marina said.

"Why would I talk to my father about it?"

She snickered. "Sorry, I don't know what I was thinking."

"I didn't mean it like that. It's just that Matty and the others are kinda like the gatekeepers here. If I can't get the idea past them, there's no chance I'm going to be able to get it past my dad."

Marina reached over to the coffee table to retrieve her glass of wine and then pulled me closer. She was the first woman I'd ever been with who I sat with that way. All other women leaned into me.

"How much do you want this?"

"It surprises me how much." I said animatedly. "I keep asking myself if it's just because the others blew me off about it. But it isn't that. I think that something really good could come out of this. It's all very romantic. You know, the whole thing about father and son forging this deep connection after all these years."

"Then it seems like you have to do something about it. And there's only one thing you can do."

I cringed. Of course she was right, but the notion of discussing this with my father directly seemed about as natural as asking the old lady down the block if she wanted to move in. In fact the old lady would probably be more receptive.

"I was kinda hoping that all of this would just happen. You want to go talk to him for me?"

"Gee, I would Jesse, but since we've never met, he might find it a little strange."

"Yeah. I'm worried about him having the same reaction if I go to see him."

"This could be a great thing for you. Even if he doesn't take you up on it, you're going to feel differently about yourself and your place in the family after you ask him."

I snuggled a little closer to her, took her free hand and kissed it.

"I could wind up feeling really empty and foolish," I said.

"You could if you decide to go into it that way. But unless you think your father is going to mock you every time you see him afterward, there really isn't anything to lose. You said it yourself: the 'gatekeepers' aren't going to let this happen. So if you strike out with your dad, you aren't any worse off. But I'll bet he'll be moved that you even brought the subject up. What parent doesn't want to be wanted by his kids later in life?"

I leaned up and kissed her softly.

"You're very good at this, you know?"

She kissed the top of my head. "You would have figured it out on your own."

"No, I think there's a really good chance that I would have just let it go and then been pissed off about it for years."

She hugged me closer to her.

"I think that might have been true if this was about something else, but you know how important this is to you. You wouldn't have gone down without a fight."

I took another sip of wine and settled into Marina's arms. Two thoughts crossed my mind. The first was how refreshing it was to be with someone who actually paid attention to what I was thinking. The other was that talking to my father was going to redefine awkwardness for me.

Chapter Three

The scent of smoke was still bad in the kitchen. It had taken the contractors only a couple of days to make the repairs, and they had done what they could to air it out. But it was still there.

Right now what Mickey really wanted was a BLT, but he settled for a ham sandwich. Mickey didn't want to be afraid of the stove. He didn't want to believe that he was going to have a hard time even boiling water without wondering if he was going to do something wrong and kill himself. It had just been a stupid thing that morning. He'd been tossing and turning in bed all night and he was still tired and he'd fallen asleep on the couch. It was an isolated incident, even if his kids were making a really big deal about it. Still, a ham sandwich would do just fine.

Mickey was slicing a tomato when his head pricked up at the sound of someone approaching the front door. *The hearing's still as good as ever.* As the bell rang, he wondered who might be there. He wasn't expecting any deliveries. Maybe Laura had sent another one of her CARE packages. He was pretty sure that Theresa wasn't supposed to come over today.

He was very surprised when he opened the door and found Jesse there. Not that it was odd for him to come over, just that he usually called first. Jess seemed to be coming around more often since Dorothy died. He was a good kid. Mickey liked telling his friends that he had a son who was younger than some of their grandchildren. It made him feel younger himself.

"Hey, Jess. I didn't expect you. I was just making myself a sandwich. You want one?"

Jesse shook his head as he walked in the door and kissed his father on the cheek.

"It's a little early for lunch," he said.

"Is it? I was feeling pretty hungry. Want some coffee or something?"

"Yeah, thanks. Coffee sounds good."

"Good," Mickey said as he worked his way back toward the kitchen. "Why don't you make it while I finish cutting this tomato?"

Jesse went over to the refrigerator, pulled out a can, and shook it.

"You're pretty low on coffee here, Dad."

Mickey looked up from the cutting board and nodded.

"Yeah, I gotta go shopping. They closed the A&P. That's where your mother used to go for groceries. All of the other places seem pretty annoying."

Jesse spooned the coffee out into the coffeemaker and then returned the can to the refrigerator.

"It looks like you could use a lot of stuff here. You want me to take you shopping? We could go out to lunch afterward."

Mickey thought he wouldn't mind a little help with the shopping. There were things that Dorothy always used to buy that he couldn't remember. He wasn't too sure about spending all of that time in a restaurant, though.

"Yeah, if you could take me to a store, that would be great. Let me just finish my sandwich first."

They didn't say much while Mickey ate. It seemed to him that Jesse had something on his mind, but if he did, he wasn't talking about it. That pretty much described Jesse in Mickey's opinion. He knew the kid was smart – all of his kids were smart – and he was at least moderately successful as a writer, so he had to be good at expressing himself. But when Mickey was with Jesse, he could never tell if his thoughts were occupied elsewhere or if he just didn't have much going on in his head. He wondered how any child of his could have turned out that way. But things had always been so different with Jesse than they had been with the others.

They listened to an all-news station on the way to the supermarket with Mickey making a comment about the Dow Jones average and Jesse saying something about going to college with the announcer. Other than that, they drove quietly.

Supermarkets had always seemed a little daunting to Mickey. Way too much selection, way too many labels calling out for his attention. This was entirely Dorothy's domain when she was alive. If they needed milk or something, Mickey would go to the convenience store about a half-mile away from the house. At least he could make his way around the A&P, having gone there enough times with his wife in their retirement. But now both Dorothy and the A&P were gone and Mickey had no idea how much broccoli he would eat in a week or how to buy enough orange juice so that he didn't run out and it didn't go bad. And then the fire happened and further complicated matters.

"What do you do with kale?" he said to Jesse, picking up a bunch after a few minutes in the produce aisle. He wondered if it was something he could eat without cooking it.

"I don't do anything with kale," Jesse said with an exaggerated grimace. "Not my kind of thing." Mickey put down the greens and turned to another item.

"What about kohlrabi?"

"Are we going to do this alphabetically? Let's see, we're on k, next is l – lemons, lettuce, lima beans. I can tell you what to do with all of those."

Mickey returned the kohlrabi to the shelf. "Thank you, Mr. Green Jeans." He looked around him, thinking he would have more salads in the future.

Jesse started walking. "Dad, I think we have a lot of produce in the cart already. What else do you need?"

Surprisingly, Jesse turned out to be more helpful than Mickey thought he would be. Jesse reminded Mickey about things like raisins and dishwashing liquid, which he had been out of for weeks but kept forgetting to buy. He even showed him all of these frozen foods that Mickey could heat up in the microwave, a prospect that seemed considerably less daunting than cooking on a stove. Jesse moved around the aisles with efficiency and purpose, as though he had a clear plan. He must have learned that sort of thing from his mother.

"Listen, Dad, there's something I want to talk to you about," Jesse said as they walked down the dairy aisle. "You know that, since the fire, all of us have been concerned about whether you should stay in the house."

Mickey's mood pivoted instantly. He threw up his arms and looked toward the ceiling.

"Don't tell me they sent you to have this conversation with me. Did they think that if they sent the kid I wouldn't give him a hard time?"

Mickey looked at his son disapprovingly while he considered how cowardly his other children were being. Jesse looked a little flustered, and Mickey realized he might have come on a little strong. It was so easy to get Jesse to back down. Mickey wondered how he hadn't instilled more toughness in him.

"It isn't the others, Dad," Jesse said tentatively. "In fact, they don't even know I'm talking to you about this, and would probably think I'm crazy if they did."

Even though he seemed to be in mid-thought, Jesse stopped talking. Mickey frowned at him. It was sometimes hard to imagine that this kid had any success as a journalist, considering how much trouble he had getting to his point.

The boy finally continued. "I'm thinking that maybe you should think about moving in with me."

Mickey's eyes widened. He certainly hadn't seen that one coming.

"No, don't be silly," he said immediately. "First of all, I don't need to move out of my house. And second of all," he hesitated, "well, we don't need to talk about second of all."

"No, I mean it, Dad. You really can't stay in the house any longer. If you don't want to believe that you aren't as young as you used to be, fine. But even if that's the case, there are certain things that Mom took care of that you just don't know how to do for yourself."

Jesse took a couple of steps closer to him. His face had already begun to color.

"Are you planning to just buy new clothes and seal off the laundry room when it starts to overflow with your dirty stuff? And let's not even get into the cooking thing. If you start experimenting with kohlrabi, the entire neighborhood could be at risk."

Jesse was smiling as he said these things, but Mickey was surprised by the intensity in his voice. He'd clearly been thinking about this. Not that any of it was convincing, but at least it was premeditated.

"Jess, I'm okay. You and your sisters and your brother underestimate me."

"Dad, none of us are saying that you're feebleminded or that you're going to spend the rest of your life huddled under blankets and listening to a transistor radio. But it's a big house, and you're all alone in it. Maybe this isn't a good time in your life to be learning new tricks."

Mickey took a step back and put his hand up to stop his son. "I don't want to talk about this anymore." He left the cart with Jesse and headed toward the checkout.

"They were talking about a nursing home," Jesse said as Mickey walked away. "The rest of them decided that an assisted living apartment would be best for you."

Mickey stopped and turned around. He couldn't believe what Jesse had just said. His children were conspiring against him without his knowledge?

"I'm not some doddering fool," he said bitingly. "They can't force me to do that."

Jesse put his arm on Mickey's shoulder and spoke in a conciliatory tone.

"Dad, after the fire, they could probably do whatever they wanted if they felt it was necessary."

Mickey felt a chill. Would his children really try to prove his incompetence in court? Would he ever let it get that far?

"I don't need an old age home."

"Which is why I suggested your coming to live with me." Jesse smiled. "Your youngest child."

Mickey gave a stiff chuckle.

"Yeah, my wild, unmarried son."

Jesse laughed loudly. "Wild and on the prowl. With his old man – and I mean that purely in the colloquial sense – riding shotgun."

Mickey smiled. Jesse was so different from the others.

"Nah, you don't want me living with you. I'll get in the way."

"Actually, I'd love it, Dad."

Mickey looked into his son's eyes. He realized he'd never figured out how to read this child. If this were Darlene or Matt or Denise, he'd be able to tell in a second if they really meant what they were saying.

What Jesse was saying didn't make sense. But the kid had put ideas in his head. Ideas about his children dragging him out of his house, of their bringing in lawyers to decide his fate. No one should have to deal with that.

"Let's go check out," he said, beginning to walk down the aisle again. "When we get home, we'll make coffee and talk some more."

Chapter Four

Sometimes the clichés just ring true. I wished for this. I got it. And by the time it started, I was already beginning to regret it. I should have known myself well enough by now. I should have known how I got when I romanticized things, and more importantly how I tended to react when things didn't turn out as I expected. I should have been experienced enough and had enough perspective to be prepared for the rocky terrain. But this was my father and I might as well have been a toddler. Once again, the simple act of dealing with my family had turned me into something less than I wanted to be.

I was fully aware that moving my father from his four thousand square-foot Colonial into my twenty-five hundred square-foot Cape was going to be a challenge, which is why I spent so much time with him trying to determine which items he needed, which others he wanted, which he was going to pass along to children and grandchildren, and which we were simply going to get rid of. Hours and hours, over days and days. I missed a deadline for the first time in my career, yet on moving day I realized that I might just as well have gone to Bermuda.

I should have expected it after what happened at the tag sale we'd held the week before. I consulted with him on every item we put on the tables. We even agreed on prices. The first time he talked a browser out of buying a basket because "my wife really loved this, I can't possibly part with it," I was touched. That was because the pattern hadn't emerged yet. Six more times that afternoon, people tried to purchase items that Mickey Sienna decided they weren't allowed to buy. Why it didn't register on me that these items would therefore be coming to my house – and that many additional items would be joining them – I'm not sure. Perhaps I simply wanted to be blissfully ignorant a short while longer.

The last couple of days before the move, I found myself uncharacteristically frenetic. I couldn't maintain a lengthy conversation, I couldn't write, I even had trouble lying in bed with Marina. I wanted everything to go smoothly. I wanted my father to be thrilled at the prospect of coming to live with me. I wanted him to move his favorite personal belongings into my house and immediately dub it his house as well. Having had so little hands-on experience, I mythologized the entire father-son experience. And yet if I had been paying any attention to the messages my body had been sending me, I would have understood how I was setting myself up for failure.

All of this was making me horribly edgy. The night before, I didn't sleep well, and in the morning I drank too much coffee. I got to my father's an hour before the movers were scheduled to arrive, then started ranting when they were fifteen minutes late. I was in no condition for even the slightest thing to go off track and I certainly wasn't ready for my father to reevaluate every item in the house.

"Pack it up carefully now. Do you have any of that bubble wrap?" he said to one of the movers. The man had taken a box into the living room and was placing ceramic swan figurines into it.

I walked up to them. "What are you doing with these, Dad?"

"We didn't pack the swans," he said with a note of disbelief in his voice.

"We weren't planning to pack the swans. You're giving them to Christina." Christina is Matty's youngest daughter.

Dad looked at me as though I'd suggested he part with one of his limbs.

"I can't give these to Christina. Your mother loved them. Remember how she used to pick up each little swan and dust it individually? Christina will break them."

"She's twenty-three."

"She won't appreciate them. You want to give them to her after I'm dead, I can't do anything about that. But I'm not giving the swans away."

I had no idea what he was planning to do with these trinkets. Certainly they weren't going on my mantle, no matter how dewy-eyed he got. He'd sort of gotten to me with that image of my mother dusting the swans, though. I must have seen her do that dozens of times over the years. I decided to let it go and to move on to supervising the packing of the truck.

A short while later, a lamp came out that I know we agreed to leave behind. I vividly recalled the conversation where I explained that table lamps required tables and how all of mine were being used already. There definitely wasn't room for another table in the living room. Regardless, I didn't say anything. But it bugged me.

Not long after, three movers made their way out of the house gingerly carrying the china cabinet.

"What are you doing with this?" I said.

One of the movers glanced over at me. "Gotta get it on the truck before we start bringing out the boxes."

"Who said you needed to get it on the truck at all?"

The mover gestured back toward the house.

"The guy inside said this was coming."

After too little sleep, too much caffeine, and too much of a sense that my father had been toying with me during the weeks of preparation, this put me over the top.

"The guy inside is severely impaired mentally. I don't want you listening to him. He probably told you that he used to live in this house with his wife, right? It's very sad. Don't move anything that wasn't marked to be moved without talking to me first."

I went back inside.

"Why did you tell the movers to load the china cabinet on the truck?" I said when I saw my father.

"How else were we going to get it to your house? Do you have any idea how much something like that weighs?"

"There's no room for the china cabinet in my house, remember? We talked about this. You're giving it to the Salvation Army along with the breakfront, the dining room table, the guest bed, and all the other furniture that also won't fit in my house."

"We never talked about the china cabinet," he said flatly.

"I think we started with the china cabinet."

"I wouldn't have said we weren't taking the china cabinet. Do you know when I bought this china cabinet for your mother?"

This was getting old for me very quickly.

"I don't know, Dad, the day you moved into the house? The day Denise was born? The day Mom told you that she wanted a china cabinet more than anything else in the entire world and that if by some chance she should die before you that you must promise to never go anywhere without taking it with you?"

My father scowled at me.

"There's no reason to talk to me like that."

I shook my head. This wasn't the image I had in my mind of the day my father moved into my house. I was thinking of something with some brandy, maybe a deck of cards, a bit of wisdom being passed down from one generation to the next. Not this.

"Take the freaking china cabinet," I said. "Floor space is overrated anyway."

I walked out of the house and down the block a bit, hoping to cool off. I tried to look at this from his perspective, then just decided I was too agitated to be sympathetic. I pulled out my cell phone with the intention of calling Matty to bitch a little. Certainly he would have no trouble understanding how stubborn and frustrating my father could be. But then

I thought better of it. I didn't want to admit to Matty that I was stressing over this move or that I was having anything approaching second thoughts. He would expect that. He was almost certainly waiting for it. He'd probably even told his assistant to hold all calls except for one from me – and then only if I sounded flustered.

Instead, I called Marina's cell. She was a third-grade teacher and there was no way for me to get her at work, but just the idea of being able to dump a little of this on her was therapeutic.

"Hi, it's me. I think I'm going to have to get rid of my bed in order to accommodate all of my father's stuff. Do you want it?" I looked skyward for a moment, and then continued. "We're not exactly having a Hallmark moment over here. Actually my father is having a series of them and it's driving me out of my mind. If he starts getting sentimental over the washing machine, I'm not going to be responsible for my actions.

"I hope your day went okay. I'm really looking forward to seeing you tomorrow night. I'll try to stay out of jail at least that long. Bye."

I decided to walk around the entire block before going back to the house. Just in time to see him supervising the move of the breakfront into the truck. I took a deep breath, tried to think happy thoughts, and decided we'd sort it out some other time.

About an hour and a half later, everything was loaded, and the truck took off for my house. We sat in the car for a moment before pulling away. The new owners wouldn't be taking occupancy for another couple of weeks, so this wasn't the final goodbye. Still, it wouldn't have been right for either of us to rush on at that very moment.

For the first time on this crazy day, I allowed myself to think about how the house I grew up in wouldn't be in the family for much longer. I thought about all the times I lay on the couch with my head in my mother's lap as we watched television. I thought about the posters I used to have up on my bedroom wall. I thought about the basement whose dark corners didn't stop intimidating me until I was fourteen. I wondered if all of the memories that I wanted to take from my time here were locked in my mind, or if I had been too cavalier with them, assuming that I could always go back to the house to retrieve them.

I can only imagine what was swimming through my father's head at that moment. If simply preparing to back out of the driveway was having this effect on me, it must have been exponentially more powerful for him. I hadn't given this enough consideration earlier. I had approached this as a task that needed to be completed. But it was a rite of passage.

We sat for a while longer in silence. At one point, I even closed my eyes to see my mother walking out to the driveway to greet me, as she always did when I was younger. At last, I decided that I needed to head off. I was getting ready to turn the key in the ignition when my father bolted up and said, "My god, I can't believe I was forgetting it." He opened the car door and headed back into the house. I called to him to ask where he was going, but he ignored me. I imagined that he was going to come out lugging some chair or vase that he'd decided he could never part with. I'd already convinced myself not to challenge him.

A couple of minutes later, he returned with a tattered and yellowed box.

"Don't give me a hard time about this," he said as he returned to the car, holding the box on his lap.

"What is it?"

"Don't try to tell me you don't have room."

I'd obviously shaken him up in some way with my earlier ranting and I was feeling pretty guilty about it.

"It's fine," I said, starting the car.

"This is important to me."

"I know. It all is. You're right."

He looked off at the house and then down again at the box.

"Come on," I said, "let's go home."

Chapter Five

My preference is to write feature pieces. I find human-interest stories fascinating. A few years ago, I did a ten thousand-word article on a single grandmother raising her triplet grandchildren by herself after their parents died in a car crash. Not only did I bond with the material, but I bonded with the subject as well. Marilyn and I still send each other Christmas and birthday cards, and I recently started an e-mail correspondence with nine-year-old Kerry, who has decided that she wants to be a writer.

Most of my work in this area has been stories of ordinary people doing extraordinary things. I'm always so deeply impressed with the way others can reach untapped reserves when required to do so. It never fails to make me just a tiny bit less cynical for a few weeks afterward. But I've also done a number of pieces with celebrities. I try to find the human story there as well and not to be too terribly disappointed if I can't find one.

The reality of being a freelance writer, though, is that feature pieces are the occasional dessert I can allow myself if I stick to a relatively healthy diet otherwise – meaning uninspiring but steady how-to pieces on subjects such as men's health, finance, and home repair. I've even ghosted a couple of pieces for experts on parenting. At the moment, I was working on an article about giving oneself regular testicular exams. There's just about no way to feel particularly motivated about work like that, even if the doctor who provided the background for the story is very dedicated, speaks with conviction, and even has you convinced that you haven't been spending enough time examining your testicles.

This should have been an extremely easy gig, and I expected to have the entire thing written in a day or so. Yet, I spent most of the morning procrastinating, laboring over opening sentences (as though anyone would be reading the article for style) and checking my e-mail on the quarter hour. It could certainly have been that the subject matter was preventing me from getting my work done. I'd dawdled in precisely this fashion when doing articles on head lice, 401K's, and installing dormer windows.

I chose instead to blame my father.

Once we had gotten him moved in and had found a place for his things in my now ludicrously overly-accessorized house, I began to get excited again at the thought of having him live with me. I'd been missing my mother a lot since she died, and having my father around alleviated that a little. When I was feeling nostalgic, I could bring her a little closer by talking to him about her. I was also excited that I would finally get to know Mickey Sienna, and that he would get to know me. There had never been time for that when I was a kid and there had never really been an opportunity since. I envisioned us evolving naturally over the next several months until we were old buddies, guys who shared both a family bond and a genuine personal connection. I imagined the next time our family all gathered together that my Dad and I would have the inside jokes and little asides that he'd always had with the others. And, if only for a moment or two, my siblings would feel a little jealous of me the way I had been of them for as long as I could remember.

Once again, though, I was romanticizing. Perhaps because I'd never had a functioning connection with my father, I oversimplified the mechanics of a father-son relationship. I assumed that there would be a natural meeting point, a place where we could sit comfortably emotionally. It had always been that way with my mother. But when this didn't happen almost immediately, I found myself getting disillusioned – even as I chided myself for becoming impatient quickly. I had so completely built this thing up in my mind that I was entirely devoid of perspective. I was angry that my father wasn't participating in my little parent-child fantasy, and I didn't care if he knew it.

It didn't dawn on me that getting to know my father meant getting to know all of the ways in which we differed philosophically and practically. I hadn't considered that we would have very different ideas about what one did with a Sunday morning, or how many times we needed to have my Aunt Theresa over for dinner, or what percentage of the available hot water was too much to use in one shower. I hadn't imagined that he would play the television so loudly that the broadcast studio in Manhattan would wonder where the echo was coming from.

"Dad, really, I'm trying to get some work done," I called from behind the closed door of my office.

He didn't respond. Of course not. How could he hear me with the television up so loud? I tried to ignore it and return to my article, but the combination of boring quotes from a physician about reducing the risk of testicular cancer and the inane exchanges that were coming through the walls from some second-rate forties movie made that virtually impossible. Finally, I walked out to the den.

My father looked up at me from his chair with an expression that suggested that he was either baiting me or that he genuinely had no idea what he had done this time to produce the annoyed expression on my face.

"It's a little loud," I said.

"I turned it down when you complained before," he said, defensively.

"And the windows in my office stopped shaking, thanks. Think you can bring it down to subway station level?"

He scowled and picked up the remote, lowering the volume.

"I don't understand why you play this so loud. You don't have a hearing problem."

"It sounds better when it's loud. Like that music you used to play at home."

I looked at the TV screen. "That's Jane Russell, not Jimi Hendrix. Not to mention the fact that you're eighty-two and not fourteen." I was actually a little surprised that he remembered the music thing at all (typical dad/kid moment: "Your father would really prefer it if you didn't play the music so loud at night"), imagining that it was one of the dozens of ways in which we barely interacted when we had previously been under the same roof.

He snapped the remote at the television, turning it off. "I didn't know you were running a library here."

I went back to my office and tried to get back into the article, but I was still peeved at our exchange and I couldn't concentrate. I finally decided that it was time to make myself an early lunch, hoping that it would kick off a much more productive afternoon.

I went back out to the den. My father was still sitting in his chair, staring at the blank television screen. I assumed he was waiting me out, staying that way until I emerged from my office so he could show me how inconsiderate I was being. I could have asked him what he was doing. I could even have suggested that he put the movie back on, since I wasn't going to be working for the next half-hour or so. Instead, I just walked into the kitchen, waiting until I got there to ask him if he wanted something to eat. He didn't answer, but he shuffled into the room a minute later.

"What I want is a BLT, but you don't have any more bacon," he said.

I opened the refrigerator and pulled out a package.

"There's bacon right here."

"That's not real bacon."

"It's turkey bacon. You eat too much pork."

"Yeah, and it's killing me. That stuff doesn't taste like bacon at all."

"That's because it's not 80% fat. You know, just because eating terribly hasn't hurt you yet doesn't mean it isn't going to."

He walked over to the refrigerator and peered inside. "I'll go shopping for myself later. What are you having for lunch?"

"I'm making a veggie burger. Want one?"

He pulled his head back from the door. "You're kidding, right?"

"Well, I was going to make a lard on rye, but we're out of rye."

He gave me that look again, the one that said that he was still surprised at the way I was speaking to him. Matty spoke to him like this all the time, and it seemed as though my father enjoyed the challenge of parrying with him. Why was it a problem coming from me? He pulled out a plate of roasted chicken from the previous night's dinner and walked over to the kitchen table with it.

As I cooked my burger, I glanced over at him eating the cold chicken. I couldn't tell whether he was angry or upset. I wondered if he was having second thoughts about moving in here, or if he just saw this as part of the process of our learning to live with one another. The thought of the former saddened me. I realized that it would be far worse to go through this and learn that we couldn't live together than to have never gone through it at all. This was the other thing that was driving me crazy – the emotional see-sawing that came from alternating good moments with my father with bad moments, switching from wanting desperately to have a meaningful bond with him to wishing he'd moved into Darlene's house instead. It was just like what happened in a romantic relationship when you cared too much. You'd think I might have learned.

I finished making the burger and sat down at the table next to him. We didn't say anything for a few minutes.

"Do you want something to drink?" I said.

"You could get me a Coke if you want."

Things were just destined not to go well. I didn't buy soda, either. I was feeling pretty displeased with myself at this point. How could I expect him to feel at home if I wouldn't let him make it his?

"We don't have any Coke. We'll go shopping later this afternoon, okay? We'll get more bacon, too."

He looked up at me with an expression I couldn't read clearly. I wanted it to say that he'd accepted the flimsy olive branch I was offering. But it might have said that this relationship was getting old quickly. He returned to his meal, and I tried to stomach mine.

"I used to have quite a thing for Jane Russell," he said after it had been quiet for a while. "It used to drive your mother crazy. Like my ogling Jane Russell was going to make her stop by the house one day and take me away."

I smiled. "Turn it back on when we're finished with lunch. I've been having a hard time with this men's health article I'm writing. I think I was just using the television as an excuse."

"Nah. I have some other stuff I want to do this afternoon. What's your article about?"

"Preventing testicular cancer."

"Jeez, really?"

"You should have seen my article on colonoscopies a couple of months ago. I think it even made my computer squeamish."

He snickered and got up to get himself a glass of water.

"You do good stuff. That article about the wheelchair basketball star last year almost made me cry."

I didn't even know that he'd read it. I felt a little catch in my throat, which I tamped down by taking another bite of the burger.

"What's that stuff taste like, anyway?" he said, sitting back down.

"It's really good. All you need is an imagination. Want a bite?"

He curled his lip. "My imagination isn't that good."

He put down his fork, which indicated that he was finished eating. At lunch, when he was done, he usually got up and went back into the den. Today, he decided to stay until I was through with my burger. We didn't talk any more, but he didn't go back to the den until after I went back to my office.

I think that qualified as progress.

Chapter Six

In the Big Book of Proper Romantic Behavior (a copy of which has never made its way into my hands), there's probably a chapter about not spending the entirety of your six-month anniversary dinner talking about your father. I certainly hadn't intended for things to go that way. I'd made reservations at a great fusion place because the idea of anniversaries and fusion seemed kind of sexy. I bought Marina a hand-painted silk scarf she'd admired at a craft gallery a few weeks earlier. I even made sure that the Richard Thompson album she loved was on the iPod for the drive to the restaurant.

But by the time the wine arrived, I was in full swing. At this point, it had truly settled on me that bringing my father to live in my house was a much bigger deal than I had expected it to be. There were the dozens of ways in which he annoyed me. There were the hundreds of ways in which I felt I was letting him down. There were the tiny breakthrough moments like that one at the kitchen table a couple of days before, when I started to believe that we might actually wind up having a relationship. There were all of those reminders of the relationship we'd never had for the past thirty-two years.

It might have been easier for me to put all of this aside and to concentrate on Marina if not for what had happened in the afternoon. I'd been working in my office and I came out to get a drink. On my way to the kitchen, I passed my father in the den. He was on his computer trading stocks, something he did practically every afternoon.

"Want something to drink, Dad?" I said as I passed by.

"Yeah, make me some of that designer coffee you like so much."

I laughed to myself as I walked to the kitchen. This was an example of where things stood in our relationship. We argued about the difference between the fair trade organic coffee beans I bought from a local roaster and the pre-ground stuff he liked out of a can. When I finally got him to taste mine, I could see that he could appreciate the difference, but rather than admit it, he made it seem as though he was conceding to drink it to spare us from having to make two separate pots every day.

A few minutes later, I brought him a mug. His eyes didn't leave the computer.

"Let me take a look at your portfolio," he said.

"I don't need you to take a look at my portfolio."

"I promise not to laugh. Do you have it online somewhere?"

"I really don't need you to look at my portfolio."

He stopped what he was doing and turned to me.

"I was a successful broker for fifty years. I've been trading for sixty. You think you know better than me?"

I could feel the tingle I felt whenever a confrontation was coming on. I wasn't particularly anxious to have this one, though.

"It isn't about that. There just isn't that much to talk about."

"Then that probably is something we *should* talk about. You have to be diversified, you know?"

I took a deep breath. I'd really been dreading this conversation.

"I have a few thousand in a mutual fund. That's it."

He looked at me as though he couldn't possibly understand what I was saying.

"Where's the rest of your money?"

"Well, there's a million or so in a Swiss bank account and I keep another couple of million in the hall closet."

He just stared at me. This was a new gambit he'd started using whenever I got sarcastic.

"I have some money in my checking account to pay bills and all that," I said. "That's it."

He rolled his eyes. "What the hell are you spending the rest of it on?"

"I don't exactly have an extravagant lifestyle, Dad. There isn't that much 'rest of it.'"

He looked back at the screen and typed something on the keyboard. "And I didn't know what I was talking about when I told you to take that magazine job," he said under his breath.

I suppose I should have been thankful that we'd lived together this long before he reminded me of that conversation. It was one of the only times my father had ever "sat me down." I'd just graduated college with every intention of heading out on my own as a freelancer. A friend hooked me up with an editor at *Newsweek*, one thing led to another, and the editor wound up offering me a staff position. It wasn't something I seriously considered, but I mentioned it to my mother just to let her know that things were already looking up for me. That Sunday morning, my father took me aside and told me that he thought I was making a big mistake not opting for the security of a job like that. He argued that I could always go out on my own after I had a few years under my belt. I told him that I disagreed. My position that I needed the freedom to write everything that excited me fell on deaf ears. Only when I suggested in broad terms that I could make more money as a freelancer did he relent. We hadn't talked about my earnings since that day.

"I'm doing fine," I said.

"If you say so."

I wanted to argue that it took time to build a writing career, that I'd received more work in the past year than ever before, that one of my pieces had been submitted by the magazine for a Pulitzer, that I would have hated working for a corporation, and that layoffs were happening all the time on magazine staffs. Instead, I simply went back to my office and had the argument with him in my head.

"I should have said something to him," I said to Marina as the waiter poured coffee. This was the third time I'd said that over the course of dinner. "He just gave me that whole superiority thing and made me feel so small-time. How can I feel that way about someone who's been only a marginal part of my life all these years?"

Marina smiled at me. Her patience was fathomless.

"He's your father. You'd feel that way if you saw him once a decade. That's just the way that stuff works."

"I feel like I'm on a roller coaster with him. We creep slowly up to some peak and then go plummeting straight down. This is not my definition of a great time."

"You might have to get used to it." She smiled softly. "You know, it's unlikely that you really had no relationship with him over the years. There was almost certainly a lot of stuff going on between you just because you were in the same house. Now you have all of these expectations about what things are going to be like with him living with you. That makes you pretty vulnerable."

"Let that be a lesson."

I took a sip of coffee and focused on my plight for a moment. I'm relatively sure this wasn't how Marina envisioned this evening.

She pointed to the wrapped box I'd placed next to my chair when we sat down. "Is that package for me, or were you going to tip the waiter with it?"

I couldn't believe that I'd been so self-absorbed that I hadn't given her the gift yet. "I'm so stupid," I said, handing it to her.

She opened the package and smiled. When she looked up at me, there was a glimmer in her eye that told me I'd chosen wisely.

"From the Artisan Shop," she said.

"I went back there a couple of days later."

"I didn't even realize that you saw me looking at it."

"You lingered over it. You don't linger over much. That seemed to be a sign."

She reached across the table and kissed me. Then she handed me my present. It was a handmade pen from the same store.

"It's a good thing we didn't run into each other while we were buying these," she said with a laugh. I kissed her and thanked her. At that point our desserts arrived.

"So what was your day like?" I said sheepishly. She looked at me with an expression that acknowledged that I had dominated the evening's conversation with my issues and that she was okay with it.

"Kendall Blevins confessed his love for me."

"Kendall Blevins?" I imagined a fellow faculty member who had been admiring her in the teachers' lounge over the years. He would bring her soft drinks and sit uncomfortably close to her. It's amazing how quickly these images can flash into your head.

"He's eight," she said, showing me once again how ludicrously transparent I was to her.

"Oh."

"It was really very sweet. When I got into my classroom this morning, there was a letter from Kendall sitting on my desk. He told me that he thought about me all the time and that he would do anything for me. That meant to him that he was in love with me. He said he wanted to marry me some day and that he knew there was a difference in our ages but that it didn't matter to him if it didn't matter to me. I wasn't entirely sure how to react to it. You know, I've gotten valentines and things like that from kids before, but never a love letter."

"Really? A babe like you?" Marina was beautiful, but she also went out of her way to keep her appearance understated while she was in school.

"I guess when a third-grader falls in love, he wants something more than just a hot chick. Anyway, at lunchtime, I asked him to stay behind. I mentioned the letter, and he turned absolutely scarlet and started fidgeting all over the place. I got him to calm down and then I got him to talk. He told me that he found out this week that his parents were getting a divorce and that his mother was moving out."

"Ouch."

"Yeah. I guess I suddenly became the most solid thing in his life. We talked for a while and he started crying, and I just sort of let him work through it. He seemed pretty upset, so we had lunch together in the classroom. We shared our sandwiches – can you tell me why anybody eats bologna? – which seemed to make him happy. I let him have my granola bar, which he treated like the most exotic thing on the planet.

"After a while, he was talking about the big flag football game some of the kids were going to have at recess and he seemed okay. Before the rest of the kids got back, I told him that he could talk to me whenever he wanted or whenever he was feeling a little upset about things, but that he was going to have to focus his romantic attentions on third-grade girls. He blushed again. I figured that meant that our fling was over."

"Boy, I wish I had you as my third-grade teacher," I said. This wasn't the first time she'd stolen my heart with an account of her interaction with her students. And it wasn't the first time that I wished I could see her in the classroom. I knew simply by knowing Marina that she had to be an inspiring and compassionate teacher. I imagined myself in Kendall's place and thought about how lucky he was to have her. My own third-grade teacher once closed a book on my face, so I knew the difference.

Several times I'd considered dropping by the school to watch her teach, even just for a moment. But it seemed a line that I shouldn't cross. It was almost certainly best to spare Marina the teasing that would surely follow from the girls who would want to know everything about her boyfriend.

We left the restaurant a few minutes later. Marina's story had taken the edge off for me, and it felt great to drive quietly back to her house, holding her hand tightly.

"I really do love the scarf," she said as we turned into her neighborhood.

I gave her hand a squeeze. "I'm glad. Six months is a pretty big deal."

"Hey, it's just a hundred and eighty days, one day at a time, right?" she said in a tone that was just a little sharper than I was accustomed to hearing from her. I looked over at her and could see that her eyebrows were arched and that her face held the slightest hint of a smirk. But then she smiled and kissed my hand.

It got quiet in the car again. I wondered if I should be saying something else. Should I tell her how much I appreciated being with her? Did she know that this was the third-longest relationship of my life? Did that matter in any way whatsoever?

Even though I didn't have that Big Book of Proper Romantic Behavior, I knew that everything I wanted to say to her would almost certainly come out wrong. I wanted to tell her that the time we'd shared and whatever time was left between us was precious to me. I wanted to tell her that, while both of us were too smart to be fooled by the implications, what we had in this relationship was fulfilling and soul satisfying. I wanted to tell her that she had made a place in my mind and in my heart that would last long after our affair had faded. I knew she would understand what I meant by all of these things and that she probably felt the same way, but it just didn't seem like the kind of thing one said under these circumstances.

I was still trying to think of something to say when she turned to me and announced, "I figured you were only good for two dates, maybe three." Out of the corner of my eye, I could see she was smiling when she said it, though I also knew that what she was really saying was "Let's skip the profundities, okay?"

We got to her house a minute or so later.

"Are you sure it's all right for you to spend the night here?" she said as we walked to the door.

"Of course."

"I'm just a little worried because of that thing that happened the last time."

Since my father had moved in, Marina hadn't spent the night at my house because I felt a little awkward about it. I'd spent several nights at hers, though far fewer than I had in the past, because I didn't want to leave my father alone regularly. A couple of nights ago, I got home in the morning to find my father in a panic. He hadn't remembered that I told him I wouldn't be coming home, and he seemed disoriented over where he was. It was the first time I had seen him like this. We all had serious concerns over his physical condition, but his mind had always seemed absolutely sound. I watched him carefully after that, but it seemed to be an isolated incident. Since then, he'd seemed sharp and capable.

"He's fine," I said. We walked into the house and I took her in my arms. "He's also gotten between us way too much already tonight."

"The night's young," she said, kissing me deeply.

~~~~~~~~

There were very few things about Marina that I found annoying. That she woke up every morning to the Beatles' "Getting Better" was one of them.

"You're going to have to explain to me at some point why you bothered to spend the money for an alarm clock with an iPod dock if you were only going to listen to the same song all the time," I said groggily.

She reached over to switch the music to a talk radio station. This was all part of her ritual and its logic was completely elusive to me. "How else would I be able to wake up to it?"

She snuggled into my embrace. That this was also something we did every morning we were together more than compensated for having to listen to a minor Lennon-McCartney composition.

"I've missed this the last few days," I said.

"Me too," she said, kissing my neck. "Do you really think your father would be weird about my sleeping at your house?"

"I don't know. I haven't been very good at predicting his reaction to anything so far. I think I might be a little weird about it, though. There's just something strange about the two of us together like this while my father is sleeping down the hall."

She kissed me again. "That's cute in an uncharacteristically puritanical kind of way. If I were a different kind of girl, I might even think you were trying to hide me from him."

We lay in bed for a few more minutes with me stroking her hair and her brushing my upper arm with her fingernails. I was in absolutely no hurry to get up. When the radio announced that it was 6:45, Marina propped herself on one arm.

"We have to get into the shower," she said.

"Call in sick. You haven't called in sick once since we've been together."

She moved over my body to get to the bathroom. "That's because I actually take my job seriously."

"I can't believe you're blowing me off for Kendall Blevins."

She turned back and kissed me on the cheek. "He's more dedicated to me. Go put the coffee on."

Once Marina was out of bed, I had no trouble getting out myself. I went down to the kitchen to make coffee before returning to the bathroom to shower with her. There was a very clear pattern to our mornings. After this we'd have a quick breakfast together before climbing into our cars and heading off in opposite directions. It was all very comfortable and comforting. Marina had organically introduced me to a way of starting the day that left me ready for whatever challenges awaited.

She wore the scarf I bought her. I was glad both that she did it and that she seemed happy to be doing it.

"Write something brilliant with your new pen today," she said, kissing me, as she was got into her car.

"I'm working on a piece about haggling with contractors."

She wrinkled her nose. "Save the pen for something else."

I leaned over and kissed her again before getting into my car. While waiting at a traffic light, I reached over and took the pen from its box. It was a beauty with a rosewood case, brass clip, and a gold-plated nib. It would be one of the most impressive in my collection.

Six months. We'd been together for half a year and still everything seemed both fresh and familiar. We fell into natural patterns. We seemed to know when the other was looking for a big night or some quiet time with a glass of wine. We always seemed to want to see the same movies. Even our newspaper reading behaviors were complementary.

I suppose the thing that made it easiest was that we were both completely willing to let the relationship unfold a day at a time. I thought for another second about the way she had used the phrase the night before, and wondered if perhaps I was missing its implications. I decided that she was just teasing me.

It amazed me that we didn't have a ponderous conversation about our future at a landmark moment such as last night. On our half-year anniversary, Karen and I even talked about it during intercourse, alternating gasps of passion with images of a domestic future. Of course two months later, on our last day together, we didn't exchange a single word.

I thought about Larry, the guy Marina had been involved with for four years. I never met him, but I had a vivid picture in my mind. By the time Marina and I started dating, she'd been split from Larry for more than a year, but he still dominated our early conversations. From the way she described it, Marina had surrendered all of herself to the relationship. He was the first guy she had dated for any real length of time and she didn't hold anything back. She became best friends with his sister and she made dinner for his parents once a week. She redecorated his house and let him reinvent her wardrobe. She even left her first school district a year short of tenure because he complained that it was too far away from where they lived.

Larry asked Marina to move in with him after they had been together for only a month. Three months later, they were engaged. Marina went into full bridal mode, scouting places

for a reception, tearing photographs of dresses from magazines, visiting bakeries and florists, even going to other people's receptions to listen to their bands. The wedding date itself remained elusive, though. First it was the next May. Then
September. Then the June after that. Through it all, Marina
approached the relationship as though she and Larry were already married. Sure, there were rough patches and times when
Larry's business trips backed up on one another and it seemed
that she never got to see him. Whether he was around or not,
though, there were always Wednesday nights with his parents
and the daily phone conversations with his sister. She was a
full-fledged member of the family.

It took four years for Marina to learn why the wedding
date never arrived. Each postponement marked a point when
Larry was starting another affair. It turned out that Larry
was in love with falling in love, and while it appeared that he
genuinely cared about Marina (certainly enough to keep her
around), he couldn't resist being seduced by a new romance.
Marina believed that some twisted sense of devotion actually
allowed him to convince himself that he truly wanted Marina in the long term, and so he kept postponing the marriage
without canceling the engagement. My own opinion was that
he knew he could keep Marina standing by as a backup.

This was of course based on nothing other than my affection for Marina, but it is supported by what ultimately happened to them. One night, Larry came home and confessed
all the other relationships. He also announced that he had met
his soulmate and that, much as it devastated him to say it, he
could no longer be with Marina. Interestingly, Larry and the
soulmate lasted only four months before she walked out on
him. Larry was smart enough not to ask Marina to take him
back.

I was only the second guy Marina dated after Larry. It took
her close to a year to even consider the notion of going out with
anyone. I have to believe that if she knew we would be together
six months later, she would have avoided any contact with me at

all. Like everything else about us, though, the circumstances just fell into place. Neither of us wanted anything more from the other than what we were already getting, and as a result, we got much more than we expected. For what must have been the thousandth time, I told myself how lucky I was to have discovered her.

Our houses were about fifteen minutes apart, and the drive back in the morning allowed me to get ready for the day. I never woke up at Marina's in the mood to work. I didn't know whether her mattress was just a little softer, the room just a little warmer, or that she was just a little more relaxed in her home environment, but I always felt like lingering. As I turned into my neighborhood, I would do the freelance journalist's equivalent of getting my game face on. I'd review the work I'd done the previous day, set a target for this day, and mentally prepare a to-do list of phone calls and minor business details that required attention. By the time I arrived home, I was ready to turn on the computer and kick into action.

On this morning, though, the smell of scorched eggs undermined my plans. My first thought was that my father had done to my kitchen what he had done to his own. As it turned out, that wasn't entirely the case. I found him standing at the stove, attempting to flip what I assumed to be an omelet (with a metal spatula on my nonstick pan, but we won't go into that). The eggs had barely begun to set and he was holding the pan off of the heat, which caused the eggs to run onto the burner. The burner diagonally across from him was also on, for no discernible reason. Plumes of smoke rose up from where the eggs hit the flame. There were also cracked eggshells at a variety of locations on the countertop and spatters of bacon grease everywhere.

"What are you doing?" I yelled as I entered the kitchen. He was obviously so bent on his futile efforts that he hadn't heard me come into the room. My voice startled him to drop the pan, inverting the rest of the eggs onto the burner.

"What are you doing?" I repeated as I rushed over to the stove to pick up the pan, turn off the gas (both burners), and use the spatula to shovel the mess.

"I was fine until you startled me," he said.

"Yeah, I noticed." I got most of the eggs into the pan and dumped them in the garbage. "Did you want to see if you could make more friends at the fire department?"

"I wasn't going to start a fire. You talk to me like I'm a total incompetent."

"Dad, you're very competent at a lot of things, but leaving you alone in a kitchen is like leaving a toddler alone with a chainsaw. Why couldn't you just have cereal or something?"

"I wanted eggs."

"And you couldn't wait until I got home?"

"I never know when you're coming home in the morning."

"I come home the same time every morning I'm with Marina. She leaves to go to work at 7:45. It takes me fifteen minutes to get here, seventeen if I hit traffic." I looked over at the clock. "See? 8:05."

"Well who the hell looks at the clock when you get home?"

I cleaned off the burner and the pan and pulled the egg tray back out of the refrigerator. There were only three eggs left in there. I was sure there had been close to a dozen the day before. I could only imagine where the others had gone.

I used the time it took me to pull out a new bowl, crack the eggs into it, and scramble them with a whisk to attempt to bring my blood pressure down.

"What did you want in your omelet?" I said calmly.

"I don't want an omelet anymore."

"Dad, just tell me what you want in the stupid omelet."

He sneered. "Surprise me."

I started cooking and he went off to a neutral corner. Neither of us spoke again until I gave him his plate and poured myself a cup of coffee. As usual, the coffee he'd made was pallid. I suppose I should have been thankful that he hadn't found a way to turn that process into a disaster as well.

I sat down at the kitchen table with him while he ate, no longer quite ready to get to work.

"It's good, thanks," he said after eating a bite.

"You're welcome."

He ate a little more. I could tell from the way he was approaching the meal that he had something on his mind.

"Why haven't I met her yet?"

"Met who?" I said, though I of course knew who he was talking about.

"The girl."

"The girl? You mean Marina?"

"Is that her name? How would I know her name?" He didn't do petulant well.

"Because I've mentioned it several times."

"Why haven't I met her?"

"I don't know. I haven't met her parents either. We're not really at that stage."

"How long have you been going out with her?"

"Around six months."

He put his fork down. "You've been going out with her for six months and you don't think you're at the stage where she should meet your father? You're sleeping with her, right?"

"No, I sleep in the guest room. We put on our feety pajamas and drink hot chocolate first, though."

He gave me the look. "If you're sleeping with her, you're at the stage where she should meet your father."

"Hmm, I've got some news for you, Dad."

"Don't be a smartass. What I mean is that if you've been sleeping with her for six months, I should know who she is."

"Why is this important to you?"

"It's what you do."

"Really? Is there an official set of rules? My game didn't come with any."

He sneered again. "Most people don't need rules. They just know that it's the proper thing to do."

I didn't want to have this conversation any longer. I didn't want to try to reconcile my relationship with Marina with his retro sensibility. I had absolutely no chance of success, and I wasn't even enjoying parrying with him on this subject.

"If you really want to meet Marina, I'll set it up. I'm supposed to see her tomorrow night. Are Thursdays okay for meeting parents for the first time, or is that exclusively a weekend thing?"

He just grumbled again and took his plate to the sink. I assumed that meant that Thursdays were fine. I couldn't wait to tell Marina about our change in plans. She was going to love this.

Chapter Seven

Mickey was never the kind of guy who ran his life like clockwork. When he was a broker, he never had distinct patterns to calling clients or checking the boards. He wasn't somebody who expected dinner on the table at 6:30 or the kids in bed by 9:00 or a Sunday drive that commenced at exactly 11:10. Mickey believed that kind of precision made you inflexible, and if you were inflexible, you were not very strong.

All the same, ever since Dorothy died, he found himself on the phone with Theresa at precisely 9:05 every morning. He convinced himself that there was nothing prescribed about this. Theresa liked watching those morning shows and they ended at nine. He didn't want to disturb her, and he also knew that she'd need a few minutes to wash up the breakfast dishes afterward. So to Mickey, he was simply calling Theresa "first thing" and nothing more.

Theresa had come into the world five years after Mickey, the last of Michael and Anna Sienna's four children. Between Mickey and Theresa had been Paulie, who had been sick from birth and passed away before Theresa was born, and Teddy, who died in Okinawa. As the only girl, Theresa was Anna's partner and a bauble for her father to adorn and admire. By the time she was four, she would spend hours in the kitchen with her mother, making pasta, kneading bread, mixing meatballs, and endlessly stirring the sauce. When the meals were ready, before she would sit at the dinner table, she would run to her room to change into one of the dozens of lace-trimmed dresses that her father just couldn't help but buy her.

Mickey could understand his father's fascination. There was just something luminous about his little sister. She was tiny, her voice was reedy and very high (something she retained even into adulthood), and she seemed to smile whenever she spoke. The result was that she appeared elfin and even somewhat otherworldly. Mickey found her mystifying and precious. There was little doubt in his mind that Theresa was the special one in the family. She got the best grades in school, made the most friends, and even somehow seemed exempt from the endless and often cruel teasing that the neighborhood boys foisted on all the other girls.

She was charming and she was charmed. Until Jackie Pandolfo came along. If Michael and Mickey could have designed the ideal man to court Theresa, it would have been Jackie. He loved his mother and he had a good job at the shoe store. He was polite and deferential, but he knew how to defend himself, and could kick back with a few beers and talk sports. Most importantly, he revered Theresa and made it clear to the entire world that he considered himself the luckiest guy on the planet to be with her.

Perhaps Jackie really couldn't believe his good fortune. Perhaps he was convinced that eventually Theresa was going to realize that he wasn't in her league. Mickey considered a lot of theories about what led up to that July night when Jackie saw Theresa innocently trading pleasantries with Victor Trulio. Victor had a reputation for stealing girls' hearts, and Jackie clearly thought that he was in the process of taking Theresa's. Mickey had no idea what snapped in Jackie, but the man he had begun to think of as his future brother-in-law swooped down and pulled Theresa away and demanded that they leave the party immediately. Theresa never made it home that night. She stumbled back in the early morning, badly beaten and sexually abused. They never found Jackie at all.

It took years of medical attention and psychiatric care to bring Theresa back in any way, and not all of her ever returned. The glimmer in her eyes, if it still existed at all, hid under lids that never seemed to open more than half way. What was left of her smile was reserved for ironic laughter. Sixty cigarettes a day eventually eroded the girlish voice.

After that, the only person unrelated by blood who was truly allowed into Theresa's world was Dorothy. As she had with so many others, Dorothy seemed to act as a salve on Theresa's psychic wounds. Dorothy was able to reach Theresa enough to let her know that she was a safe harbor, that she wouldn't threaten Theresa in any way, and that she wouldn't ever inflict the well-intentioned torture of trying to bring out the magical creature who once resided in her body. For years, this played out as long sessions across a kitchen table with coffee and crumb cake and quiet conversation. It moved Mickey to see Theresa responding to anyone and he adored Dorothy for making the effort. Eventually, Dorothy brought Theresa into her afternoon social circle. Theresa started cooking again. She got a job that she held for thirty years at a candy factory. She and Dorothy even went on a cruise together – just the two "girls" – for Theresa's sixtieth birthday. Theresa's smile never again electrified the way it had when she was young, but at least it was now something more than an embittered reflection of the past.

Theresa called Dorothy her sister, never appending it with "in-law." They saw each other or talked on the phone practically every day for the last forty-eight years of Dorothy's life. As a result, Mickey associated his wife's memory more closely with his sister than he did even with his children. At first he called Theresa daily just to continue the tradition, doing it, in effect, for Theresa's sake. But he soon learned that talking to Theresa gave him access to a part of Dorothy. He could almost hear her on the line with them.

"I think I'm going to go to the movies this afternoon to see 'Affair of the Soul,'" she said. "That stiff man with the bad hair on TV made it sound good. Want to come with me?"

"What guy with the bad hair? They all have bad hair. The one on 'Good Morning America?'"

"No, the one on the 'Today' show. What's wrong with the man's hair on 'Good Morning America?'"

"You think that's the way hair is supposed to look? It's like he's wearing a helmet."

"You never have anything nice to say about celebrities. Have you noticed that? So do you want to come with me or what?"

Mickey thought he wouldn't mind going to the movies, though he didn't feel particularly safe in a car with Theresa anymore. She had never been a careful driver, and lately her declining vision had exacerbated the problem.

"What's it about?" he said.

"It's a love story. About these two people whose souls touch until a tragedy tears them apart. It sounds very sad."

"Yeah, just my kind of movie. I think I'll pass."

"Suit yourself. I was just looking for a little company. Did I tell you that Maggie is in the hospital?"

"No, what's wrong?"

"They don't know. They're running tests. She went to the doctor because she wasn't feeling well, and they decided to keep her for a few days."

Mickey rolled his eyes. He knew this kind of story all too well.

"I hope the doctors know what they're doing," he said. "Did her sons come in from Baltimore?"

"I don't think she's told them about it yet. You know Maggie. She doesn't want anyone to worry about her. Except me, of course. She tells me everything."

Mickey laughed. In the last few years, Theresa had become something of a confessor for all of the seniors in her apartment building. He got the impression that she enjoyed it, though she would never admit that. To Mickey it was a sign that, all these years later, the healing process still continued.

"So how's Jesse?"

"Great. He's bringing his girlfriend over for dinner tonight."

"Now that's interesting. Is he serious about her?"

"I guess he must be if he's bringing her to meet me. You know what he's like."

Mickey could imagine Theresa nodding on the other end of the phone.

"So you're settling in over there?"

"Pretty much. Jesse can give me a headache sometimes, but he's a good kid. I can tell that he's really going out of his way."

"You're lucky. Dorothy raised her children right."

"Thanks for the compliment."

"I guess you did okay, too. What have you heard from Darlene lately?"

"Ah, she's so busy. She's got the garden club to run and she puts that program together at the library. I guess she has extra incentive now that Carla is having a baby. It's still hard to believe I'm going to be a great grandfather. I wish Dorothy were around for this. She'd love it. Darlene told me the other day that Earl is in line for a promotion and that they might be traveling to Asia together on business later this year. She's made quite a life for herself."

"When was the last time you talked to her?"

"The other day, I don't know, a couple of weeks ago. She's been trying to get me to sign up for this Facebook thing. She says we would be in better touch that way. Seems ridiculous to me."

"And Matthew is good?"

"He sounds great. Rings in almost every day. He'll call a little before ten when he gets to the office out there. He always sounds like there are a hundred things going on in his head, even though he's just walked in the door. He's taken on a lot of responsibility at that place. I certainly hope they appreciate what they have with him. I told him he should come back to New York, that they'd pay a guy like him three times what he's making."

"He certainly knows what he wants."

"Always has. Never had to worry about that one. He'll never earn what Denise makes, but he does okay."

"Is Denise still working for that company in Manhattan?"

"Has an entire division reporting to her now. She's going to make president some day if she plays her cards right. Though I don't know how Brad is going to feel about that. He's probably going to be the head of a company himself in a few years, but I wonder how he'll take having a wife that successful. Lotta guys can't handle it."

"Well, how would you have felt if it was Dorothy?"

Mickey hesitated for only a moment and then said, "I would have been fine with it. Not that it ever would have been Dorothy. But if she had been interested in that kind of stuff, it would have been fine with me."

It hardly mattered to Mickey that he had virtually the same conversation with Theresa every morning. It was all part of the ritual – talk about the kids, talk about what you were going to do that day, sprinkle reminiscences of Dorothy throughout. It was as welcome a morning habit as that super-gourmet coffee his son had him drinking these days.

"So are you coming to the movies with me or not?" Theresa said.

"You're really going to see that affair movie?"

"We could see something else if you want. It just sounded good."

Mickey thought a moment longer and then said, "Nah, you'd better go without me. If I'm meeting Jesse's girlfriend tonight, I don't want to be tired from being out all day."

He got off the phone a few minutes later after hearing about Ted Cranston's gall bladder problem. Once he hung up, he wondered if maybe he should have told Theresa that he'd go to the movies with her. She hated to go anywhere by herself, and she'd probably wind up not going at all now that he said he wouldn't come along. But how could she possibly think he'd be up for that "Affair of the Soul" thing? Theresa more than anyone should know that wasn't his kind of movie.

Mickey made his way from the den to his bedroom. The knees were killing him today. If his kids didn't get so hysterical every time he mentioned an ache or a pain, he'd get Jesse to take him to the doctor for some pills or something. It didn't really matter, though. It wouldn't hurt as much in a day or so. That's the way it had been for a long time.

He walked over to the wrought iron sculpture that sat on the night table and touched it for a moment. After the move, Jesse asked him about it as though he'd never seen it before, even though it had been in the house the entire time he lived there. It had been in the china cabinet – easy enough to miss, Mickey supposed. It was one of the few times that Jesse had complimented him on his taste. Of course it was a backhanded compliment. "It's so unlike you," he recalled his son saying.

The box was on the floor in his closet, which meant that he was going to have to go down on his knees to get to it. He tried to do this as slowly as possible, but it still felt like the freaking Inquisition. Mickey really wanted to talk to her today, though. To hell with the pain. He felt like talking to her on most days, but he was less inclined to go through the physical rigors on some than others. Theresa got him going this morning, though. Talking about that stupid movie. Like anyone in Hollywood had any idea of what they were talking about. He never saw a love story that ever got it right, and he doubted very seriously that this one would be the first.

The photograph sat on top of the pile as it always did. He pulled it out and then slowly uncoiled himself to stand up. It probably would have made more sense to just sit there with the picture so he wouldn't have to go through this again when he replaced it, but he didn't want to be on the floor with her. He sat on the bed.

Mickey took a moment to admire her beauty. She was still the most stunning woman he had ever seen. The years couldn't change that. Certainly no starlet on a movie screen could ever compare. Then he closed his eyes. He sometimes wondered why he bothered to pull out the picture if he wasn't going to look at it while he talked to her, but the connection just felt stronger this way.

"You want to know something funny?" he said to the image in his head. "I've been thinking a lot the last couple of days about Jenny Hirschberg. You remember her? She worked in my office and she always used to come by to say hello when you visited. Remember how she used to have a new boyfriend just about every week? She just kept going through men, trying to find a husband.

"'I'm just looking for someone to grow old with,' she'd say. Remember that? I'm sure I told you because she said it to me so many times. 'I'm just looking for someone to grow old with.' Like that was all there was to love and marriage. Find someone who you'd be comfortable talking to about your arthritis or your failing vision or your creaky knees. Boy, if that was all she was looking for, she probably could have gone out and picked someone off the street.

"Anyway, I've been thinking about that lately because I've been wondering what people are really looking for anyway. I never gave it much thought myself because it just happened. But, you know, I'm meeting Jesse's girlfriend tonight, and he's just never seemed to have any idea of what he's after. I guess I'm just wondering if you ever really know. I certainly didn't know that I was looking for you."

Mickey tilted his head back further, his closed eyes pointed toward the ceiling.

"Do you ever get tired of hearing me tell you how much I love you? Do you ever think that I'm boring because I say the same things to you over and over again? If you do, I'll stop.

"No, that's not really true. I wouldn't stop even if you wanted me to because I can't stop. I could never stop."

Mickey opened his eyes and admired her picture again. How could anyone ever have been so beautiful? What would he trade to have her here now?

He was looking directly at the photograph now. "So I wonder who this girl is, anyway. I hope she's nicer than that last one he brought home. What a nightmare she was. Not that it would have mattered, but I was getting ready to say something about the way she treated him when they broke up. The kid doesn't seem to have a lot of common sense when it comes to women.

"Well, I'll know a whole lot more by the end of the day. I'll tell you all about it tomorrow. I'll try not to be too judgmental. I know you don't like that."

He gazed upon the picture a few moments longer. Then he labored to his feet and carefully put the photo back in its place in the box. He lingered over it for several minutes, not as much looking at it as absorbing it. At last, he moved the box flaps back into position.

"Save a place at the table for me," he said before he closed the closet door.

Chapter Eight

This being a big night, I chose the menu carefully. I'd quit working early in the afternoon so I could spend the necessary hours making the mole poblano. I chose the mole with my father in mind; I knew he didn't like Mexican food.

I was still peeved about the conversation that led to my planning this whole dinner. It wasn't as though I was deliberately keeping him away from Marina. I just didn't want to make a big deal out of it. I figured he'd ultimately meet her at Easter or something like that if Marina and I were still together. Or maybe she'd just stop by after school sometime. Something casual, unrehearsed, decidedly not an event. I'd meet her parents – or not – in a similar fashion. Now, of course, it had turned into a major thing. My father had mentioned it to me half a dozen times that day alone, asking me about Marina's background, her family, and what she did for a living. When he finally asked my opinion of the shirt he was considering wearing that night, I began to wonder if he'd called CNN. I'm not sure what had him so wired. I'd made it as clear to him as I could that he wasn't meeting his future daughter-in-law. Still, he was bubbling with anticipation. There were so many things about him that I didn't understand.

Marina was decidedly more relaxed about coming to dinner than I was about her coming.

"Well, I was sort of wondering when I was going to get to meet the legendary Mickey Sienna," she said when I told her about the tiff that had led to the invitation.

"Hopefully he'll be frustrating and confounding for you. If he isn't, you won't have really met him."

"Don't worry, Jesse, even if he isn't I'll still take your side." She kissed me on the cheek and added, "Unless, of course, he's nicer to me than you are. Then I might have to switch alliances."

"Yeah, well, while we're on that subject, there's something you need to know," I said seriously. "I'm different when I'm with members of my family than I am at other times."

She looked at me bemusedly. "Do you use baby talk?"

"Anything is possible. I just tend to get out of character. A lot of times it means that I get really quiet. It used to be like that with my father, too, although lately I tend to get into these verbal sparring matches." I thought about it for a moment and added, "To the casual observer, this could be interpreted as being mean-spirited, though I know you know that I wouldn't be deliberately mean to anyone."

"No, I think that your making a dinner that you know your father is going to hate is an extremely compassionate act. I don't see how anyone could interpret it differently."

That night, Marina arrived at 6:30. She'd changed from work clothes to jeans and the white sweater I loved beyond anything else in her wardrobe. There was something about the way her black, shoulder-length curls fell against the soft white sweater that I found incredibly appealing. She kissed me and I drew her into a hug. I held her longer than I usually did, partially because I was so turned on by the way she looked, and partially because the longer I held her the longer it would be before we got on with the rest of the evening. Before we separated I whispered in her ear, "Excuse yourself to go to the bathroom. I'll meet you outside in fifteen minutes. He'll never know what happened."

With that, she gently pushed me away, gave me a little kiss, and turned to my father, who was treading up to the door. He was wearing a smile on his face I had never seen before. Certainly I'd never seen him smile like that when I'd introduced him to other women.

"I've been so looking forward to meeting you, Mr. Sienna," Marina said, extending her hand.

"It's Mickey, dear," my father said, "and the pleasure is all mine." He grasped her hand and held it with both of his. He didn't let go immediately.

"Jesse's told me so much about you."

"Well, he talks about you all the time." My father glanced at me to make sure I understood that he was exaggerating for my benefit. He still hadn't let go of Marina's hand. "But I'm sure there's so much more to know. Why don't we sit down and you can tell me all about yourself." He slipped his arm into hers and brought her over to the living room couch. I walked with them, but my father turned to me and said, "You have cooking to do or something, don't you?"

I could swear he was speaking in a different register. His speech even seemed to have a different cadence. Was this my father's idea of being smooth? Was this how he chatted up the ladies at Senior Citizens meetings? I couldn't believe he was putting on an act for Marina. It dawned on me that he was doing this as a way to invalidate whatever he assumed I'd told her about him. He probably figured if he was charming enough, she'd never believe me when I bitched about him in the future.

Though I wanted to stay to see the next act in my father's performance – especially since he had all but banished me from the room – I actually did have responsibilities in the kitchen. Of course, I could hear most of what they were saying anyway. My father rarely spoke quietly, and this was true of his new alter ego as well. It sounded as though Marina was also speaking a little louder than usual so I could hear her. My father let Marina do most of the talking – about school, about her students, about her family – interrupting only to ask another question or to make an observation such as, "Dedication is one of the most admirable qualities in a human being. But obviously I don't need to tell you that." I had never heard him speak this way before. With Mom, he had always been respectful but commanding. With us kids, he had always been provocative and challenging. He treated Matty's wife Laura the way one might treat a favorite niece, with smiles and appreciation masking the fact that he didn't consider her to be an equal. But he was fawning over Marina. He was either mocking me in some subtle way, or he was trying to make a move on her.

This went on for a while and I stayed in the kitchen getting dinner ready. I was increasingly glad I'd made the mole. That would draw him out of this character. If the past couple of months were any indication, my father just couldn't pass up the opportunity to suggest that nothing of value had ever come from any cuisine other than Italian or French.

Eventually, Marina excused herself to check in with me.

"You didn't tell me he was so handsome," she whispered as she walked into the room.

"He's craggy and stooped and twenty pounds overweight. You go for that?"

"He has gorgeous eyes."

"It figures you noticed that. Has he broken eye contact with you once since you walked in the door?"

Marina laughed. "Your father is very charming."

"That's not my father. It's his body out there, but his soul has been whisked away on an alien starship. Don't get too close to him. God knows what their mission is on our planet."

She pulled the wooden spoon out of my hand and put her arms around me. I kissed her softly, and our heads stayed close together afterwards. It was one of my favorite ways to talk to her.

"You look spectacular tonight," I said.

She smiled. "Your father has better lines."

I pulled her a little tighter. "No, I mean it. Will you wear this sweater every time we're together?" I kissed her again, more passionately this time.

She purred a little. "I was about to dump you for your old man. Maybe I'll reconsider."

I kissed her one more time and then said, "You'd better get back out there. If not, he'll come in here looking for you and it really is best for all of us if he spends as little time in the kitchen as possible."

She gave me another peck on the lips and left. I watched her as she walked into the living room. I'd always thought of Marina as attractive, but she seemed to be getting even more beautiful to me. I'd never had that experience before.

~~~~~~~~

I should have known that my father would love the mole. That was the way things were going to be this night. I kept looking for signs that he was hiding his food in his napkin or throwing it on the floor, but it was obvious he was really enjoying it.

"This is really excellent, Jesse," he said. "Never had chicken like this before."

Marina nodded. "I love Mexican food. There's nothing like it in the world."

My father smiled at Marina. "Yes, it's wonderful. I've been meaning to try more of it."

I choked back the urge to remind him about the guacamole he'd rejected the first week he was here or the salsa verde that he told me tasted like soap. I also resisted the urge to snicker when he followed this up with, "I think it's critical that you keep exploring new things. It keeps you young." Marina of course had no idea how bull-headed and stuck in his ways he could be, so she missed the irony.

"I couldn't agree with you more," she said. "It's even true for people my age. You have to keep yourself open to everything that's around you. I wish more people understood that as they matured."

"They just haven't had the right teachers." My father was practically crooning. I figured the aliens had taken his soul all the way to Pluto by now.

I reached out for Marina's leg under the table and gave it a gentle squeeze. It was partly to comment on my father's performance. But it was also simply because I wanted to touch her. I'd been doing it all night. There was something going on here. It could have been my own reaction to getting the two of them together. It could have been relief that – as ludicrous as his display was – he obviously liked Marina (I'll never forget the disastrous day when he met Karen for the first time). It could have been the way she looked that night. Or it could have been the arousing qualities of chocolate and chiles. But I found myself being much more openly affectionate with Marina than I normally was. I liked sitting at a dinner table with her and my father. I liked having her entertain him while I finished the meal. I liked the fact that she was my girlfriend and welcomed my touch. It was all very exciting to me. Like when Jill Somers came to my family graduation party after I'd taken her to the senior prom.

For dessert, Marina brought out the apple pie she'd made, and served it with her own caramel ice cream. Just in case my father wasn't already convinced that she was the most perfect woman in the world, she gave him an extra scoop of ice cream after she brought out the plates. His expression redefined the term "goofy." At that moment, he looked like the oldest pre-adolescent on the planet.

It probably would have been a good night to break the ice regarding the sleeping arrangements, but we had definitely not planned ahead for this. There was no way of really knowing what my father was going to be like, and I had envisioned a scenario where things had gone so badly that I wound up going back to Marina's house with her. The upshot was that about an hour and a half after dinner was over, Marina told us she had to leave.

"Don't go on my account," my father said, standing as she did. "I'm going to go to bed soon anyway, so the two of you can have the house to yourselves."

Marina took his hand and smiled. "Thanks, but I really do have to go. I have some tests to grade before I go to sleep tonight."

"I hope those children know how lucky they are," he said. He then kissed her hand and I was certain a reptilian thing was going to leap out of his chest at any moment. Marina pulled him toward her and pecked him on the cheek. I could swear he blushed a little.

I put my arm around Marina's shoulder and walked her out to her car.

"That went okay, huh?" she said.

"I think he's gone back to his room to write you into his will."

"He's a nice guy."

"He sure was tonight."

She pulled me close to her. "I had a good time."

"Yeah, me too. Imagine that."

"I'm glad we did this."

We kissed for a long time. I didn't want her to leave. In fact, I didn't want anything but to stand there and kiss her. Eventually, she pulled back and informed me that she really did have tests to grade. We kissed once more, and then again after she got into the car. I waited until she drove down the block before going back into the house.

My father was waiting for me just inside the door.

"That's some woman," he said.

"She's pretty great, isn't she?"

I walked toward the kitchen to clean up. My father didn't clean. He didn't feel it was in his job description. He did what he often did, though, which was to sit at the kitchen table while I cleaned.

"So what are your intentions with her?" he said.

"Intentions?"

"Yes, what are your intentions?"

"Dad, I think people stopped using that term about three days after the invention of the wheel."

"You know what I'm saying. What are your plans?"

I shrugged. "We don't talk about plans, except for restaurant reservations or movie schedules. We're just taking it a day at a time." Again, I was reminded of the way Marina had said those words a few weeks back. I was going to have to start using a different phrase.

"You do realize that this is a very special woman, don't you?"

"I could see that you liked her."

"It would be a mistake to let her get away."

"I'm not letting her get away, Dad. We're just not really doing 'plans' or 'intentions.' You know most relationships eventually don't work out. We're just being realistic."

"Don't be a fool."

He said this so sharply that I turned off the faucet and looked at him.

His eyes narrowed as he spoke. "Are you telling me that you think that Marina is just another woman?"

"Dad, if I thought she was just another woman, I wouldn't have been with her for the past six months. I just think it's silly to get caught up in a bunch of romantic notions."

"Like that would be the worst thing that could happen to you."

"It's just not necessary. Marina and I really like each other. We have a great time together. We've managed to continue to have a great time together without making any promises to be together until the end of the world."

He waved his hand at me dismissively, got up from the table, and walked away. I turned back to the sink. A few moments later, he was back and he reached over to turn off the faucet.

"I've got something I want to tell you," he said abruptly.

I tilted my head toward him and gave him my best look of impatience. "I can't wait."

His gaze held mine for a moment. There was so much disapproval in his expression. I started to feel a little chastened.

"Nah, you don't deserve it."

He walked away again.

I stood there for a short while awaiting his return. When it became clear that he wasn't coming back, I resumed cleaning the dishes.

Chapter Nine

Tom Postron is a friend and, in the loosest definition of the term, a colleague. Six years ago, we did a panel together at a writer's conference. Afterward, we had a drink and wound up hanging out for the rest of the weekend. Back then, Tom was simply a hot young assistant editor for a major newsmagazine. Within a couple of years, though, he had signed on as Features Editor for the online startup *Tapestry*. It seemed to be a risky move, since he was fast-tracking at his other job, online magazines were an unknown quantity, and no one could tell how long the new magazine would keep publishing. But *Tapestry* captured the imaginations of a great demographic group and Tom's decision looked pretty shrewd. It looked like genius two years later when the Editor-in-Chief decided to move to Montana and Tom was handed the mantle. Three years older than me, he controlled what most writers of my generation considered the best outlet available for feature pieces.

I'd done exactly one item for Tom, and it was little more than a sidebar as a follow-up to something another writer had done a few issues before. I took it at the time as a way in the door with *Tapestry*, but while the door remained open, I hadn't found the legs with which to walk through it. I'd pitched Tom on dozens of stories, several of which I ultimately sold elsewhere, but I couldn't seem to find anything that clicked with him. Still, we stayed in regular e-mail communication, talked on the phone fairly often, and had lunch three or four times a year. Which was the agenda for that morning's call.

"Hey Jess, what's up?" he said when he came on the line.

"Just calling to see if I can get on the jam-packed Tom Postron lunch calendar sometime before the turn of the next century."

"No exaggeration allowed this early in the morning, Jess. You know I'm never booked more than a year or so in advance."

"Yeah, your accessibility is obviously one of the keys to your whirlwind success."

Tom laughed and then paused. I assumed he was looking at his calendar.

"How's the eighth?" he said.

"The eighth of what month?"

"The eighth of next month. Or was I being presumptuous? Are you booked-out several months yourself?"

"Well, I am in incredibly high demand, but let me see if I can move a few things around."

"Great, I'll pencil it in. So what are you working on these days?"

Just then, I heard my father on the other line. I assumed that Tom could hear him as well, and that he probably didn't need the phone to do so.

"Hey Theresa, how're you feeling today?" Dad said. He used the same line every morning, delivered at the same booming level. It was hard not to be distracted by it, and I usually didn't make phone calls first thing in the morning because of it. But with Tom, if you didn't get him before 9:30, you stood little chance of talking to him that day.

I focused back on the call. "A couple of things to pay the bills. I'm working on some more significant stuff, though. That's one of the reasons I wanted to get together."

"Well, I'm always interested in hearing your pitches. If you want to e-mail me some notes before we get together, go ahead."

"Yeah, well if you have a couple of seconds, I'd like to tell you about this one thing I'm thinking about."

"Shoot."

I stopped for a second to gather my thoughts. I always did this before pitching a story. Nothing frustrated editors more than hearing someone say, "Oh, wait a second, I forgot to mention" or, "Oh, right, there's this other thing."

As I was thinking, I heard my father say to my aunt, "It was great. He's got himself someone completely different this time."

He was obviously relating the details of the previous night's dinner with Marina. It threw me off for a second, but I shook it off.

"I'm thinking about doing a piece on Percy Kescham, the Newark kid who was drafted by the NBA right out of high school."

"Didn't he last for ten games or something like that?"

At the same time, my father said, "She's quite a looker and she seems very warm. I liked her right away."

It was impossible not to cock an ear toward the den under the circumstances, but I reminded myself that I was talking to *Tapestry* magazine.

"He actually stuck for the entire year," I said into the phone, "but by midseason he was something like the eleventh man on the roster. The Bucks cut him before the start of the next season, even though they had to eat a huge contract."

"So what's the story?"

"What do you mean 'what's the problem?'" my father said. "Why do you think there was a problem?"

I continued, though I was now extremely distracted by my father's conversation. "You flash forward a few years. The guy decides he's going to do something with his life. He gets his commercial real estate license. Last month he gets arrested for fraud. The kid's got a couple of million dollars in the bank, and he still gets messed up in a dirty scheme."

"That's it?" Tom asked.

At which point my father said, "Oh, it's just that Jesse is getting ready to screw things up with her, I can just tell. I can't believe he thought about marrying that crazy girl and he's playing it cool with this one. It's like he's learned nothing."

"Yeah," I said to Tom. "I'm seeing it as a cautionary tale. Here's a guy who believed he could do no wrong even, after the biggest thing in his life came crashing down. So he still acts like he's exempt from the rules and he gets busted."

"And why is my reader interested?"

My father's voice was getting louder, though one might have thought that was physically impossible. "I'm *not* getting excited about it. But you weren't here, Theresa. You didn't see them. I just can't believe he's gonna screw up with this great woman." He let out a bellow of exasperation. He seemed way more worked up about this than he should be. "It's like he wouldn't know love if it bit him on the leg."

I wasn't sure which conversation was going worse for me.

"I think this works on a few levels," I said to Tom. "You know, there are always issues about whether these kids should come right out of high school or not, and, you know, I think there's a certain segment that responds to icons – even little ones – going down."

"I'm not seeing it, Jess. That story has been told a million times before. If you dig deeper and learn something more about his character and what drove him in this direction, there might be something there, but you have to look at the story from that angle. It's a little bit like what I was telling you the last time we got together." He hesitated for a moment. "Jess, can you hang on a second?"

"Yeah, sure."

Tom got back on the line a minute or so later. "I've gotta run. The drama is starting a little early this morning. Should be a great day. I'll see you on the eighth, right?"

"Yeah, thanks."

I hung up the phone and heard my father talking to Theresa about someone from her apartment building. Both he and Tom had moved on.

~~~~~~~~

I almost wondered if my father had intended for me to overhear the conversation, though I overheard every conversation he had with my aunt. I was tempted to go out to talk to him after he got off of the phone, but I had a feeling that I wasn't going to enjoy the confrontation. I decided instead to try to get back to work on my article. It wasn't particularly easy to concentrate with his voice and Tom's still in my head, though.

Tom was probably right about the Percy Kescham story. There wasn't enough there that hadn't been presented in other ways at other times. I of course found this a little ironic considering that I was currently working on a piece that had probably appeared – in only somewhat different form – in hundreds of magazines over the years. However, feature writing was different and, while I saw myself long-term as a feature writer, I'd had a fair amount of trouble coming up with stories on my own. I'd only published about a half dozen major feature pieces in my career and they were by far the toughest pitches for me. A story idea would come to mind, I'd spend some time with it and I would think that I had something substantial. But for whatever reason, it wouldn't play out that way. I didn't want to believe that I was destined for a career of how-to stories, but every time a pitch went badly for me, I started to think that this might be where I was headed.

My father wasn't wrong about my romantic history, either. Back when I was actually looking for a life mate, I hadn't been particularly effective at choosing my partners. Both Georgia and Karen had been women whose greatest contribution to my life had been that they allowed me to express myself romantically. In retrospect, neither had offered me nearly as much in return, though this didn't mean that my own feelings were any less genuine. The other women I'd dated before Karen tended to be beautiful and emotionally unavailable. I just seemed to gravitate toward that kind of person.

Since Karen, the rules had changed for me as I retrofitted my view of romance to connect with the kind of woman I was drawn to. It no longer mattered that I went out with women who gave little of themselves, because I wasn't looking for much. Companionship, sex, something to get me out of the house. I was more sanguine about my romantic life than I had ever been before. I dated interesting women, we had a good time for a while, we moved on, and no hearts were injured during the filming of this production.

My father was too much the child of another era to understand how this could work for me. To him, guys were supposed to find mates, create families, make castles that they could be king of. Just as they were supposed to go to offices, collect paychecks, and build diversified portfolios. In my father's time, the only men who were single in their thirties were closet homosexuals and relentless womanizers, and "freelance" was code for "unemployed." About three or four years earlier, I'd told him that he shouldn't ever expect grandchildren from me and he looked at me like I had nine heads. To him, I wasn't playing the game the right way.

I'm sure I threw him off with Marina. Looking back on our conversations about her, I thought I'd made it clear that things were "committed casual" with us. But I'm sure he drew his own conclusions from our seeing each other several times a week for half a year.

There was no effective way for me to explain to him what I had with Marina. I wasn't fluent in the language, and he didn't know what most of the words meant anyway. How do you explain to someone who grew up with a very narrow definition of love and family that you agreed with him that the woman you were seeing was extraordinary but that you had prepared your heart for the end of the romance? How could he possibly understand that I assumed Marina would be my lover until the inevitable happened, after which I was hoping that she would be one of my best friends for the rest of my life? How could I think that he would see that as not only desirable, but preferable to a marriage that was likely to be filled with quiet desperation and at best would be nothing more than comfortable?

So I decided not to try. If my father wanted to bitch at my aunt about how I was missing the point, so be it. I wasn't going to bang my head against the wall trying to explain a healthy twenty-first century relationship to an antiquated mind like my father's.

It took me more than an hour, seven e-mail messages, and a couple more phone calls, but I finally got my head back into the article I'd been writing. At lunchtime, I walked out of my office to find him sitting on the couch watching the television with the sound practically off.

"Do you want some lunch?" I said.

He glanced up at me briefly and then returned his gaze to the television. I assumed that was his way of saying "no" and I went into the kitchen. When I got there, I saw a pot on one of the burners with less than an inch of furiously boiling water in it.

I called out to him. "What are you doing with the water?"

"I'm making something for myself."

"Something that has to do with boiling water until it evaporates completely?"

"I was just about to go in to take care of it. You need more pasta, by the way."

He shuffled toward me, avoiding eye contact as he did.

"Dad, I thought we agreed that I'd do the cooking in the house."

"I'll cook for myself. I don't like the way you cook."

"You didn't have any complaints last night."

"I was putting on a show for your 'girlfriend.'"

"No kidding. And it was a hell of a show. But I think she probably would have been convinced after your second helping. You didn't need to eat a fourth."

He grumbled. "I'll do my own cooking."

"Thanks for letting me know. I'll make sure the insurance on the house is up to date."

I started to make myself a sandwich. While I was at the refrigerator, I pulled out the container of bolognese (or "meat sauce," as my father referred to it – we didn't discuss the fact that the meat was ground turkey) that I'd made a few nights earlier. He was so damned set in his ways. Pasta came dressed with either meat sauce or marinara. God forbid I try anything else with him.

Meanwhile, he threw pasta into the water and walked back into the den. As much as I wanted to prove a point to him, I didn't feel like cleaning burnt pasta out of the pot, so I decided to wait around until it was ready. I put it in a dish for him with the sauce and left it on the kitchen table.

"Your lunch is ready," I said as I walked back into the den on my way to my office.

"I told you I'd take care of it."

"I know what you told me."

He got out of the chair slowly. Regardless of how peeved I was at him, I always felt a pang of sympathy watching him try to move on his failing legs. The doctors had told us that his only option was joint replacement, something my father had flatly rejected.

"I can take care of myself," he said as he walked past me.

"You're welcome," I said and started toward my office. I stopped and turned toward him. "By the way, I'm going to Marina's tonight. I'll be leaving around six. There's stuff in the refrigerator for you. If you're going to cook for yourself, I'd prefer if you did it while I was on the premises."

He stopped and looked back at me. "You spending the night over there?"

"Yes, I am."

He muttered something as he turned away. It wasn't until after I walked back to my office that I realized what he said.

It was, "You don't deserve her."

Chapter Ten

It was 7:43. Mickey sat at the kitchen table thinking that Jesse would be home in a few minutes. He was probably kissing Marina goodbye just about now, not appreciating her any more than he ever did.

Mickey wasn't sure exactly what it was about Marina. Sure, there was the passing physical resemblance, but you had to look awfully close to recognize it. The shape and set of their eyes. The tiny creases there. But there was something much deeper than that. It was the way that Marina seemed to embrace you simply by saying hello. The way she held Jesse when she greeted him. The way she regarded him when she first walked into the room that said she was thankful for his presence and that she cherished it. There is nothing more satisfying than having a woman look at you that way.

If Jesse couldn't identify that for what it was, Mickey felt sorry for him. "We're just being realistic," he had said. Was it possible for a second that Marina was as blind to this as he was? In some ways, Mickey hoped that was the case, because it would be less painful to her if his unenlightened son never came around. But Mickey really wanted things to turn out differently. Marina was a rare woman. That much had to be clear even to the casual observer. And Mickey wanted her to stay with his son – for both Jesse and himself.

Mickey appreciated the fact that Marina let him be a little flirtatious with her the other night. He didn't get the opportunity to spend much time around gorgeous women in their early thirties, and the encounter had tickled him. It was the first time he'd talked to a woman like that since Dorothy died. She used to tease him mercilessly about doing that kind of thing when she was alive. Even pretended to be jealous every now and again, though she knew without a doubt that she had nothing to worry about. From the moment he first talked to Dorothy, Mickey was sure about where his life was headed, and he wouldn't have compromised that for anything on Earth.

Mickey took another sip of coffee. So damned strong. He couldn't understand how his son could drink coffee like this all the time. Where the hell were his taste buds? Normally, if he got up before Jesse, Mickey made the coffee his way, but not this morning. He didn't want the conversation to get off track because Jesse was preoccupied with the "dirty water." The extra caffeine was probably beneficial, anyway. If he was going to get this story out, he was going to require a little additional stimulation.

A few minutes later, Jesse walked through the door. As usual, he bounded into the kitchen. How could he not notice that he even walked differently after spending the night with Marina?

"Hey Dad. Sleep okay?"

"Yeah, it was great," Mickey said. The fact was, he'd hardly slept at all in anticipation of this morning, but that was beside the point. "Grab a cup of coffee. I just made a pot."

"Ooh, Dad's secret recipe," Jesse said as he took a mug out of the cupboard. "I don't know how you get so much flavor into every drop."

Mickey bristled, but held back. His reward came moments later.

"Hmm, good," Jesse said, his brows arched. "Looks like the old man has made a breakthrough." He started to walk out of the kitchen. "I've got a ton of stuff to do today. I might have to work late tonight."

"Jess, come sit down for a couple of minutes."

Mickey could tell by Jesse's reaction that his son had picked up the nuance in his voice. He could also tell that Jesse wasn't enthusiastic about "a talk."

"Dad, I have a ton."

"I heard you the first time. There's something I'd like to tell to you about. Come sit with me for a few minutes."

From the expression on Jesse's face, you would think that Mickey had been holding a foot-long hypodermic needle in his hand when he'd extended his invitation.

"Can we do this tonight? Like maybe after dinner or something?"

Mickey appraised his son thoughtfully. Jesse held his gaze, but Mickey could tell that he was looking to run, and for more reasons than simply the deadline he needed to meet. Mickey knew that the handful of father/sons they'd had over the years had tended to go badly. But they'd never discussed anything like this before.

"Give me a few minutes now. This isn't what you think, I promise you that much. It isn't about you – at least not directly. It's about me."

He had Jesse's attention now. His son seemed less evasive and more apprehensive as he reluctantly sat down at the kitchen table.

"It's nothing like that. I'm not dying or anything. I just have a story I want to tell you, something that I haven't told your sisters or brother about. Something I haven't told anyone in a very long time. After seeing you and Marina, I realized you needed to know about this."

Jesse's expression changed again, and Mickey could tell that his son was expecting a lecture.

"Relax. This'll be painless. But you're going to have to keep an open mind because I know how close you were to your mother."

Jesse's eyes opened wide.

"And it's not that, either. I was always faithful to your mother. I don't believe that you can be any other way and still look at yourself in the mirror. But I think if you're lucky, you're blessed with one great love in your life, one person who makes the world a completely different place for you." He looked over to Jesse, a little less sure about how his son was going to receive this story.

"That person came to me before I ever met your mother and I want to tell you about her now."

~~~~~~~~

Manhattan was a place teeming with possibility. The war was a couple of years in the past, the country was on the road to unprecedented prosperity, and Manhattan was the beating heart of America, if not the entire world. For a young man with an education and a good head for numbers, the doors were wide open. Mickey Sienna was just such a man.

A problem with his right knee had kept Mickey out of active service during the war, though it hadn't kept tragedy from his family's doorstep. Mickey had made as much of a contribution as he could working in the communications office at the Brooklyn Navy Yards. While doing so, he had enough time on his hands to get a degree in business administration. He was the first person in his family to graduate college, which brought him their admiration but also set him apart from them. When the war ended, a friend mentioned that the brokerage firm of Quick, Banks, and Kay was looking for bright candidates for their training program and Mickey applied. Within six months, he was building a modest client base. The brokerage field was a natural for someone with Mickey's keen understanding of how different people regarded various levels of risk and reward. Soon, Mickey had earned the approval of his superiors, the respect (and some closeted envy) of his colleagues, and enough money to allow him to rent an apartment in a townhouse on Gramercy Park.

This elevated life suited Mickey well. As the son of a modest shopkeeper, he'd grown up in a home where there was always food on the table, but few luxuries. Now Mickey found that he enjoyed the taste of white Burgundy and the way his Brooks Brothers shirts draped his frame. He ate out regularly and danced to live jazz at least once a week.

The move from Brooklyn to Manhattan was more than a sign that Mickey was doing well at his job, though. It was also a symbolic step from his old world into a new one. There had been clouds over his family from the time Paulie died, but Teddy's death and Theresa's attack had cast a pall over his mother and father and seemingly the entire neighborhood. Mickey continued to visit his parents at least once a week, and he saw Theresa every two or three days, but he also knew that he needed to create a life for himself or he would wind up trapped by the despair.

Mickey found it easy to make friends within the quickly evolving financial community. There were so many young men in his same position and so many bright, attractive women to spend time with. There was always another dinner party to attend, always another Vassar graduate to walk arm-in-arm with. Settling down was the last thing on his mind, and he truly believed he could go on like this indefinitely.

Among his better friends at QBK was Carl Ceraf. They had gone through the training program together, and there was initially some competitive tension between them. But once they realized that there were plenty of clients to go around if you were aggressive enough and good enough, they began to socialize outside of the office. They'd double-dated on several occasions, went out for drinks together regularly, and spent many summer days at the Polo Grounds cheering on the Giants. Carl still lived in his family home because it was "the best deal in town." Mickey knew that the Cerafs had lived in Manhattan for three generations, that Carl's father was a professor at Columbia, and that Carl's sister was "the resident genius," but beyond that he knew very little. That all changed the night Carl invited him and "a couple dozen of our closest friends" to a cocktail party at the family house.

Mickey took Jessica Fain to the party. He had only a passing interest in Jessica, but she was the most sophisticated woman he dated and, while Carl himself was always casual in his demeanor, Mickey knew that this evening demanded the highest level of decorum. He was actually very excited, if a little intimidated, at the prospect of meeting the estimable Professor Ceraf. Little did he know that a far more fateful introduction awaited him.

Mickey and Jessica arrived some twenty minutes or so after the party had begun. There were probably twenty people already milling through the living room, where the bar was set up, the dining room, where various cold hors d'oeuvres were laid out on a table, and the den, where soft jazz played and people sat and talked. When he came through the door with Jessica, Carl broke away from a conversation to greet them.

"Mickey, great to see you," Carl said. "Jessica, you're looking statuesque as always." Mickey shook Carl's hand while Jessica offered a demure smile and a faint peck on the cheek. Carl escorted them into the house. Mickey knew several of the people there from work and was introduced by Carl to several others as "my partner in crime at QBK." They moved to the den, where Carl's father stood telling a story to two women in their early twenties.

"Dad, I'd like you to meet my friends Mickey Sienna and Jessica Fain," Carl said as they walked up. Daniel Ceraf turned, took Jessica politely by the hand, and welcomed her to his home. He then gripped Mickey's hand and said, "My son tells me that you're an absolute wiz at the Market."

Mickey made solid eye contact with Professor Ceraf. "That's kind of him, sir. Actually, he's taught me everything I know."

Carl laughed. "Right, which is why Mickey's commissions are a third higher than anyone else's in our group."

"That's very impressive, Mr. Sienna," the professor said. "To what do you attribute such significant success?"

Mickey felt a little flushed. "I just try to give people good advice, sir. In my business, if you do that often enough, it gets around."

"That's very sound thinking, Mr. Sienna." He turned to his son. "Carl, Mickey tells us that you've taught him everything he knows, but it seems that he might have a few things to teach as well."

"That's why I watch his every move like a hawk, Dad."

Carl, Mickey, and Jessica walked away to meet an old college buddy of Carl's and his new wife. As they were talking, Mickey glanced over to the sofa where two young women were chatting and laughing. The one on the left was very pretty, but the one on the right was stunning. Lustrous black hair, enormous blue eyes, a smile that electrified. Mickey found himself utterly distracted. It wasn't simply that this woman was beautiful. Mickey had been in the presence of any number of beautiful women. Jessica was beautiful herself in a sculpted sort of way. It was that this woman's beauty projected itself. Mickey hadn't even met her and he felt as though she'd gifted him with a bit of her radiance.

He might even have been staring, because Jessica eventually tugged on his arm to bring him back into the conversation. Mickey made a moderate effort to stay focused on it, but his mind was elsewhere. He wondered if there was a discreet way to suggest to Carl that he introduce him to the two women next.

It turned out not to be necessary. After one final burst of laughter from his own group that Mickey might have appreciated if he'd been paying any real attention, Carl pulled Mickey and Jessica away and said, "Gotta introduce you to Sis." They walked over to the couch where Carl first introduced the woman on the left – Mickey forgot her name instantly – and then the woman on the right as "my horribly spoiled sister, Gina."

Mickey shook her hand while he swam in her eyes.

"Carl has told me so much about you," he said, adding to himself that Carl had failed to mention that his sister was the most gorgeous woman in the free world.

Gina smiled for both Mickey and her big brother. "I'm sure at least some of it was true and perhaps even a tiny bit complimentary."

Mickey quickly began to rummage his mind to think of something that would elicit another smile.

"Oh Sis, you know I only say the nicest things about you," Carl said. He turned to Jessica and added jovially, "I'm an excellent liar."

Mickey couldn't see Jessica's reaction because he steadfastly refused to look in any direction other than Gina's.

"Well, I can't vouch for whether he was telling the truth or not, but I can tell you that Carl said you were bright, talented, and much, much nicer than he is," Mickey said to Gina. "I'm guessing he understated it."

As Gina transfixed him with the glint from her eyes, once again Jessica pulled on Mickey's arm. "Do you think we could go get a drink? I'm very thirsty."

Mickey allowed Jessica to steer him away, but only because he knew that not doing so would be impolite. A short while after they went to the living room, Jessica headed off to talk with some friends who had just joined the party. Mickey, as casually as possible, made his way back toward the den. The room had gotten more crowded, and while he looked for Gina, another broker at the firm accosted him, seeking his opinion on a textile stock. Mickey gave the man a modicum of his attention while his eyes scanned the room. He wondered if Gina had moved to another part of the house or even left the party altogether. He was about to excuse himself when suddenly Gina was standing beside him. Mickey made one additional comment about the stock and the man walked off.

"Are you the kind of person who talks about business all day and all night?" Gina said.

Mickey turned to her to get a better view. "There's a time and place for everything."

"And now?"

He smiled. "Now, we can talk about anything you'd like."

"Even if I wanted to talk about the stock market?"

"We could talk about the telephone book if that interests you," Mickey said, reminding himself to avoid appearing too obviously charmed.

"How gentlemanly. I don't want to talk about either the stock market or the telephone book. I think both are boring."

"Then I'll leave our topic entirely up to you."

Gina made a display of giving this serious attention before her face brightened again.

"Cocktail parties. What do you think of them?"

"It all depends on who you meet," Mickey paused and looked around the room. "I'm enjoying myself very much at this one."

"Was that intended to be a compliment?"

"I was thinking of your father," Mickey said with a grin, congratulating himself on eluding the too-obvious opportunity to flatter her.

Gina laughed and her eyes flashed up to embrace Mickey again. He'd never been so drawn into a woman's expression before.

"Would you like to sit and talk for a while?" Gina said. "Or is it critical that you mingle?"

"I've mingled enough for the night. I think it's critical now that we sit and talk."

There were no seats available in the living room, dining room, or den, so Gina and Mickey moved to Professor Ceraf's study.

"Your father won't mind that we're in here?"

"As long as we keep the conversation intellectually stimulating, he'll agree that the room is being put to good use."

They did precisely that. For a half-hour that seemed to define the beginning and end of time for Mickey, they talked about Gina's education, the President's latest speech, an editorial in *The New York Times*, the theatre, and even their favorite comic strips. A few minutes into the conversation, Mickey realized that he was genuinely fascinated with what Gina had to say – not simply because she was beautiful, but because she spoke with authority and dedication. He wanted to know her in a way that he'd wanted to know few people in his life. The party could not possibly last long enough.

"I have to admit," Gina said, "I was hoping we would meet tonight. Carl speaks highly of you. And since he has so few nice things to say about anyone, I was anxious to get to know someone about whom he was so consistently charitable."

"I hope I haven't disappointed you."

"No, not at all. In fact you've surprised me. Carl is usually a terrible judge of character and his other broker friends have a tendency to be – how should I say it? – single-minded."

"You mean they're focused entirely on money?"

"Entirely," she said, rolling her gorgeous eyes. "One of the most boring of all possible topics in the world."

Mickey looked around at the mahogany-paneled room and the leather furniture they were seated on. "I think it might be more boring to those who have always had money than to those to whom it is all very new."

Gina's lips turned upward ever so slightly. "You may be right about that." As had been the case with everything else they discussed that evening, she seemed to be giving his comments serious consideration. "You're a fun debating partner."

Mickey smiled and was about to suggest something else they could debate when he heard a voice from outside of the study say, "Oh, there you are." It was Jessica. She didn't seem pleased. "I was wondering where you'd gone."

"Jessica, hi. Sorry, there was no place to sit, so we came in here. You remember Gina, don't you?"

Jessica's expression was flat. "Yes, of course."

Gina stood and walked toward the door. She touched Mickey's date on the shoulder. "I apologize, Jessica. I won't monopolize Mickey any longer." Then she left the room quickly.

Mickey immediately felt empty. He was completely unprepared to do anything other than continue talking to Gina. He knew it would be horribly rude to say as much to Jessica, but chatting up strangers and associates with a woman who was only marginally interested in him was so much less appealing than the alternative.

Regardless, if he didn't want to be impolite, he really didn't have any choice. They stayed at the party for another hour. Jessica didn't seem particularly concerned about spending time with Mickey and didn't even involve him in many of the conversations she brought them into. All the same, she didn't seem inclined to let Mickey drift off again. Several times during the hour, Mickey caught glimpses of Gina talking to other party guests. Twice, their eyes made contact and Gina smiled before returning her attention to whomever she was speaking. Mickey desperately wanted to go back to the study to learn more about her, but he feared that not only would he incur Jessica's wrath, but that the moment with Gina might have passed.

Their coats on and ready to go, Mickey and Jessica said goodbye to Carl and several others at the entrance to the apartment. While they were doing so, Gina walked up to them.

"Leaving?"

Mickey tipped his head toward her. "Yes, sadly. We both have busy days tomorrow."

"Perhaps my brother will invite the two of you over again sometime so we could get to know each other a little better."

Jessica placed her arm inside Mickey's. "That would be very nice."

With that, they walked out the door and into the hallway. As they rode the elevator down to the lobby, Mickey could think of nothing other than Gina's eyes. When the elevator door opened, he walked out after Jessica and then turned and said, "I forgot something, I'll be right back."

Jessica looked at him quizzically as the elevator doors closed. A moment later, Mickey was back in the apartment asking the man that Gina was talking to if he could excuse them for a moment.

"I need to see you again," he said.

Gina smiled, underscoring the point for him. "But what about your girlfriend? She seems very possessive."

"Jessica's just a friend. In fact, since I have her waiting in the lobby, she might not even be that anymore."

"I wouldn't want to get between the two of you."

"I promise you it's not like that."

Gina held Mickey with her eyes for an eternal moment.

"In that case, you can take me to dinner next Saturday night."

Saturday? That was an entire week away.

"I'd like that," Mickey said, though he had no idea how he was going to wait that long.

~~~~~~~~~

It took three days for Mickey to get a reservation at La Coquille. Finally, a client was able to procure it for him, though Mickey felt a bit guilty about asking the favor or for even bringing up his personal life. Under any other circumstances, he would have gone to Carl for this. Carl had the remarkable ability to free up tables, theatre seats, and hotel rooms, and had become Mickey's source for the necessary things. Mickey didn't want to tap his friend for this assignment, though. He wasn't even sure how to raise the subject of dating Carl's sister with him.

"So where are you taking her, anyway?" Carl said out of the blue on Thursday afternoon.

"Coquille," Mickey said, certain the awkwardness he felt was clear on his face. "Do you think she'll like it?"

"Coquille, huh? Were you planning to go there with someone else already? It's impossible to get a table without a month's notice."

"You just have to know the right people," Mickey said, repeating a phrase that Carl had delivered to him several times after doing favors.

"Good to see you're taking this seriously."

Mickey hesitated before speaking again.

"I'm sorry I didn't say anything to you before this. You don't mind, do you?"

Carl smiled. "That you're dating my sister? No, not at all. You've given all indications of being a gentleman, Sienna, and

I'm sure you'll continue to be so with Gina. Besides, as long as you're dating her, I'll be able to get her to do whatever I want. Anything to prevent me from telling you about the scandalous tutu affair when she was five years old."

~~~~~~~~

Saturday night could easily have been intimidating if it hadn't felt so natural. Gina was dressed in a black chiffon dress that made her look at once completely irresistible and utterly refined. Mickey had dated many sophisticated women, but he had never been with anyone as sure of every movement and inflection as Gina. At the same time, she made it unmistakably clear to Mickey that she wanted to be with him. In fact, she made him believe that she would rather be with him than anyone else in the world. It was a heady feeling.

The restaurant was less inviting. Darkly paneled, dimly lit, and filled with rigid, tuxedoed staff, La Coquille announced itself as unavailable to all but a select few. Fortunately Mickey, dressed in his finest suit, accompanying a woman like Gina, and with a ten-dollar bill tucked in his palm, felt worthy of entrance. He'd eaten in many of the City's best dining rooms and would not be daunted by the forbidding aura of this French establishment.

"Do you take all of your first dates to places this impressive?" Gina said after they were seated.

"You mean this little neighborhood joint? I thought it was best if we started out casually."

"Very sound thinking. So are the hamburgers good here?"

Mickey smiled. In his mind, he and Gina were sitting on a park bench eating hamburgers. Over the past week, he had imagined himself and Gina in a variety of situations. It seemed that any sight or snippet of conversation prompted a vision of a life in which Gina was the center. This was all very new to him. Mickey had been smitten before. He'd certainly been impressed by physical beauty before, but Gina was the first woman who had ever caused him to dream about the future even ahead of their first date.

At this stage in his life, Mickey was performing a balancing act between honoring his upbringing in a neighborhood comprised mostly of first generation Italian-Americans and striving for the more urbane and worldly air of the New York financial community. He never wanted to forget the warmth and nurture of where he came from, but he couldn't help but gravitate toward the appeal of the cosmopolitan Manhattan life. Mickey felt that he could appreciate quality and, since he had recently been blessed with the means to surround himself with it, he felt that it would be wasteful not to make the most of the situation. On this night, the refinement that Mickey was cultivating would serve him well. The wine steward complimented his selection. Gina agreed to let him order for the two of them and offered a satisfied smile when he made his selections. When the captain came to their table to check on them, Mickey engaged him in a conversation about a mural on the far wall that coaxed the man into temporarily shedding his blank expression. Mickey wanted to seem polished and wise to Gina, and he actually appeared to be accomplishing that.

At the same time, everything about Gina impressed him. That she knew the Puligny-Montrachet he had chosen, that she could talk passionately about issues in the day's news, that she could be amused by things like the little scallop-shell shapes both carved into the walls and embossed on the linens. What impressed him most about Gina, though, was her ambition. Gina didn't go to college for the sake of an education and the possibility of meeting a husband, as so many other women did. She went because it was a stepping stone toward getting things done.

"Why the Mayor's office?" he said as they ate their entrees, hers a pressed duck and his a rack of lamb.

"I thought about a few things when I got out of school. My father was trying to convince me to do something at Columbia. He said he thought it would make the best use of my skills, but I think it was really because he'd be able to keep an eye on me if I was there. I thought about newspapers, but I had a feeling that they'd try to make me write an advice column or something like that. That tends to be what they do with women. You might think this is odd, but I even thought about going into television."

"Television?"

"Yes, I know. Who knows if it's going to last or if anyone is going to care about it? But I have a feeling that people are going to respond well once they figure out what it is. And I think it might be a good way to do something meaningful."

"I can't say that I've paid much attention to it. It's not like going to the movies."

"You're right. But in the future? Anyway, I asked myself a lot of questions about what I wanted to do with my life, and I realized that, much as I'm not convinced that O'Dwyer is the right person to run New York, the City has a lot of programs that could really help people if those involved make a genuine commitment. When I found out I could get assigned to the women's shelter project, it just seemed perfect for me."

"These are women who have been abandoned by their husbands and can't support themselves?"

"That's a piece of it. But we're really trying to create a place where women can feel safe and come for refuge. We want these women to know that they don't need to stay in abusive marriages any longer."

It dawned on Mickey that this was yet another way in which Gina was different from other women he'd dated. Most of them had no political opinions at all, and even if they did, they would never consider sharing them on a date.

"That's pretty progressive thinking," he said.

"It's time for progressive thinking. Men can be awful to women sometimes."

The image of Jackie Pandolfo immediately flashed into Mickey's mind. Any reminder of the attack on Theresa still wounded him.

"I've learned that," he said quietly.

Gina took a sip of wine and looked down at her plate. It appeared to Mickey that she was trying to restrain herself.

"I must sound strident to you," she said. "My father tells me that I can get on a soap box faster than anyone he's ever met in his life."

"No, not at all," Mickey said, brightening. He didn't want Gina to think that his suddenly darkened mood had anything to do with her. "It's very stimulating."

"Do you really think so?"

"Yes, very much. It's inspiring. It makes me want to enlist in community service."

Gina smiled. "Stick with me and I'll have you handing out flyers on street corners in no time."

Mickey thought anything that involved "sticking with" Gina seemed utterly appealing.

"Sign me up."

The conversation shifted at that point to lighter subjects. Gina seemed to have an encyclopedic knowledge of film celebrities and their personal lives, and admitted sheepishly that when she read the newspaper she turned to the funny pages first.

"Slapstick," Mickey said, almost in a whisper, while he ate his raspberry soufflé.

"Pardon me?"

"I love slapstick." Mickey was very surprised to be admitting this to a woman he wanted to impress. "I know I'm not supposed to. I realize it isn't the sign of an educated mind. But I just love it."

Gina laughed. "I think that's great."

"You think it's great that I find it funny to watch people bop each other over the head and fall down?"

"I think it's great that you find anything especially funny. I mean, I already know that you are smart, a hard worker, and up to date on most of the issues of the day. I also know that you can be a little mysterious, but you're too mysterious to explain that just yet. I think it's great that something always makes you laugh – even slapstick. Not that I can say I'm a fan myself."

She smiled at him again. And this time she was smiling because he had admitted something that he'd been too intimidated to mention to any of his other Manhattan friends, something that he thought pegged him as an ignorant Brooklyn boy. Instead of reacting badly to the admission, though, Gina had rewarded him with the greatest gift she had given him to date: that remarkable smile.

As they left the restaurant, Mickey felt like he was airborne. The night was young and he had no desire to see it end anytime soon.

"Would you like to go dancing?" he said while Gina took his arm as they exited La Coquille.

She squeezed his arm softly. "I'd like that very much. Someplace quiet, though. I'd rather not go anywhere noisy tonight."

"There's a great trio that plays at The Plaza on Saturday nights."

"Sounds perfect."

Mickey had thought the night couldn't get any better, but as he put his right arm around Gina's waist and clutched her left hand for their first slow dance, he realized he had been pitifully wrong. There had never been more delicate fingers, never been a softer cheek, never been a form that fit more naturally against his. Cole Porter had never written a song to describe this feeling. How could a woman he had only begun to know possibly thrill him this way?

"And you can dance as well," Gina said as they moved across the floor.

"My mother taught me, if you can believe it. She said 'the ladies' would like it."

"And do 'the ladies' like it?"

"I'm only interested in the opinion of one lady."

Gina set her cheek against his and whispered, "I think your mother might have been right."

They danced until after one. Mickey wasn't sure that he would ever have stopped, but Gina told him regretfully that she was expected at breakfast early the next morning and needed at least a bit of sleep. In the cab back to Gina's apartment, she laid her head on Mickey's shoulder and neither said a word. When they arrived outside the door, they lingered on the street for several minutes.

Mickey turned toward her. "I'm sure this is obvious, but I had a wonderful time tonight."

Gina swept him up in her eyes for perhaps the twentieth time that night. "I'm glad. I did as well."

"Can I see you again?"

"I'd like that."

"This week?"

"I'd like that, too." Gina thought for a moment. "Do you like the opera?"

"I don't think Laurel and Hardy have ever been in one. I can't say I know much about it."

"Come with me Tuesday night. My mother and I have a subscription at Lincoln Center. I think I might be able to convince her to give up her ticket."

"The opera would be wonderful. It will be like exploring a new world."

"That's as it should be." She looked over her shoulder. "I should really get inside."

With that, Gina leaned forward and placed a delicate kiss on Mickey's cheek. While she was just barely touching him, her lips lingered at the spot for several moments.

Then she pulled back, smiled, and walked into the building.

~~~~~~~~

"It was like an angel had kissed me," Dad said. "A living, breathing angel." He looked off into the distance. "I can still feel it, Gina." He cast his eyes downward.

Jesse hadn't spoken since Mickey had begun the story. At first he had thought to interrupt his father with questions, but he hadn't even noticed when he made the decision to simply sit and listen. Jesse was stunned that his father was telling him this story, and he had to admit that he was completely hooked. He waited now for his father to continue, but Dad didn't say a thing. A shadow had passed over his father's expression. He had been beaming only minutes earlier, but now he seemed lost in thought – or was he lost in time?

The suspense was killing Jesse. "There's more, right?"

Mickey seemed to return from wherever he had gone. He regarded Jesse as though he had forgotten his son was in the room.

"There's more, yes. But not right now. I think I'm going to lie down for a little while. And you have a lot of work to do."

Chapter Eleven

This story was stunning to me on so many different levels that it was hard for me to even comprehend just how stunned I was. I of course wanted to hear more, but since things had been pretty awkward between my father and me the last few days, I also didn't want to appear overeager. When he rose from the table, I got up as well, saying something inane like, "Yeah, really, gotta get to this article." But my mind was reeling.

Who was this woman who had so completely captivated my father? Did she turn out to be someone very different from who he thought she was? Did she turn into some overbearing freedom fighter, leaving my father in the lurch? Perhaps Gina wasn't her real name and she was really a major political figure whose identity he was forbidden from revealing. I, of course, immediately began to wonder about what broke them up, because that's where my mind went whenever I thought about love stories. It was clear that talking about Gina took a lot out of my father, and that suggested to me that she ultimately broke his heart. Did they burn intensely for a short period, or did things decline slowly, leaving my father to grasp at what might have been?

Then there was the shock of hearing my father speak this way. Until a couple of days before this, I had never once thought of my father as a romantic. He and my mother filled their roles, partners in the enterprise. He didn't bring her flowers, sing her love songs or do anything else that Neil Diamond might have suggested – at least not while I was around. Then he put on his little display with Marina, which was strange enough. When he talked about Gina, though, his entire demeanor changed. He was like one of those professional storytellers who become possessed by the characters they're playing. He was transformed from Mickey Sienna, eighty-two-year-old grumbler, to a lovestruck young man with dreams in his eyes. When he talked about the intoxicating qualities of attraction, I could identify with what he was saying. But this was because of what I knew of it myself rather than because I had seen him talk this way before. While he was telling this story, I believed that the most important thing in the world to my father was the love between a man and a woman. This was a nearly complete disconnect from the guy who talked portfolios, career choices, and bacon. At least I recognized the part about slapstick. There had been several times since he moved in when I nearly buried my head under a pillow because he was guffawing over some stupid comedy in the next room. He'd had that guilty pleasure for as long as I could remember. But not only had I never heard him prioritize romance before, I'd never even seen him put it in the top ten.

Meanwhile, who was this guy he was describing in this story? Not only was the Valentino someone I'd never met, but neither was the Cosmopolitan. I always knew my father was very intelligent and he certainly liked to surround himself with quality. But designer suits? Four-star restaurants? Posh nightclubs? Prime beef, Stickley, and Lincoln were in character. Puligny-Montrachet, though? Not any Mickey Sienna I'd ever seen.

I couldn't wait to tell Marina about this, but of course I had no choice. She was in school already, so I'd have to wait until I saw her that night.

"This is incredibly sweet," she said after I'd begun telling her the story. We were sitting on her couch, even though we were going to be late for a movie. I simply couldn't help but spill the details the moment I saw her. "I can just see your father all doe-eyed and gushy."

"Therein lies the difference between you and me."

"Oh, come on, Jesse, you're going to have to admit one of these days that your father is a thinking, feeling person. I could have told you that two minutes after meeting him. But now after hearing this story, how can you have any other opinion? Heartless people don't carry torches for fifty-something years."

"I never said he was heartless. Closed-minded, demanding, a world-class pain in the ass, I've said those things. But I never said heartless."

She pulled me closer to her on the couch and kissed me on the cheek.

"I can't believe he's telling you this huge secret after all this time. Do you think your mother knew?"

I shook my head. This was one of the dozens of questions I'd been asking myself all day, the biggest one of course being why he was telling me this story at all.

"I don't know. He made it clear that none of my siblings had heard it, but he didn't say either way about my mother. These days, as you and I are very much aware, someone like Gina would come up in conversation during a first date. But back then, maybe you didn't talk about things like that."

"So when do we get to hear the rest of the story?"

I smiled up at her. "Got you hooked, huh?"

She smirked. "Unlike you, right? Feel free to take off your coat anytime you'd like. By the way, I think the movie started seven minutes ago."

"No, I absolutely admit my fascination. Not to him, of course, but I'll admit it to you. I don't have a clue when he's going to tell me more, though. He looked exhausted at the end of this part, like it had taken this huge effort. The few times I saw him the rest of the day, he seemed completely lost in thought, like he was reliving the whole thing. He didn't say a word about it, though. It might be a while. It could even be that this is all he's going to say."

Marina considered this for a bit. I wondered if I would feel disappointed if he never mentioned Gina again and I realized that, especially now that Marina was interested in it as well, I would be.

"It makes you think of him in a totally different way, doesn't it?" Marina said.

"It does, amazingly enough. Do you think that's why he told me?"

"I think he's reaching out."

"Maybe. If that's the case, his timing is awfully strange. He'd been in a lousy mood since the day after you came for dinner."

"Maybe the story was a peace offering. He wants you to know that he's really a good guy even though you two don't always get along."

"I suppose anything is possible. I mean, who would have thought that Gina was possible?"

Neither of us said anything for several minutes. I nuzzled further into Marina's arms and thought about the details of my father's story. I'm sure Marina was doing the same. I wondered how my father and Gina held each other. I'd been doing that since I walked in the door, juxtaposing my father's and Gina's life with Marina's and mine. Did he excitedly come to her home to tell her things? Did they miss movies because he did? Was he especially fond of certain things she wore? Did she have any endearing little habits like Marina's lightly brushing the hair at my neck while we sat together?

When some time had passed, I returned from my time-trip to my father's past to acknowledge how comfortable I felt here on the couch with Marina. It had been more than a week since we'd had any time to simply sit with one another, and it was a welcome respite.

"We don't have to go anywhere tonight," Marina said.

"You're okay with not seeing a movie?"

"No movie is going to beat the story you just told me."

"What do you want to do instead?"

"We'll think of something."

I settled back a little more comfortably in Marina's arms. I was thinking about how much better that felt than I would have felt going to the local multiplex. I closed my eyes and the next thing I knew it was 1:00 a.m. I startled when I saw the time on the clock and my doing so awakened Marina.

"What happened?" she said, rising to a sitting position.

"It looks like our date tonight was a nap."

Marina laughed. Her arms were still around me and she pulled me a little closer. "That was a great date."

"Yeah, it was. I didn't even know I was tired."

I was surprised that I felt that way. I had never simply fallen asleep on a date before. I think if I had done it with any of the other women I'd dated over the years I would have been scandalized, concerned that I, or at the very least our relationship, was losing vigor. Instead, I felt deeply satisfied, like we had spent all night talking in a quiet café. This had been much too impromptu to suggest that we plan on its happening again, but at the same time, I looked forward to the possibility.

As much as I regretted it, I said, "I need to get back. I shouldn't be away from my father two nights in a row."

"I know. You don't want him getting mad at you now when you haven't heard the rest of his story."

"Hmm, so maybe that's what this is all about. Maybe this is his new way of keeping me in line."

Marina got up from the couch, which caused me to get up as well. I realized as we headed for the door that I had never taken off my coat.

"Kind of a weird night, huh?" I said as was stood in the doorway.

"It was nice."

"Do you really think so?"

"I really think so."

"Me, too."

"Give your dad a kiss for me."

Chapter Twelve

By the next Sunday, my father still hadn't said anything more to me about Gina. While I had suggested to Marina the possibility that he would never say another word about it, I hadn't begun to take that notion seriously until then. He wasn't reticent in any other way. If anything, he seemed a little more relaxed, a little more familiar with me. Surely, though, he had to know that I was expecting him to finish. I remembered how tired and worn down he'd looked when he got up from the kitchen table that morning, and I wondered if telling the first part of the tale had taken so much out of him that he hadn't yet fully recovered.

But that wasn't what this Sunday was about. Not when a visitation from royalty – at least in their eyes – was upon us. Denise, Brad, and Marcus had chosen this day to make their ceremonial visit. It would be the first time Denise had set foot in the house since my father had moved in. In fact, it was the first time she'd made the crossing in nearly two years. Everything about this had the aura of fulfilling an obligation, from the scheduling ("An afternoon meal would be best, Jesse. You know the traffic can be hell on Sunday evenings. I'll have a dozen things to do to get ready for Monday, and Marcus will need to study") to direction over the menu ("We're trying to avoid red meat, so it would be best if you didn't serve that," she told me, though I had stopped eating red meat five years earlier) to the pre-screening of topics of conversation ("It would be best if we didn't over-discuss Mom, don't you think? That can't be good for Dad"). My father was, of course, excited that they were coming.

"Do you think Denise will bring her Blackberry, her tablet, and her laptop?" I asked as we were getting things ready. "Or do you think she'll just bring an assistant along with her?"

"Why do you talk that way about your sister? She was always very good to your mother and me."

"Dad, she took a call during the funeral."

"It lasted thirty seconds. She forgot to turn the phone off."

In a complicated kind of way, I was excited about Denise coming to the house as well. As much as I saw her for who she was and disagreed with many of the things she stood for – like endless devotion to career advancement, raising your child from the time he's two to be a valedictorian, and systematically marginalizing your parents – I had never stopped looking up to her. She was sharp, she was polished, and if she could bother to concentrate on me for any length of time, she was actually very valuable at dispensing advice. I always felt that I needed to be on my toes with her, that I needed to report to her on my progress in life. While that lent our infrequent visits a relatively high level of stress, it was also invigorating.

Though we were expecting them around noon, they arrived at 1:15 in a flourish of protestations about the hassles of getting over the George Washington Bridge. Denise kissed me on the cheek and then put her arm around my father's shoulders and walked him through the house. Brad shook my hand, nodded stiffly, and moved deliberately into the living room. Marcus also shook my hand (he'd hugged me once a few years back, but I'm pretty sure it was an accident) and immediately began to pepper me with questions about an article I'd published in the summer on male pattern baldness. While I didn't want to be rude, the prospect of discussing this with an eight-year-old seemed absurd and I had an ear cocked in the direction of the den, where my sister was discussing the placement of several items from my parents' old house.

"Things look pretty well incorporated," Denise said to me when she returned. "You've fit a lot into this space."

I wanted to mention that I would have been able to "incorporate" things even better if I had a five-thousand-square-foot lakefront second home at my disposal as they did, but I bit it back. Another complicated thing about our relationship: I knew she earned the massive amount of money she made, but I still couldn't help feel a little envious about it.

"Dad was a trooper about making decisions on what to bring here," I said instead. "And of course no one will ever be able to go into the basement again."

"Under the circumstances, the house looks good."

"Thanks," I said, feeling that little thrill I got – decidedly involuntarily – whenever she gave me even the vaguest compliment.

"Jesse's got me eating Mexican food," my father said. Denise turned to me with a look of surprise on her face.

"Well, twice," I said.

My father continued. "And turkey meatloaf. Did you even know you could make meatloaf with turkey?"

"Can't say I've given it much thought, Dad."

My father smiled over at me as if to say that he was impressed even if Denise was unmoved.

"So what are you working on?" he said to her.

Denise rolled her eyes. It wasn't clear whether it was as a prelude to her recitation about her overwhelming workload or as a way of thanking God that the subject had moved off meatloaf.

"Ugh, a million things. When am I not working on a million things? The quarter's winding down, I'm putting together a summit with the London office, I've got two people who completely aren't cutting it . . .."

"Come tell me about it," my father said, taking her by the arm and leading her back toward the den. I knew that the next half-hour at least would be a skull session between the old financial pro and his brilliant protégé. Denise would pretend to pay attention to my father's observations, while at the same time trivializing every one of them. My father would interpret this as the pupil surpassing the teacher, but it was hard for me not to interpret it as the pupil being so full of herself that there wasn't room for any opinion other than her own.

Gladly choosing to skip this exchange, I walked into the living room with Marcus right behind me. Brad was hardly scintillating, but we at least had a bit we could talk about. He was a senior vice president at a corporation that included a few magazines in its holdings. As a result, he knew some of the people I worked with and we could patch together a conversation even as I cringed over his posturing as an expert on the industry.

"Hey, how's it going?" I said as I walked into the room. Brad had fixed himself a drink (I was surprised he even knew where the liquor cabinet was) and was sitting in an armchair looking toward a window.

"Good, good," he said as he glanced over at me briefly. Marcus walked up to him and he touched the boy lightly on the head. Marcus then quickly surveyed the pottery on the breakfront and left the room.

"How's life at Lynch these days?" I asked.

"Fine," he said, again making momentary eye contact. "Busy, you know."

"Hey, did you hear that Ken Hurley is leaving *Alive* to take a television gig?"

"No, I hadn't heard."

"What do you think about the management changes at *American Week*?"

He shook his head and said, "They've been coming for a long time."

After each exchange, he turned back toward the window, just to make clear that he wasn't planning to take the discussion further. I'd used my two opening gambits, meaning I was tapped out of conversation-starters with my brother-in-law. Usually, Brad had a lot more to say. I assumed he would spend an hour talking about *American Week*, including how he believed their problems stemmed from taking writers too seriously. As far as Brad was concerned – "all due respect" – writers had only slightly more to contribute to a magazine's success than the clerical staff. It was all about management and the ad sales team. This time, though, he was skipping an opportunity to take an easy shot, since overpayment to writers was at least part of the reason that *Week* had been so unprofitable. If we weren't going to talk about the industry, I wasn't sure what we were going to talk about.

After a couple of minutes of uncomfortable silence (at least it was uncomfortable for me; Brad seemed perfectly relaxed with his drink and his view of my driveway), the words "have you seen any good movies lately" were actually forming on my lips when Brad spoke, still looking out the window.

"How much do you know about Gruenbach Communications?"

"Didn't they buy Hesson last year?"

Brad offered an unamused laugh and said, "Yes, they did."

"I don't know, they're like the third or fourth largest media conglomerate in the world, they have all of those women's service magazines and the children's cable channel, and of course they own Chimera Studios and Chimera Records. Why?"

"Do you know anyone over there?"

"Well, Ted Ream records for Chimera and I always loved his stuff," I said, joking.

"I meant do you know someone personally over there."

I thought about it for a minute. "Sally Oxford, who I used to work with at *Optimum*, went over to *Senior Woman* last year. I haven't stayed in touch with her since I don't have many credentials for writing pieces on grandmotherhood."

Brad shook his head. I'm sure he was thinking, "Just another useless writer."

"Why?"

He put down his drink and turned to me.

"I have it on good authority that Gruenbach is trying to buy Lynch."

"Wow. That would be major news. What's the point, though? Don't you guys own things like and drug stores and car washes?"

"We own no car washes," Brad said in a voice much more animated than normal. He wasn't usually this easy to rile. "They want the magazines. They'll sell everything else off."

"Proving once again that I'll never understand the corporate world." I let the notion roll around in my head a bit. "So if that were the reason they were buying Lynch, they would basically need none of Lynch's executive management."

"That's what one would think."

"Got a good contract?"

Brad looked at me scornfully then picked up his drink again. At least I now knew why he was less willing to lecture me on my chosen profession than usual. I felt a little sorry for him. While I never had very much respect for people whose job it was to supervise people who were supervising people who were actually doing something, I could sympathize with his fear for the future of his employment – though given Denise's salary, he was hardly going to be panhandling anytime in the near future. When it was clear that Brad didn't want to talk about business anymore and I couldn't think of any way to effectively change the subject, I excused myself to check on the food.

A little less than an hour later, we were all seated around the dining room table. My father seemed flushed from his exchange with Denise, as though he had just completed a vigorous match of racquetball. Marcus, noting that I had included paprika in the chicken dish I'd made, offered a brief dissertation on the origins of the spice and its uses in various cuisines. If ever a child needed a videogame system, it was Marcus. The thought flashed in my mind that there was probably no one in the world who called him Mark. Brad remained sullen and distracted. I would have interpreted this as smug if we hadn't spoken earlier. I tried to imagine what he was thinking. Did he see the same energy in my father's face after he'd had his session with Denise? Did he feel somewhat disenfranchised from it, knowing that his wife had been regaling my father with the vibrancy of her professional efforts while he himself

was facing an uncertain career future? Was he wondering if
my father (and by extension, the entire world) was going to
see him as a hanger-on if he lost his position when Lynch was
acquired and he couldn't find another executive spot quickly?

"You do realize that that company has been grossly over-
valued for years, don't you?" my father said. It seemed like a
non-sequitur, but it was probably a continuation of something
he and Denise had been discussing earlier. "The stock is certain to tumble."

Denise shook her head. "It's never that simple, Dad.
When you know as much about their operations as I do, you
realize there are more subtle indicators."

"You mean like there were with Dodd?"

Denise picked up her salad fork to help her emphasize her
point. "I never said that Dodd was going to show long-term
gains."

"I think you called them one of the most solidly con-
structed companies in the entire sector."

Denise waved her fork in the air. "I doubt that I said it
that way. And who could have anticipated that the old man
was going to crash on his way out with the only risky move he
made in his entire career?"

My father laughed. "Served him right. And I'm sure it
taught you a lesson, even if you don't remember all the details."

"I never said anything about the long-term," Denise said
again, but with a small smile of concession. It always surprised
me to see her in an exchange like this because she gave ground
to absolutely no one else. I'm sure she had just spent forty
minutes explaining to my father how antiquated his observations about commerce were. But he was still the only person
I'd ever seen call her on her mistakes and he was certainly the
only person with whom she actually seemed a bit entertained
when it happened.

I could tell that my father took special pleasure in eliciting
that smile. I'm sure he cherished his position in Denise's life and
the knowledge that she would concede things to him that she

conceded to no one else. It was precisely this kind of exchange that left me so envious of the relationships he had built with my siblings. I began to react to it the same way I always did: a flicker of appreciation followed by brush of melancholy. I was surprised to discover that there was a third component to my response this day, though: a flash of inclusion. For perhaps the first time in my life, I could actually relate to the feeling of being an "insider" with Mickey Sienna. Denise might have Dodd Petrochemical with my father, but I had Gina. It made it so much easier to accept Denise's dismissal of my dinner as "bold," and her appraisal of *National Voice*, the first issue to which I had contributed, as "too narrow to find a meaningful readership."

When dinner was over, I went into the kitchen to clean the dishes while the others went into the den. This was another family tradition I'd somehow remained outside of. My father and the other kids would talk while my mother cleaned up. When I was about six, I started helping her perform this task. She always seemed surprised when I did so, would suggest that I join the others, and then come to appreciate it as the time passed. I was in the kitchen alone for about ten minutes when Denise came in and put her hand on my shoulder.

"So how's Dad holding up?" she said.

"I think he's doing great. Why, are you concerned about something?"

"No, not at all. He looks good. He seems relaxed. He seems to be walking more stiffly, but what are you going to do about that? If he doesn't want to do the knee thing, he doesn't want to do the knee thing. So he hasn't blown anything up?"

"We probably would have gotten around to calling you about it already if he had."

"Well, I can't say that I thought this was going to work out, but I guess you guys haven't tried to kill each other yet, so it can't be as much of a disaster as I guessed it would be."

I simply smiled and returned my attention to the dishes. Obviously they escaped Denise's notice because she didn't offer to lend a hand.

"And how are you doing?" she said after a minute.

I glanced over at her. "I'm fine."

"You know, I'll tell you right now Jess that if you're worried that this is too much for you but you don't want to 'admit defeat,' no one is going to give you a hard time."

"Really, Denise, I'm fine. I like having Dad around."

She shrugged, as though the notion was simply inconceivable to her.

"Dad tells me you have a girlfriend."

"He mentioned that to you?"

"For several minutes. I guess he thinks she's pretty cute. She's a schoolteacher?"

"Third grade, yeah."

"Are you serious with her?"

"Why is that always the next question? Would you like to know her name?"

"I know her name already. Does that mean you aren't serious?"

"It means we're not preoccupying ourselves with whether we're serious or not."

"Well, that's very sophisticated."

"Is it? I just thought we were being realistic. It's nice to know it's also refined."

"It is. Very postmodern. Of course, when you're fifty-five and doing this for the twentieth time, it'll just be pathetic, but it's cool now."

She patted me on the back and walked back toward the den. Under my breath, I thanked her for her help.

We had coffee a short while later, and not long after that the three of them left. My father and I returned to the den after saying goodbye to them. For a while, he talked about how smart Marcus was and how he was teaching the kid about P/E ratios. Then we turned on the television and watched the end of a basketball game. As the game went to commercial in the fourth quarter, my father hit the mute button on the remote and turned to me with a huge boyish grin.

"Okay, I promised myself that I wasn't going to say something, but I've got to tell you this."

"What?" I said, smiling because he was smiling.

"While Denise and I were talking in here this afternoon, she pulled out her Blackberry, called her assistant, and talked to him for ten minutes. And – get this – the assistant was in her office because Denise insisted on a report being ready when she returned this evening."

I rolled my eyes and smiled, as much at the pleasure with which my father was telling me this as what he was telling me.

"I'd like to say I'm surprised, Dad."

My father snorted. "She's something else."

"That's one way of putting it."

He was still smiling when he pointed his finger at me and said, "And she has always been very good to your mother and me."

Chapter Thirteen

Mickey knew that he had had Jesse's full attention when he told him the first part of his story, and he knew that Jesse would have sat there listening for as much of it as Mickey was willing to tell. Mickey still didn't feel like he could read his youngest son as well as he read his other kids, but in this instance the expression on Jesse's face made his feelings easy to decipher. Mickey also knew that it was important that he get out the rest of the story of his life with Gina, because Jesse needed to hear it. After that first session, though, Mickey felt as though he had spent twenty hours on the trading floor of the Stock Exchange. How could it be so different to talk about Gina than it was to simply think about her all the time? Whatever the reason, Mickey could feel the effects days later and only now, more than a week after the first time he'd sat down with his son, did he feel that he had the emotional strength to continue.

Jesse had breezed in and out of the kitchen that morning, wolfing down a bowl of cereal and mumbling something about parquet floors. The kid certainly wrote about many different things, even if most of them seemed inconsequential. Mickey had his morning conversation with Theresa, learning that the doorman in her building had suffered a heart attack and that Maggie was back from the hospital and feeling well enough to eat three pieces of the apple pie Theresa made for her. He put on the television after that, but as happened four times out of five, he couldn't find anything that held his interest. It never ceased to mystify him that with everything that had been filmed since the moving picture was invented the sum total of worthwhile entertainment wouldn't fill a week's worth of television programming. He snapped the remote at the screen and sat in silence for a few minutes. Then he pulled himself up slowly from the couch and made his way toward Jesse's office.

He knocked softly on the closed door and then peeked his head in. Jesse hadn't turned around and seemed intent on holding down the backspace button of his keyboard to erase whatever he had just written.

"This is a bad time," Mickey said quietly.

Jesse lifted his finger off the key and leaned his head back without turning around. "Dad, do you know what the fascinating thing is about parquet floors?"

Mickey took a step into the room. "What's that?"

"I have no idea! That's the problem. I took this stupid fifteen-hundred-word article for practically no money and a tight deadline because I thought it would be a piece of cake, but there is nothing worth saying about parquet floors."

Mickey took a step back and put his hand on the doorknob. "This *is* a bad time."

Jesse swiveled his chair around. "No, I'm just having my daily crisis. What's up?"

Mickey took his hand off the doorknob. "I just thought, if you had a little time, that I'd tell you some more about what we were talking about last week."

Jesse's eyebrows inched upward and he sat back further in his chair.

"Yeah, definitely," he said, signaling to Mickey to sit down. "It's gotta be better than what I was doing in here."

Mickey settled into the other chair in the office. Now that he'd told Jesse what he was going to do, he wasn't sure where to start. It wasn't like the first time when they were sitting at the kitchen table and Jesse had no idea what was coming. There were so many things that Mickey wanted to say, but he wasn't sure where he should go next. Without realizing it,

Mickey allowed his mind to drift in a way that he never did when others were present. He was standing outside of Gina's apartment building, her face pulling back but still so close that he could feel the warmth of her skin.

"I didn't kiss her on the lips that first night because it didn't seem like the right thing, but after our second date, we kissed and my knees actually buckled. Where the hell does that come from?"

~~~~~~~~~

Manhattan is made for springtime, Mickey thought as he walked up to Gina's building that night. In the summer, the pavement sizzles and makes you weak. In the winter, the wind cuts right through you and you can't walk more than a couple of blocks without wanting to go inside. But in the spring, Park Avenue is like one long welcome mat, inviting you to stroll for as long as you wish, admire the architecture, appraise restaurant menus, take note of the tens of thousands of things for sale. The weather is fine; no need to hurry in the springtime. Unless of course you're on your way to seeing the most beautiful, most fascinating woman you've ever met.

Mickey had been to the opera exactly once before in his life. Right after he'd arrived at QBK, he went out a few times with a woman named Marla. Just coming to terms with his new environment, he had taken her to see "La Traviata" on their third date, believing that this was something the person he wanted to be would do. He spent the first act trying to convince himself that he would be more impressive if he became passionate about opera, and the second act convincing himself that it was acceptable for him to find it all incomprehensible. By the end of the evening, he'd decided that both opera and Marla were incapable of maintaining his interest.

However, if attending the opera meant seeing Gina dressed like this, he would gladly go every night of the week. She was wearing a cream-colored dress made of raw silk, her

hair was pinned up, and she wore a cream hat that drew attention to her shimmering eyes. She looked as elegant as a movie
starlet, but with a smile and bearing that made her eminently more approachable. As they left the apartment, Gina took
Mickey's arm. Was it his imagination, or was she walking just
a little closer to him tonight, leaning just a little bit more in
his direction?

"Do you know 'Pagliacci?'" Gina said as they settled into
a cab.

"That's the one about the clown, right?" Mickey had meant
to learn a bit about the performance they were attending earlier in the day, but he couldn't get away from his office to do so.

Gina smiled amusedly. "Yes, the clown."

Mickey felt a bit of awkwardness about his ignorance, but
when he saw nothing in Gina's expression to suggest that he
should feel that way, he relaxed. "I told you the other night
that I'm pretty uneducated when it comes to this subject."

Gina patted him on the arm. "I promise I'll make it easy
for you."

I'm sure you will, Mickey thought. *You would make lifting
the Empire State Building easy for me.*

The Metropolitan Opera House bubbled with the energy of a community celebrating something it loved. While he
could not at this time count himself among those who had
strong feelings for this art form, he could certainly appreciate
what it brought out in others. Here in this auditorium, the
wealthy and the well bred gathered to wear their finest clothing and witness an act by performers at the very tops of their
fields. And while Mickey was certain that some members of
the audience were here only to placate others in their party,
and some others were here exclusively because they believed
it to be an accessory of their station, most were here because
there was no form of entertainment in the world like this one.

Until about halfway though the show, Mickey found his
attention wandering. The singing was impressive, if utterly
foreign, but Mickey found it difficult to follow. Compounding

his distraction was the fact that Gina's arm was still around his, and she would squeeze it during dramatic passages. While this could have focused his attention more closely on the performance, it drew his mind instead to consider the excitement of her nearness, the sculpture of her ankles, the sweetness of her perfume.

At some point, though, perhaps inspired by the rapt expression on Gina's face, the opera began to transform for Mickey. Its language began to clarify itself for him, the emotional power began to work its way into his heart. Mickey found himself moved by the swells in the music and the torment in the singers' voices. When he turned to Gina to find her openly crying, the performance took on a greater force. After the final curtain, Mickey looked at Gina again. She turned to him, eyes glistening, and smiled in corroboration. It was only then that he realized that there were tears in his own eyes.

Mickey rose with the rest of the audience in applause, but then sat back down as others began to file toward the exits. He was overwhelmed.

"Did you enjoy it?" Gina said, sitting back with him.

"More than I ever would have thought I would. Thank you for bringing me here tonight."

"My mother will be delighted that her ticket went to good use. It's nice to see that you were so comfortable crying like that. Most men in the audience spend a lot of time wiping their eyes and pretending it's dust."

Mickey wiped at his own eyes at that point. He had no idea that the tears had run down his face. Gina threaded her arm into his again and they sat silently while the theatre slowly emptied. Eventually, they were alone except for the ushers and the cleaning crew.

"I'd like to come back here again soon," Mickey said after a long period of quiet.

"We can come here whenever you'd like."

This thrilled Mickey on a number of levels. "They probably want us to leave now though, don't they?"

"Probably. I've never been here so long after a performance."

When they headed outside, they saw a daunting line of people waiting for taxis.

"I guess we shouldn't have taken so long to get out of the theatre," Mickey said, wishing he were in a position to hire a limousine to drive Gina anywhere she wanted to go.

"Let's walk."

"You don't mind?"

"Do I appear too delicate to you? It's a beautiful night. Let's make the most of it."

They walked toward Fifth Avenue and then slowly south. There was no question now that Gina was nestled more closely into him as they strolled. Or was it that he was nestled more closely into her? Regardless, Mickey walked with no real desire to get to their destination. He would have been perfectly happy walking this way to the end of the Earth.

As they headed downtown, Gina said to him, "If a man really wanted to make an impression on a girl, he would know exactly what to do right now."

Mickey was baffled. He wanted to make an impression on Gina more than he wanted to breathe, but he had no idea what she was talking about. The confusion must have shown on his face, because Gina broke into laughter and temporarily loosened her grip on his arm.

"Schrafft's," she said.

"Ice cream?"

"Is there anything better?"

"There is, actually." He tipped his head toward her. "Schrafft's with you."

Mickey was in for yet another surprise when Gina ordered: three scoops, hot fudge, walnuts, and double whipped cream. He had been on many dates with women who would barely eat for fear that he would find it unladylike.

"There's a tiny morsel of fudge at the bottom of your dish," he said after watching her eat with gusto. "Did you not like it?"

Gina grinned at him. "I love ice cream."

"I never would have known."

"You should probably know right now that I can't walk anywhere near Schrafft's – well, any ice cream place, really – without stopping for a sundae."

"So your suggesting we walk from the theatre was an elaborate invention to get us here."

"You've seen right through me. Does that make me naughty?"

"Inconceivable."

When they walked back outside, Mickey stepped toward the curb. "I suppose you'll want a taxi now that you're finished duping me into buying you ice cream."

Gina reached for his arm. "No, it's lovely out here and I am very happily filled with butter pecan and whipped cream. Now I just need a handsome man to walk me the rest of the way home."

Had Mickey been by himself, the walk to Gina's would have taken him no longer than twenty minutes. Instead, it took more than an hour, Gina pulling on his arm to explore a shop window, asking his opinion on dresses and hats, imagining out loud what he would look like in a certain suit or blazer, revealing little secrets gleaned from colleagues in the Mayor's Office about certain shopkeepers.

"Four Board of Health violations," she said, pointing to a pricey restaurant across the street.

"You must be confusing this place with someplace else," Mickey said, remembering a meal he had there a few months back.

"No doubt about it. They're probably working on their fifth right now. Let's go in and tell the Maitre d' that we're with the Mayor's Office just to see the expression on his face."

"I take it back. You are in fact very naughty."

A minute later, they passed a toy store window where an enormous stuffed bear resided. Gina giggled at it and revealed that only a few years earlier she had cajoled her father into buying something similar for her.

"That was shamelessly manipulative of me, wasn't it? I really do love it, though. I think of my father and get this warm feeling inside every time I look at it. I don't suppose you have anything like that, being a man and all."

"No, no stuffed bears for me."

"Anything that has sentimental value?"

"I'm not really the sentimental type."

"Come on, there must be something that makes you go all soft inside when you look at it."

Mickey considered the statement briefly before answering.

"There's a tie," he said softly.

"A necktie?"

"Yes. It's a beautiful thing, really." Mickey saw the tie clearly before him and felt the tenderness he always felt upon seeing it. "My sister Theresa has been very troubled in recent years, but when I started working at QBK, she somehow managed to go out shopping for me and bring me a present of this beautiful necktie. I wore it only once and got a little spot of sauce on it. Now I won't wear it anymore for fear of staining it. Every time I go to pick out a tie, though, it's there, and it 'warms my heart a little' as you would say."

Gina squeezed his arm toward her. "That's sweet. Your sister must mean a lot to you."

"Always," Mickey said, nearly to himself. "No matter what happens to her."

After that, they walked slowly and quietly, with perhaps ten blocks passing before they spoke again. Mickey wondered briefly if his talking about Theresa had cast a pall on the evening, but a glance at the expression on Gina's face suggested otherwise.

When they finally arrived at Gina's building, she turned to him and took each of his hands in one of hers.

"It's okay to be sentimental," she said. "It shows that your heart is open."

Mickey smiled at her. "I think I could come to appreciate that."

"There aren't many men who are willing to be that way. You're lucky to have that in you." She hesitated and looked down. "And so am I."

Gina squeezed his hands and then looked up at him, her eyes again shimmering. "So where are you taking me this weekend?"

Mickey laughed. "You certainly are sure of yourself, aren't you?"

"Do you mean you don't want to go out with me this weekend?"

"Oh, I definitely didn't say that. I'm just accustomed to being the one to set the dates."

"I'm terribly sorry. I'll hold my tongue in the future."

"That would be an awful shame."

Gina offered Mickey a sly glance. "So you still haven't told me where you're taking me."

Mickey considered a number of options and then said, "Dinner and dancing at the Carlyle. How does that sound?"

"Absolutely lovely. I accept."

They stood quietly, looking at each other and holding hands, for a lengthy moment. Mickey considered the fact that nothing in his dating experience had compared to what he had been feeling these two nights with Gina. He couldn't wait for next Saturday and for all the days with her that would follow.

At last he reached over and kissed her lips. That they were indescribably soft and inviting was something he had been expecting. What was completely unanticipated was the wave of emotion that washed over him as their lips touched. Mickey felt at that moment that something had been released within him, that he had just reached down into a new level of feeling that he had never before known. He wanted to spend the rest of his life like this. They lingered over the kiss, neither seemingly willing to separate from the other. When at last their lips parted, Gina hugged Mickey close to her, their cheeks resting together. When she pulled back, Mickey memorized the closeness of her face, the brush of her skin, knowing that he would keep that memory with him forever.

"Until Saturday," she said softly.

"Saturday."

Gina took a step toward her building and then turned back to Mickey, gifting him with one more smile. Mickey wasn't at all sure that his legs would support him when he turned to walk toward his apartment.

~~~~~~~~

He sat in the chair in Jesse's office, fully immersed in the memory of those moments. He was drained. It felt like he had walked back half a century. He looked over at Jesse's face and knew that his son was rapt. Jesse would be disappointed if he was expecting Mickey to continue, though. There was no way that he could tell any more of this story today.

Chapter Fourteen

After presenting me with the second installment of his saga, my father spent a great deal of time in his room. This story-telling seemed to sap him of so much energy. Was he upload-ing the entirety of his relationship with Gina before he talked about her, the sheer volume of the memory requiring him to suspend other functions? Was it possible that after he talked about her for a while, he flashed forward to their breakup and the memory of that bitter event wore him down?

For the first time, I considered the possibility that perhaps he could even be making up the entire thing. Perhaps this was some sort of allegory, the moral of which I would come to un-derstand in time. Maybe the reason he couldn't tell me more in one sitting was because he hadn't invented it all yet.

Whatever it was, I was absolutely mesmerized. I couldn't get over how interesting it was to hear my father talk about a love affair and all of its accoutrements this way. The New York of another era. "Pagliacci" at the Met. Schrafft's (we had gone to the last one in the City when I was a kid – that mem-ory would certainly take on a new cast in the future). I knew something about all of these things, but never before had I considered them from the perspective of my father as a young man. A young man in love.

The reason I knew that my father was in his room for much of the day was that I spent a good portion of it wan dering through the house seeking inspiration to work on the damned parquet floor piece. By the early afternoon, I realized that this story was no more inane than any other I'd written, and that I had been entirely aware of what the assignment was before I accepted it. That it had hung me up – and that I was having an increasingly harder time getting started on even the most rudimentary articles – had little to do with the articles themselves and everything to do with my having done nothing but this kind of piece for several months now. I know a number of people who make a good living vacuuming up assignments such as these from a variety of magazines and spitting them out, sometimes several in one day. It required a certain kind of demeanor and, I'm sure, a certain kind of talent, but I couldn't help but feel that it was the writer's equivalent of flipping burgers. It wasn't in any way why I had chosen my profession and I was beginning to fear that by taking work that wasn't challenging or edifying I was losing the ability to imagine challenging or edifying stories. My pitches were flopping regularly. Hence half a year of wondering if the editor wanted fries with that story.

I eventually belched the parquet article into existence. Once I succumbed to the reality that not a single reader of this piece was going to care about cadence or nuance, it only took a couple of hours.

Around 4:30, with my father still in his room (I assumed he was sleeping), I decided to go to the fish store to pick up something for dinner. They had Dover Sole available, which they almost never did, and I decided to splurge.

When I got home, my father was sitting in the den watching the news. This was unusual, since he did most of his trading in the afternoon. The online brokers offer the opportunity to keep going after the closing bell, so he usually did so until around 6:30. The television was of course blaring.

"Hey, Dad," I called over the din. "I got some fish for dinner."

"Sounds good."

"No trading?"

"The market can do without me for a day."

Were I more of an alarmist (like my brother, for instance), I might have found reason to be concerned about that last comment. I just took it as another indication that he was a little off his game.

I went into the kitchen, put the fish in the refrigerator, and began to think about the various ways in which I could prepare it. With a tarragon vinaigrette. Some olive oil and capers. A few chopped tomatoes and basil.

Then I remembered that my father loved Sole Amandine. My mother would make it regularly, and I regarded it in the matter-of-fact way that kids regard so many things they grow up with. When I started eating out and becoming interested in cooking myself, though, I realized the dish was bland, unnecessarily rich, and horribly old-fashioned. The fact that my father loved it so much was just another indication of how one-dimensional his tastes were. Considering this in the context of the stories he was telling about the life of a man living on the town after World War II, though, my perceptions changed. I realized that it was the kind of thing he would have grown fond of eating in those lavish New York restaurants of the time. Suddenly, he wasn't an elderly man with too much affection for butter, but rather a gourmand from a different era.

I decided to make the dish for him that night. I pulled out a French cookbook I had taken from the house after my mother died. I probably could have figured out the preparation on my own, but I wanted to make sure I got it right.

When I served it, the look of satisfaction on my father's face made it clear to me that I'd succeeded. I could almost see him drifting back, if not to tables with white starched linens and equally starched waiters, at least to his own dining room. I wondered if traveling back in time twice in one day could be bad for his health.

"You can cook like this?" he said.

"On occasion. Since we're having soy meatloaf with ancho peppers and dried bonito flakes tomorrow night, I thought I'd try something different."

He offered me an amused smirk and then returned to his plate. As much as he'd come to appreciate some of my cooking, I could see that he was comforted and relieved to have this dish in front of him. He practically hugged it to his chest.

"You are kidding about the meatloaf thing, right?" he said after a few bites.

"Yeah, of course. We're out of bonito."

I had another bite of the fish. It really was good. At least as good as my mother made it. I could see how one could become enamored of food like this, especially if one chose to remain blissfully ignorant about nutrition.

The thought of my mother's cooking took me in an almost entirely different direction from where I'm sure my father's mind was. I started to have little nostalgic pangs over seeing my mother laboring lovingly in the kitchen, which led me to the hundreds of after-school conversations we'd had there. My mother was smart, she was open, and she was quintessentially maternal. Other than a couple of months after I got my driver's license and a short time during my insane Karen phase, I had never rebelled against her. To me, she was the safest person in the universe.

However, she was not in any way like how my father described Gina. She wasn't worldly or elegant or capable of clever banter, all of which the Great Love of my father's life had been. My mother was caring and responsible and monumentally goodhearted, but these attributes obviously didn't add up to Great Love status in my father's eyes. I was surprised to realize in some way that they wouldn't have in mine if I were still looking for that sort of thing.

I suddenly felt a little disloyal to my mother for being so intrigued with my father's story. I wanted to ask him a million questions, starting with how he could have moved from Gina to my mother, but I wasn't sure how to ask them and I wasn't entirely sure that I wanted the answer. Instead, I chose a ridiculously circuitous route.

"So Dad, how come you didn't decide to stay in the City after you and Mom got married?"

My father dipped a bit of baguette in the butter sauce and looked up at me.

"I was done with the City by then. Except for work, of course. And your mother really wanted to move out to the country."

The notion of the congested streets of Northern New Jersey ever being considered "the country" made me laugh, but I understood that it would have seemed that way back then, especially after Manhattan.

"But you loved the City, didn't you?"

"I was okay doing whatever your mother wanted to do. There's only so much of New York you can take, you know? She just didn't think it was the best place to raise kids."

"So coming out here was all Mom's idea?"

"Pretty much, yeah."

"And you were fine with it?"

He looked at me quizzically. "I trusted your mother. I believed she knew what was right for us."

Spoken like a true partner. The CEO leaving the operational work to the COO. I was getting the answers I had expected to get but not, I realized, the ones I was hoping to get. I wanted there to be some romance to the story. I'd always assumed that there had been some in their relationship somewhere along the line, and I really wanted to hear it. I feared, though, that if I asked directly my father might interpret this as meaning that the Gina story was disturbing to me in some way and he would stop telling me more. Again I felt as though I were betraying my mother in some way.

Our dinner finished, my father uncharacteristically got up to take both of our plates to the sink.

"So did you make chocolate mousse for dessert?" he said. Another of my mother's regular dishes.

"Dream on. There's some cantaloupe."

~~~~~~~~

I knew that my father was having more and more trouble with his knees. It also seemed to me that he was flexing his fingers more often, as though trying to improve the circulation. We'd gone to the doctor about the former and learned that there was little to do short of replacing the knees completely, which my father rejected. I knew that there would come a time when he was going to be less mobile, perhaps even requiring a walker or a wheelchair, but his thought processes were still crisp, as our multitudinous verbal exchanges confirmed. I had every reason to believe that he was as sharp-witted as he had ever been. Except for that morning when I returned home to find him disoriented. And then the night that followed the second Gina story.

I tended to be a very deep sleeper, which explains why I didn't hear my bedroom door open that night or why I probably missed the beginning of the episode.

"Teddy . . . Ted," I heard my father saying as he shook my shoulders. "Get up, will you? I've gotta talk to you."

I paddled up from sleep and slowly sat up in bed. My father kept one hand on my shoulder.

"Dad . . . .."

"Ted, I'm sorry to wake you, but you're the only person I can talk to about this. I stayed out really late to make sure that Dad was asleep when I got home. He's driving me crazy."

"Dad," I repeated more firmly. He still was holding my shoulder and he was looking in my direction, but even in the dim light I could tell that he was looking past me.

"He wants me to start working for him at the shop, Ted. You're the only one I've ever told how much I hate that place. I don't want to wind up there for the rest of my life. You gotta give me some advice."

I thought that perhaps he was sleepwalking, and tried to think of a way to get him back to his bed without waking him. I started to get out from under the sheets.

"I know you're the younger one, but you're just so much better at talking to Dad than I am. What can I say to him?"

"Dad, listen . . . .."

"Yeah, 'Dad, listen.' Like that's really gonna help."

That caught me by surprise. To the best of my knowledge sleepwalkers weren't responsive to outside stimulus.

"Dad, I'm not Teddy."

"You want me to tell him that I'm not you? He knows I'm not you. I'm not the muscle man. I'm not gonna be the big war hero. He wouldn't ask *you* to do this."

I was flat-out frightened now, completely unprepared for this.

"Do you want me to talk to him for you?" I said, wondering if it would be useful to play along.

"He'll think I'm chicken if you talk to him for me."

"I won't let him know that you said anything to me. I'll just ask him about what he's planning to do with the store, and when he tells me I'll tell him that I think it's a bad idea."

"Do you think that would work?"

"It could work. You know I've always had a way with Dad."

He hugged me then and looked directly into my eyes. I wondered if he could see the tears there.

"I love ya, Ted. I don't know what I'd do without you. You won't let him know that we've talked right?"

"I won't say a word about it."

"And you think this will work?"

"I'll do my best."

He stood up walked toward the door. He turned back. "I don't know what I'd do without you, Ted." He was beaming.

He left the room and I sat in the same position for what must have been a half-hour. *My God*, I thought, *what if my father is losing his mind?*

Chapter Fifteen

For obvious reasons, I didn't sleep particularly well that night. The next morning I called Marina from my bedroom to tell her about my episode with my father. She talked me through a number of possible reasons why it might have happened and tried to ease my mind, but she wasn't nearly as successful this time as she usually was.

By the time I got off the phone with her, I could hear my father moving around the house. I walked out to the kitchen, more hesitant than I had ever been in my own home. I half expected his hair to have grown wild overnight and for him to be spouting random proclamations like some street corner preacher. Instead, he looked relaxed at the table, drinking coffee and reading the paper.

"Hey, Dad."

He looked up from the paper and made the same sharp, clear eye contact he'd made with me on every other day (except, of course, for those days when he wasn't making eye contact with me at all).

"Hey, Jess. Did you have a good night's sleep?"

"Not great, actually. How about you?"

"Ah, you know me. I always sleep well until about 5:30 and then I just lie there until I decide to get up. If that's a good night's sleep, then I guess I had one."

There was nothing on his face that suggested he was hiding anything from me. He obviously had absolutely no memory of "talking" to my late uncle last night.

I poured a cup of coffee and sat down next to him.

"How are you feeling lately, Dad?"

He put down the paper. "I'm not doing the knee replacement thing. Give it up."

I held up my hands defensively. "I'll never mention it again. Is that the only thing that's bothering you?"

He cast his eyes downward, the universal language for *I haven't been entirely honest with you.*

I leaned closer. "What else?"

He looked back up at me and flexed his right arm. "I don't know what's going on with my arm. Sometimes it tingles. Sometimes it just feels cold. Right now it's perfectly fine."

No, he had absolutely no memory of the night before.

"Want to ask Dr. Quigley about it?"

"What's he gonna do, recommend arm replacement surgery?"

"You always liked Dr. Quigley, Dad. You know it is his responsibility to explain all the alternatives to you when he diagnoses a problem."

"And it's my responsibility to tell him to go to hell if I don't like his alternatives."

"Something like that."

He moved his arm again. "I don't want to see Dr. Quigley. If the arm gets worse, we'll go, but I'm okay right now."

He picked up the paper again. I made breakfast and observed him for signs of mental impairment. Other than his opinion about a standardized testing issue that was the subject of a front page article in the *Times*, I found none. Wanting to assure myself that he was going to be fine, I went to my office a half-hour later that morning. By the time I got there, I'd convinced myself that he was at least okay for now.

I wasn't expecting it to be a promising workday. I had an interview with a CPA for an article at 1:30, the anticipation of which was hardly releasing adrenaline. I couldn't start on the piece until I spoke to him, and had decided to dedicate the morning to getting my office in order, doing a little filing, maybe running a Quicken report for the quarter, maybe calling a few editors for lunch dates. After all of that excitement, I figured I'd have no trouble getting a nap in before the accountant to make up for some of the sleep I'd lost the night before. Marina and I were going to a chamber concert that night, and I didn't think she'd appreciate my snoring on her shoulder.

I was piling papers over various open spaces on the floor when Aline Dixon called. Aline was a senior editor at *Food and Living* and we'd hooked up on a few pieces over the years, though not nearly as many as I would have liked. I loved writing for the magazine as both food and living were things that interested me, but I was definitely on the taxi squad with them. I'd never been able to establish myself as a "foodie," and found that the work was tough to come by when you weren't in the inner circle. Every now and then, Aline would throw me an article after she'd exhausted the A-list. ("I'm not sure why the readers want another article on cheddar cheese, but they seem to. Do you think you could bang out 3,500 words?") As with *Tapestry* and any other magazine I would have liked to be working with more often, I always took these tidbits very seriously, always delivered ahead of deadline, and always gave the subjects way more attention than they deserved.

"What do you know about Grant Hayward?" she said.

"The rock and roll winemaker?"

She laughed at my use of the nickname the media had given him. "The very same."

"I know that he started in Sonoma something like twenty years ago making some good boutique wines and that he somehow became the hot thing among West Coast celebrities. I know that when he got into the business he was around two hundred and fifty pounds and that when he began hanging with pop stars he went on this intense diet and started wearing Versace. Then he organized that summer concert series and I think he's in TMZ as often as he's in your pages. The wine is still good, though, and I've always heard he was a solid guy."

"He's been very nice the few times I've met him," Aline said, "and the wine, in my opinion, is better than it ever was. You're right about the media attention, though. I think sometimes that gets in the way of how people perceive what he does. Have you heard about the New Collective?"

"Got me there. Is this a hot band he's discovered?"

"Maybe, but not of the musical variety. It's pretty amazing. As I'm sure you know, the change in the economy has been rough on the little California wine guys. A lot of small vintners have either gone out of business or had to sell to much bigger wineries. Hayward has pulled a group of these guys together, subsidized their operations, essentially taken care of all of their financial concerns, and has them all working together to craft the next generation of great wines."

"Really? I can't believe this hasn't been reported on every celebrity show in America."

"That's the most interesting thing about it. Hayward is shunning publicity on this. He doesn't want reporters getting in the way of the art. It took us six months to convince him to let us send someone there to do a piece."

"Wow."

"Yeah. The same Grant Hayward. So, do you want the gig?"

I literally started sweating when she said it. Editors didn't call me with offers like this.

"Me?"

"Hayward asked for you."

"He *asked for me?*"

"It was because of that 'Pancake Quest' piece you did for us last year."

"I loved writing that piece."

"Well, he loved reading it. He liked the way you talked about the dedication of the great pancake makers. He tore it out."

I couldn't believe I was hearing this. The very fact that someone like Grant Hayward had even read one of my articles was flattering. That he had torn it out and was now asking for me to write about him was borderline inconceivable.

"Yeah, I think I'd like to do it."

"Great. Our idea is that you would spend a week with him and the Collective to get into the true day-to-day of it. We want you to talk about Hayward, of course, but the other vintners are as much of the story as he is. This is a big coup that Hayward is giving us this access and we're going to promote the hell out of it, so we want the story to have as much depth as possible."

"When?"

"This is ridiculously short notice, but he's willing to have someone come out there next week."

My first thought was, *Next week? No problem. I'll be out there next flight if he wants.*

Then I had my next thought. My father. I certainly couldn't leave him alone for a week.

"Is that a problem?" Aline said.

"No, no, I'll work it out. I have some stuff I have to deal with, but I'll get it done. Let me call you back this afternoon and we'll figure out the details."

I got off the phone, wiped my brow, and considered the options. Saying no to this assignment was not one of them. This would be the highest-profile piece of my career, the kind of thing that could lead to more big-time assignments, including more from the editorial team at *Food and Living.* I called Denise at the office and, in a break with tradition, she was available for my call.

"I've gotten a huge writing assignment," I said when she got on the line.

"Hey, good for you," she said with a trace of enthusiasm.

"The thing is that the job is in Northern California and I'm going to be gone for a week."

"How are you going to do that with Dad?"

"Hence my call."

"What do you mean?"

"Do you think you could give me a hand with this?"

"How could I give you a hand?" I was sure she wasn't being intentionally dense. She had no idea how she could help.

"Like maybe let Dad stay at your place while I'm away?"

"Oh, that would be a terrible idea."

"What's so terrible about it? He loves you and he'll do anything you say. You talk to him about a stock or a merger or two and he'll think he's on vacation. Other than that, you just need to give him a place to sleep and eat."

"Do you have any idea what my life is like?"

"Of course I do, Denise. You tell me every time I see you."

"Well, then how could I possibly fit taking care of Dad into it? I can't believe you're even suggesting it."

"Never mind. I'll figure something else out."

"Hey Jess, this was part of the deal. You know, if you'd agreed with the rest of us to have him put in one of those assisted living homes you wouldn't be having this problem right now. I'm surprised you didn't realize that."

"Thanks for the valuable advice, Denise. I'll let you go. I'm sure you have more important things to do."

I got off the line and called Matty, but the message was the same. He had too much going on to drop everything and fly in from Chicago (at least there was something reasonable about that), and this was exactly the kind of thing he was worried about when I said I wanted my father to live with me.

"It's a big responsibility, Jess."

Frustrated, I cut the conversation short and considered other options. It was ridiculous to even think about asking Darlene. My Aunt Teresa wasn't exactly hale herself. Leaving him alone was flat-out unthinkable, especially after what had happened the night before.

As absurd as it seems, I don't think I fully realized how much I had taken on by having my father move in with me until that very moment. I was practically chained to the house. I could get out for a while for a business meeting or a night at Marina's, but anything beyond that would be subject to the

mercies of my siblings. And they weren't going to be especially forthcoming with those. Did this mean that Marina and I
could never go away for the weekend? Did this mean that I
would only be writing articles I could research from home for
the rest of my life?

Did this mean I was going to have to turn down the hot-
test assignment I'd ever received?

I was beside myself. I was feeling claustrophobic. I envisioned my entire career dissipating before my eyes. I saw
my fifty-year-old self sitting with my hundred-year-old father,
the two of us staring blankly at a television screen, his verve
dimmed by time, mine dimmed by the lack of opportunity.

I needed someone to vent to, but there was no one available. My siblings were less than sympathetic. I didn't have a
single friend who would be able to relate. Marina was teaching. I knew instinctively that I had to avoid seeing my father
while I was feeling this way, because I would almost certainly
say something hurtful to him, and he didn't deserve that. I
didn't call Aline right away because the idea of making that
call was devastating to me. I tried to continue filing, but my
thoughts were so clouded that I could barely remember the
alphabet.

Marina called a little after noon. A few weeks back, she
had taken to calling me during her lunch break, and it was a
welcome way to make the transition out of the morning. The
moment she said hello, I dumped the entire story on her.

"I can't believe I have to make this phone call," I said toward the end of my tirade. "I did a five-thousand-word article
on butter for her once just so I could get an opportunity like
this, and now I have to call her to say, 'Thanks, but no thanks.'"

"I'll stay with him," Marina said when I took a breath.

It took a second for the words to register. "What do you
mean?"

"I'll stay with your father. You don't think he'll have a
problem with that, do you?"

"He doesn't get a vote."

"He *definitely* gets a vote. Why, do you think he'll have a problem with it? He seemed to like me."

"He loves you. I think he wants to marry you. You would really do this?"

"Of course I would. Unless you think his being alone during the day will be an issue after what happened last night."

I thought about this for a moment, but the image of his being his clear-eyed self this morning (not to mention a significant amount of my desperately wanting this not to be an impediment) persuaded me.

"No, he's been great today. I have no idea what that was last night."

"So talk to him and make sure he's okay with it, and then book your flight to San Francisco."

"I can't believe you'd do this for me."

"Why can't you believe it? You'd do it for me, wouldn't you?"

I didn't have to think about this, even though I had never thought about it before. "Yeah, of course I would. I guess it just seems funny that you're coming through for me when my brother and sister couldn't be bothered."

She chuckled. "Well, he was *very* nice to me when we had dinner."

"Just make sure you keep your distance from him. He's pretty slick and I don't want to have to worry about the two of you while I'm away."

"Hey, you never know what might happen. But I'll try to remain faithful as long as I can. I guess it depends on how much of a commitment he's willing to make."

"Maybe this isn't a good idea after all."

"Sometimes you just have to take a chance."

I laughed. Marina's lunchtime calls often gave me a lift, but never before had one catapulted me like this one.

"This is world-class great of you, you know?" I said.

"I'm sure you'll think of some fabulous way to thank me."

"I guarantee that."

We got off the phone a few minutes later. I called Aline to follow up and confirm plans, but she was out to lunch. I went out to see my father. Given how dumbstruck he had been about Marina the first time he met her, I figured this news was going to make his day nearly as much as it had made mine.

Chapter Sixteen

Northern California – particularly the wine country – simply does "quality of life" better than anyplace in the Northeast does. *Food and Living* put me up in an inn that was relatively modest by the luxe standards of some lodging available in the vicinity, but still there were aromatherapy bath beads for the tub, a collection of herbal teas on the sideboard, fresh fruit and chocolate-dipped strawberries, and a CD player with a selection of recordings from local musicians. I hadn't been in the area in several years and yet from the moment I touched down in San Francisco, I felt a rare sense of comfort. I felt like I belonged here.

I landed in the early afternoon. As soon as I hit the freeway, the combination of topography, sunlight, bright music on the radio, and excitement about my assignment inspired me. Rather than go directly to the inn, I decided to take a couple of side trips. I walked along the waterfront in Sausalito for an hour, eating an ice cream cone and exploring different stores. Then I remembered a craft shop in Yountville and drove to see if it was still there. I bought a coffee mug for my father (assuming that his drinking coffee in a handmade mug would be the next step in his coffee-drinking evolution) and a pair of silver earrings for Marina.

I'd been to the area four times previously. The first was with friends while Georgia was in Europe. I gained my appreciation for California wine on that trip, and learned that it was possible to feel more sophisticated while stumbling around if you got drunk on the better stuff. The second was with a fellow journalist in an attempt to drum up business with West Coast magazines. I came away with a pretty clear sense that I didn't have the voice to write for them, but the experience subtly altered my writing style, making it more sensory and less narrative (which of course was particularly useful when writing about hedge funds). The third was with Karen and like everything else with her it was a bacchanal. Prodigious amounts of food and wine, lovemaking on a beach, in a garden, in a Jacuzzi, even a wicker chair. (It dawned on me that there was a very real possibility that Karen was somewhere within a hundred-mile radius of where I was lodging on my current trip. I didn't attempt to look her up.)

The fourth was a few years ago. Having a bit of a crisis in terms of where my professional and personal lives were going, I headed out there on my own. I stayed in a tiny bed-and-breakfast and drove and walked for hours every day. The trip was restorative beyond all of my expectations. I made many discoveries in terms of shops and restaurants, and nearly as many in terms of where I was headed in my life. This was the first time I became genuinely comfortable with my solo-ness. I could go to a concert unaccompanied. I could spend an entire day talking to no one. I could do something that I had previously enjoyed doing only in the company of others, and still enjoy it. I returned from that trip feeling for perhaps the first time in my life that, while having friends, lovers, and relatives was welcome, it wasn't a prerequisite to living well.

It was the memory of the last trip that suffused the first day of this trip, undoubtedly because I was there by myself. There was a lightness to my mood as I wandered around, remembering the things that I did and the things that I thought. Just before going to the inn, I took a drive to Calistoga and walked up to the playhouse there. On my last trip I had bought a ticket to the Edward Albee play being performed. It was the first time I had ever felt comfortable entering a theatre by myself, the first time I didn't have any concerns about other people seeing me alone and thinking, "Poor guy, can't get a date." It was a significant turning point, and since it was Albee, the play was profound as well.

I eventually got to the inn and settled down. The next morning, I made my first trip to the vineyard where Hayward was putting his New Collective together. The company and the wine were not going to be called "New Collective," but Hayward liked the idea of keeping the name a secret until the first bottles were released in two years. Everything about this winery differed dramatically from the Hayward image. I'd been to Hayward Vineyards on one of my previous trips and recalled it as a buffed monument to the triumph of wine-making for the educated masses. Hayward wines were quite good mid-level wines, the kind of thing I might have served (and had) at a dinner party. I thought they deserved most of their popularity. It was clear from the look of their operation, though, that their goal was to put a bottle or two in the wine rack of every home in America. It was a Machine.

The new setting was stripped down and unpretentious. Of course, they wouldn't be receiving the public for another couple of years and they had plenty of time to get their façade in place, but one would have thought that if Grant Hayward, The Rock and Roll Winemaker, was going to be spending any time here at all, he would have insisted that the trappings be flashier. I of course leapt to the conclusion that the spartan environment was all very consciously designed by Hayward and his PR people. I assumed they had spent months deciding how stripped down to make the place in order to suggest the proper level of monk-like dedication to craft.

There were very few rules governing the piece I was writing, which surprised me given how controlling Hayward tended to be with the media. I have to admit that, as excited as I was about the prospects of doing this article, I was also more than a little dubious about the way I expected my interviews to proceed. I fully expected Hayward to spin this into ten thousand words of promotion. I assumed that my first meeting (or perhaps even my first several) would be with publicists and gatekeepers who would explain to me not only what I would be allowed to observe, but also what my observations were going to be. Instead, on that very first day, Hayward himself came out to greet me.

He was much smaller in person than I expected him to be. At the same time, he radiated much more presence than he did on a television screen or the pages of a magazine. I had only begun to stand when I saw him enter the reception area, and I swear he lifted me to my feet when he gripped my hand. Looking him in the eyes (which required looking down, as he was actually a few inches shorter than me), I could see that he did not perceive my arrival as a burden but that he in fact seemed to be glad to have a representative of *Food and Living* here. He led me through a door and we walked off at a brisk pace.

"We've set up a home base for you –" He stopped and looked around and then shook his head. "– somewhere around here. But if it's okay with you, I thought we'd walk the vineyard first."

"Yeah, fine. Lead the way."

We stepped through another doorway and out toward the grapes. We were walking at a pace I'd reserved exclusively for midtown Manhattan, far brisker than the one I'd set for myself the day before.

"I like your work," Hayward said.

"Thanks. Aline mentioned that you read the pancake story."

He nodded. "I did. I'm a bit of a pancake junkie myself. I'll have pancakes for dinner sometimes. Name a major American city and I'll tell you the best place to get pancakes."

"I guess I could have saved myself a lot of time if I'd just called you before I wrote the article, huh?"

"Nah, you always want to do the work yourself. Besides, you were absolutely right about Detroit, and I would have given you bad information there. And I didn't even know about that place outside of Portland. I completely disagree with you about Kansas City, though."

"I'll leave room in this article for a rebuttal, if you'd like."

He laughed. "Yeah. I'll keep that in mind. I like your other stuff, too. That grandmother piece was a knockout."

"You read the grandmother piece?"

He threw me a knowing glance. "I like to be informed about the people I grant interviews to."

I nodded. I was impressed. Of course he had his staff pull the articles together (unlikely they gave him any of the searing investigative work I'd done on wallpaper), but he'd still bothered to read them himself. And he even liked them. Like the vast majority of the population, I find it incredibly endearing when someone thinks highly of me, and I was already starting to like Grant Hayward.

Once we got to the vineyard, Hayward's pace slowed considerably. We spent more than an hour there while he explained to me the Collective's choices in fencing, their approach to irrigation, the various sub-strains of grape chosen to grow in different locations, even the subtle decisions they'd made regarding the spacing between rows of vines. The entire time, at Hayward's request, my tape recorder stayed off and my notebook remained in my backpack.

"Not that any of this would be easy to steal," he said, "but as you can imagine, it's all rather proprietary."

"You know, you probably could have glossed over this and I wouldn't have had a clue about any of it."

"I figured that. But it's important for you to know. If you're really going to write about what we're doing here, you need to understand what goes into what we're doing here."

A short while later, Hayward brought me back inside and introduced me to his assistant, who showed me the office they'd set up for my visit. He excused himself, saying that he had some things he needed to attend to. It was only then, while talking to his assistant, that I learned that Hayward was located at this facility full-time, having turned the day-to-day task of running

Hayward Vineyards over to his COO. He'd even given the management of his annual summer concert series to someone else.

I spent much of the rest of the day on the premises, meeting with various members of the staff and conducting interviews with groundskeepers, designers, even the receptionist. At around 3:30, I packed up my laptop and headed out. Hayward caught me in the hallway as I was leaving.

"Hey, Jesse. I'm sorry I didn't get a chance to talk to you more today," he said. "The working life, you know? We have a bunch of people lined up to sit down with you tomorrow."

"That would be great. I got some good stuff today."

"I'm glad. What are you doing for dinner tomorrow night?"

I shook my head. "I haven't made any plans."

"Great. I think I can pull the entire Collective together. We'll go into town and you can get to know everybody."

After that, he turned, throwing out something about "details," and heading off at his sprinter's pace.

~~~~~~~~~

I got back to the inn around 4:15 and figured it would be a good time to call home. My father answered the phone.

"Hi, Dad. Everything going okay over there?"

"I don't know, Jess," he said softly. "Didn't you say that your girlfriend was going to come over here again today?"

I felt a chill and immediately began wondering about flights back to Newark.

"What? She's not there? Did she call?"

My father laughed and then answered in his normal booming voice. "Are you kidding? Do you think Marina would ever abandon me like that? I just wanted to see how you'd react. Yeah, everything is great here. I was just finishing up the dishes."

"Finishing up what with the dishes?"

He spoke to me as though I were seven. "Washing them, Jess. They tell me that it's nicer to eat off of dishes after they've been washed."

"You're doing the dishes?"

"Do you think I can't handle the job?"

"Oh, I'm sure you're great at the job, Dad. Keep up the good work."

He chuckled, for a reason that escaped me. "So? Are you getting anywhere out there?"

"I think I'm doing okay so far. I had a lot of good interviews, and I have a bunch lined up for tomorrow. This is going to be an interesting story."

"Hey, you travel across the country for a story, it had better be an interesting one. Want to talk to Marina?"

I told him I did, and a moment later she got on the line.

"He's doing the dishes?"

I could feel her smile across the line. "Yes he is. I didn't have to bribe him or anything. He got up from the table when we were finished eating and told me to go relax while he cleaned up."

"I just realized that I've had it all wrong. *You're* the alien. You've blasted him with your hypno-ray, haven't you?"

"Found me out."

"Is it permanent?"

"We haven't perfected the technology yet."

I settled back in an overstuffed chair and brought a box of potpourri to my nose for a sniff. "So I guess asking if everything is okay is superfluous, huh?"

"He seems to be enjoying himself." I could envision Marina pulling her hair back to expose one side of her neck while she spoke. She did it all the time when she was on the phone, and I found it ridiculously sexy. "He's eating. And I think he's sleeping okay. We haven't had any events."

"That's great. Have I told you how much I appreciate your doing this?"

"The eighteen times you said it before you left for the airport got the message across."

I played with the dried flowers in the potpourri box. "I just want to make sure you know."

"It's nothing. When my mother comes to town again, you can live with her for a week to make up for it. So how's it going out there?"

"I think it's going great. I really like Hayward, which is nearly as much of a surprise as my father doing housework. He's nowhere near as slick as I expected him to be, and he didn't drop a single name the entire time I was talking to him today."

"Will you get a good story out of this?"

"It's anybody's guess, but this was an encouraging first day."

"That's great. So what's on the agenda for tonight?"

"Well, first I think I'm going to take a bath with these sandalwood bath beads while listening to a CD of dulcimer music." I took one more sniff from the potpourri and put it back on the nightstand. "Then I think I'm going to drive over to a little place about fifteen minutes from here to eat dinner in a garden."

"It's so nice that you don't feel you need to pretend to be working your fingers to the bone for me."

I laughed. "That sounded pretty 'lap of luxury,' didn't it? I guarantee you that I'll be thinking about the Collective's platforming plan the entire time I'm soaking."

"I'd rather that you were thinking about my being in the bathtub with you."

"Mmm. Much better idea." I wished I could kiss the naked skin on her neck.

"I've got a few more homework assignments to read. Then I promised your father that I'd watch Myrna Loy with him. He made me watch a Three Stooges movie with him last night. What was that about?"

"Ooh, Dad's dirty little secret. Yeah, the educated and erudite Mickey Sienna is a slapstick junkie. I'm surprised he let you in on it."

"I thought he was going to throw his back out, he was laughing so hard."

"Jeez, The Three Stooges and Myrna Loy. They're setting aside a special place in heaven for you as we speak. Hey, he hasn't told you any more of the story of Gina, has he?"

"Does he even know I know about it?"

I thought about whether I'd mentioned that I told Marina, and realized that I hadn't. "No, I suppose not."

"I don't think he likes me that much, yet. Maybe tomorrow."

~~~~~~~~

The interviews the next day were productive and gave me a significant amount of background on the Collective and the plan for introducing its wine to the public. During dinner that night, I began to get a sense of what was really happening with this group of vintners and where the core of the story was.

As we ate artisan pizzas and bulgogi (a combination unavailable in New Jersey) and drank the restaurant's last remaining bottles of a pinot noir created by one of the Collective's members at his now-defunct boutique winery, the conversation ranged widely. The impact of the economy on the wine industry. The impact of the economy on real estate prices. The need for one of the members of the Collective to buy a new house now that his third child had been born. The need to learn how to throw a curveball now that another's child had turned ten. The need for a particular San Francisco Giant to learn how to throw a curveball because batters weren't supposed to hit pitches as far as they had been hitting them off of him.

But it was a side comment about "lingering effects on the palette" that allowed me to truly see the Collective at work. Suddenly, they were "talking wine" and the passions, philosophies, and music of their collaboration emerged. These were not business people. These were not creators of a product. These were people who could look at an armoire and imagine how its design could somehow influence the construction of a great Cabernet. The conversation veered toward a sampling at the vineyard three days before of a wine in progress. Perhaps a few more grapes with thicker skin. Perhaps one more day on the vine. Perhaps five more days in the barrel. A degree here. A quarter of a percentage point of humidity there. Any and all of this could be the difference between a wine someone like me would admire, and one that would be heralded for the ages.

Hayward didn't lead this conversation, but he was a lusty participant. It didn't matter that his main vineyard was fifty times bigger than the vineyards of the rest of the Collective combined. It didn't matter that he counted actresses and rock royalty among his close personal friends. It didn't matter that there wouldn't have been a writer from *Food and Living* at the table if Hayward hadn't been there as well. He was "talking wine" and he was doing it with utter conviction and joy. For all any of us knew, something great could come of this exchange. Or nothing of any use at all. In either case, I was sure there would be another conversation like this every time these seven people sat in a room together.

I left the dinner with a level of inspiration I hadn't felt in years. It was as though I had been privileged enough to gain a seat at the Algonquin Round Table. In fact, it would be that image that would serve as the spine of my story. The quest for art in the making of wine. Though I knew I wasn't prepared to start the actual article, I went back to my room that night and wrote for nearly three hours. Much of this was personal impression. A lot of it was far more emotional than my writing tended to be, and in all likelihood much more so than the editors at *Food and Living* would find comfortable. But I was driven by the need to write, the need to express my own creativity, to seek a vision of my own. I hadn't felt this good about writing in a very long time, and for the first time in recent memory, I regretted that I was too tired to continue when I finally turned off the laptop and climbed into bed.

My major interview with Hayward was the next afternoon. We sat in his office, which looked shockingly like the one they had put me in, with the exception of hundreds of pieces of "work debris," as he described it. I wanted to thank him for what I'd witnessed the night before, but I thought doing so might compromise me. Still, I found myself laughing easily at his little jokes and allowing him to direct the interview far more than I normally would. We covered a lot of the essentials: the origins of the Collective, the timeline for release, production expectations, that sort of thing. I let Hayward talk about what was going on at Hayward Vineyards in his absence and to promote the talents of the new master winemaker there. I allowed Hayward to express his excitement for this new venture and to talk about its lofty aims. It was a good story, and one I was much more willing to believe than I had been a few days earlier.

"But how does this make any sense?" I said after we'd been talking for more than an hour.

"What do you mean?"

I made a small gesture with my hands. "How does it make sense for you to do this at this point in your career? Hayward is on the verge of becoming a major brand name in the field, you yourself are the closest thing to a pop star the industry has ever produced, you've gotten merchandising offers from everything from frozen food companies to t-shirt manufacturers. This is not when most people would decide to turn their main business over to their second-in-command so they could start an entirely new company out of their own pocket, subsidizing a bunch of guys who were about to go out of business, to pursue an ambition that will be examined with the most powerful microscopes the media can get their hands on."

Hayward laughed and sat back in his chair. "Gee, I hadn't thought of it that way. I'd better close this place down now before I get into big trouble."

I was a little embarrassed and concerned that he thought I was presuming to tell him how to run his life. "Sorry, that was probably going over the line."

He held up a hand to let me know that he'd taken no offense. "I thought it was your job to go over the line. Trust me,

I completely understand that this isn't exactly a safe move and maybe not even a smart one. If Hayward were a public company, the stockholders would have ridden me out on a rail. Fortunately, it's not a public company. Equally fortunately, I can pretty much handle any financial hit that comes from this."

"And the psychic hits?"

"You mean if I go out there and say 'I'm creating the greatest wine in the world' and everyone gags on the stuff?"

"Something like that."

"I'm pretty sure I can handle being a laughing stock. When I get to know you a little better I'll tell you about starring in my high school's performance of 'Jesus Christ Superstar.'

"But there's something important for you to understand – especially since you're the first guy writing about this place: I'm not saying that we're creating the greatest wine in the world. That would be ludicrous. Even for me. The idea here is to try to find out how good the wine can be when you have lots of resources available but no business considerations. There are some amazing people on this Collective. Eric Schumpf is one of the most artful guys in the industry, but he couldn't put all of the care into his wine that he wanted to and still make a profit. Leanna Prine was well on her way to establishing a national reputation for SunCrest when a flood just about wiped her out. There's a different story with every one of these people, but what brings them together is that they live and breathe wine, they are dedicated students of the craft, they're all remarkably talented, and they're all lousy business people."

"Except you."

He laughed again. "Yeah, except me. Though as you yourself pointed out, perhaps I'm not as smart about business as some have suggested I am.

"There's no way to say this without sounding like I'm spinning, but at some point you have to close your eyes and just decide that you're going to do the thing that's most important to you out of love. Everybody on the Collective knows the risks. We all know that the media is going to be paying an absurd amount of attention to what we do here once we go public. We all know that this vineyard could shut down for any number of reasons.

"But we also know that we would all rather be doing this than anything else in the world. That's worth taking a chance on."

I let his last words hang in the air for a moment before saying, "You're right; that could easily sound like you're spinning."

Hayward shook his head. "And you've gotta write it the way you see it."

I made eye contact with him and held it for a moment. "When I get to know you better, I'll tell you about what I did after dinner last night. I think I get it."

~~~~~~~~

I flurried some more that night. It would be pretentious of me to call it writing. In fact, it would be accurate to call it pretentious. I wrote in a blind heat for twenty headlong minutes, then stopped to pace the room, sniff something aromatherapeutic, and then change direction. Too consciously literary. Too affected. Too florid. I would stop, scold myself for my pretensions, and then move on to another approach. I always saved the other approaches, though. Something told me that I wanted a record of this article, even the discarded portions of it.

For the first time in years, I imagined people reading the finished version of an article I was writing. I saw them turning to the first page and settling in with it. I saw three faces: Grant Hayward's, Marina's, and my father's.

It was nearly 10:00 before I finally stopped to go to get something to eat. It was clear to me that I hadn't written much that would remain in the actual published article, but I felt as though I'd accomplished something anyway. I found a place to pick up a sandwich and drove while I ate. I didn't have a destination in mind, but I was intent on moving. I harmonized (very well, I might add) with the radio, even switching to a classic rock station to guarantee that I would know the songs and could therefore sing along with them.

As I continued to drive, it eventually registered that I was headed toward San Francisco. I gave some thought to driving into the city, maybe finding some live music. But as I approached the Golden Gate Bridge, I changed my mind. It was getting late, I had a lot more work to do on the story tomorrow, and I wasn't really in the mood for a city.

I pulled off to the side of the road just before I got to the bridge. It was a magnificent structure, its design the result of true dedication. I turned the radio down, but not off, and sat on the hood of my rental car for several minutes, admiring the view. I was staring at achievement, what could be done if you cared deeply enough to make it happen. I thought not only about the designers of this bridge, but the designer of the very first bridge and the level of risk and ignoring the odds that that must have required. It was stimulating.

Eventually I got in the car and headed back toward the inn. A short while later, I even changed the radio back to the progressive station I'd locked into a few days earlier.

The moment came along with me.

Chapter Seventeen

Having spent a good deal of time around children, Marina knew more than a little about letting people win at games. Eight-year-olds were just on the cusp of being able to compete with adults, and they were very aware if you weren't trying hard. As a result, she had gotten pretty good at appearing to be giving a game her full concentration while also managing to commit a critical blunder or lose focus at just the right time. Because of this, she was relatively certain that Mickey didn't know she was letting him win at checkers.

At the same time, by the end of the second game, she was also sure that going easy on Mickey wasn't particularly necessary. He'd beaten her without much trouble in the first game, and just then had completely surprised her with a triple jump that effectively ended the match.

After that move, Mickey looked at her proudly. "I haven't played checkers in years. I guess it's like riding a bicycle."

Marina grew a little fonder of the elder Sienna with every night they spent together. He was clever and his smile was almost exactly the same as Jesse's, but other than that, the two men were completely unalike. Mickey obviously wanted to please her, and she found his attentions charming. He flattered her cooking (though he'd promised to take her out to dinner the following night), her wardrobe, her approach to her profession, even her choice of music. He did it in a way that was slightly flirtatious, but also unmistakably paternal. Marina wondered if Jesse would be this way when he reached Mickey's age.

And then, entirely unbidden, the thought came to mind that she almost certainly wouldn't be around to find out.

"One more game?" Mickey said, his voice boyish.

"Sure," Marina said, reminding herself to try to win this time.

During this extended stay, Marina had felt closer to and more distant from Jesse than ever before. There were details about him that she hadn't picked up during her previous nights in this house. The way he arranged his pantry by category. The fact that a Little League baseball trophy had as prominent a place on his mantel as a college journalism award. The photograph of his mother that hung on the wall of the guest room where Marina slept, and the group shot of his brother and two sisters that sat on the dresser in that same room. All of these things added definition to her image of the man she'd spent the last six months with. But at the same time, they indicated how far she had to go before she could feel truly incorporated into his life. Why hadn't she met any of his siblings? Why didn't she know the story behind that baseball trophy?

Marina reminded herself that there were probably several things in her own house that would lead Jesse to similar questions if he studied them. He knew the code to her house alarm, but she never told him what the code represented. Her cousin Ally had managed to slip in and out of town a couple of months ago without gaining an introduction. It wasn't necessary for them to share on this level given the relationship they had. It just seemed that lately it was getting harder to convince herself that she really felt this way.

In the past couple of months, Marina had been thinking more and more of Jesse as a fixture in her life. God knew it wasn't the way it had been with Larry. She would never be that unguarded again. But she'd stopped wondering what she was going to do when she wasn't with Jesse anymore. This didn't mean much by itself, but living with your boyfriend's elderly father for a week so he could do an assignment implied certain things.

Was Jesse thinking the same way at all? He was easily the most sensitive and stimulating person she'd ever been with, and if anything he seemed more sensitive and more stimulating as the days went by. The fact that they'd stopped talking about the "inevitabilities" might actually suggest something about the way he was thinking. But then she would look at a photograph of his family and be reminded once again that he hadn't come close to fully inviting her in.

Even though her mind was wandering, she managed to offer Mickey considerably greater resistance during their third checkers match. In the end, she even prevailed, which seemed to give Mickey great pleasure and led Marina to wonder if perhaps *he* had let *her* win this time. The thought made her laugh.

"I'm going to get myself just one more scoop of that ice cream," Mickey said, standing, after the match was over. "Can I get you anything?"

"Do you eat three helpings of dessert every night?"

Mickey waved a hand. "Nah, but we're on vacation here."

Marina chuckled as the phone rang.

Mickey looked at the clock. "Probably Loverboy if you want to pick it up."

Marina moved toward the phone and answered it.

"How are things going over there?" Jesse said.

"You didn't mention that your father was a checkers shark."

"Yeah, I don't know how I could have forgotten that. Is he behaving himself?"

Marina glanced over at Mickey, who was adding a *second* scoop of ice cream to his bowl.

"He might be a few pounds heavier the next time you see him, but yes, we're having a great time. How's the story going?"

"I'm not sure it could be going any better." Marina could practically hear Jesse beaming on the other end of the line. "I guess there's a chance that I'll get home and realize that I was deluding myself out here, but this feels really good. I can't wait for you to read it."

Marina was surprised. He'd never said that to her before. She always had to ask to read his work. "I'd love to read it. Anytime you're ready to show it to me."

"I think you'll be impressed. God, I hope so. I hope I'm not kidding myself. I even think I'm kinda making friends with Hayward. He spent fifteen minutes talking to me about his first marriage today."

"Pretty different from what you were expecting, isn't it?"

"There's an understatement. I can't believe I've got to go back to writing stories about spackle and ingrown toenails after this."

Marina laughed. "The assignments were never that bad."

"I know, but they certainly felt like it sometimes. How's everything going at school? Is Cassie still throwing up in class?"

"Thankfully, no. The big news on this end is that we began rehearsals for the musical this afternoon. There are some kids who can actually sing. Melissa Parks is a fifth grader, and I knew I could count on her. But there's this little second grader with a voice like Ethel Merman's. You should have seen the expressions on the other kids' faces when she opened her mouth."

"Wow, your first diva. Has her manager contacted you yet?"

"Not yet. That reminds me, your brother-in-law Brad called and asked you to call him before you get back."

"I'm not going to ask how Ethel Merman reminded you that my brother-in-law called. Is my father still doing the dishes?"

"Every night. I don't even bother to pretend that I'm willing to do them anymore."

"You know that he won't lift a finger when I get back there, right?"

"Well, I am much cuter than you are."

"You'll get no argument from me about that." Jesse paused and she knew that he was imagining her in his mind. Probably with that white sweater he got all worked up about.

"I should get going," he said after the pause. "I'm meeting some of the marketing people for dinner. I'll call tomorrow night."

"You might want to make it a little later. Your dad's taking me out to dinner tomorrow night."

"I *knew* he was going to make a move on you."

"Hey, we never said this thing was exclusive."

"Don't even joke about that."

"I'll talk to you tomorrow night. Have a great day tomorrow."

"Thanks, you too. I miss you."

Marina's eye settled on the Little League trophy again. She was definitely going to ask him about it when he got home. "Yeah, I miss you too."

Marina put down the phone. As was so often the case when she started pondering her future, a simple conversation with Jesse seemed to quell any concerns.

Mickey was eating his ice cream when Marina got back to the table. "He didn't want to talk to me?"

"Sorry, I monopolized him. He had to run off to a dinner."

Mickey shook his head. "Better he talk to you." He took another spoonful of ice cream. "I still can't believe you made this stuff. I've had some great ice cream in my time. But this . . .."

Marina touched Mickey on the hand. He was so easy to please. He ate quietly for a moment and Marina played idly with a couple of checkers.

"Jesse's doing okay out there?" Mickey said.

"He sounds like he's doing great. He seems so excited about this story and about the winery itself. I've never heard him talk this way before."

"This is good for him. Hopefully he'll get more stuff like this." He looked up at her meaningfully. "He isn't a lot of fun to be around when he's writing stories he doesn't like."

Marina nodded. "So I've heard. At least he's honest about that kind of thing."

Mickey snorted. "Yeah, my son is big on honesty."

Marina wasn't entirely sure what Mickey meant by that, and she didn't respond. For a few beats, it didn't appear that he was going to say anything else. Then he put his spoon down (with at least a quarter of a scoop left in his bowl) and sat back in his chair.

"I don't know what to make of you two," he said.

Marina tilted her head. She didn't know where Mickey was going with this.

"I mean, the two of you look all cuddly when you're together and a doorknob could tell that there are real sparks between you, but according to him you don't have any plans."

Marina wondered if Mickey had been this blunt with Jesse. If he had, Jesse hadn't mentioned it. "Jesse and I care a great deal for one another. That's more than I can say about a lot of couples who profess big commitments."

"So you actually buy into this?"

This was not the time for Marina to confess what she had been thinking about only minutes earlier. There would probably never be an appropriate time to confess such thoughts to Mickey, no matter how well they got along. "I'm fine with it. I think one of the reasons Jesse and I connect so well is that we've both had some tough times in relationships in the past."

"You and the entire rest of the world. Everyone has to deal with heartache."

"That's true. Of course. But Jesse and I have chosen to deal with it the same way. Or at least in a similar way. I think it's been a big help in our relationship."

Mickey grunted. "So neither of you believes in long-term relationships, which allows you to have a really good relationship, but you can't sign on for the long term because you don't believe in that."

Marina had to admit to herself that Mickey's presentation made it seem a little silly. "I guess you could put it that way."

"And this doesn't make you crazy?"

Mickey seemed to be getting agitated. Again, Marina touched Mickey's hand. This seemed to calm him down quickly. "It really doesn't."

"You should have more than that," he said, half under his breath.

"It's okay, Mickey, really. It's more than okay. It's good. This is the healthiest relationship I've ever been in. And we're not saying it *isn't* going to be a long-term thing. You know, you take things day by day and sometimes the days add up."

"But my son claims to be convinced that all love dies eventually."

Marina nodded. "And for all we know, he could be right about that."

"He's *not* right about that."

He said the words softly, but Marina could feel the conviction behind them.

"Whether he's right or wrong, we'll find out in time. And either way, we won't waste a lot of energy worrying about it."

Mickey looked up at her. It was obvious to Marina that he knew it was time to drop the subject, but it was also obvious to her that nothing she had said during this conversation had changed his mind in any way.

"And I'll make you a deal," Marina continued. "Even if I wind up dumping your son, I'll still come around to bring you dessert every now and then."

Mickey smiled. "Well, if that's the case, you can bounce his ass tomorrow."

~~~~~~~~

Marina had kissed him on the cheek before he went to his room. She really was something. It was hard to believe that she could have convinced herself of some of the things she was saying to him an hour or so before. Why would a woman like Marina ever need to compromise?

Lying in bed with the light still on, Mickey had to admit that he wasn't as good at understanding people as he once had been. He'd made it a point to keep his eyes and his mind open long after most of his contemporaries had begun to complain about the dim-wittedness of the younger generations. But despite his best efforts, his grasp had weakened over time. First,

it was the music that he couldn't abide. Then the preoccupation with money and then the more annoying preoccupation
with designer/gourmet/premium everything. There'd always
been a distinction between the best and the run-of-the-mill,
but coffee, t-shirts, telephones? Who cared? Maybe this was
one of the downsides to having a son so much younger. You
had to try to stay in touch with the way the world was changing long past the point when you wanted to.

But some things shouldn't ever change, and Mickey knew
this wasn't the old man in him talking. Love and romance
wasn't any different now than it had been sixty years ago. Not
the real stuff. That had been the same for centuries, millennia.

Why was it that his conversation with Marina left him
feeling so unsettled? It could just be that he had gotten it
wrong about her and Jesse. Maybe they really didn't have that
thing between them that he thought they had. It was the only
logical explanation.

While it was unusual for him to do at night, Mickey felt
a strong need to talk to Gina. As he struggled out of bed, he
remembered why he never got up to walk around once he was
down for the night, even if he couldn't sleep. It was just too
much work.

He got the picture out and sat back down. It dawned on
him that he could probably keep the picture out of the box
now that Jesse knew about Gina. He should probably even
show the photograph to his son. But keeping it on his dresser
would probably make Jesse uncomfortable, even if he almost
never came in here. Jesse and Dorothy had been so close.

"The kid's making me feel old tonight," Mickey said to the
image of Gina he had in his head. "After all this time, it turns
out that your man is out of touch. Did you ever think that
would happen? I'm sure it hasn't happened to you. You always
knew what was going on before I did. And you always saw
people differently. It'd be great for you to meet Jesse. Maybe
you would understand him.

"This girl of his is a real prize. That much I know for sure. I always was a great judge of substance in a woman, and this one is really substantial. I don't think he sees it, though. And what's even more surprising is that she doesn't seem to mind. Could you imagine if I had been that stupid with you?

"I gotta tell him some more about you when he gets back from his trip. It really wears me out, but I know I have to keep on doing it. I'd just cut to the chase with him, but I don't think he would understand what I was trying to say to him if I did it any other way. Matty maybe, but not Jesse. Of course, I couldn't tell Matty the story at all because he would overreact to all the wrong things, so I guess I shouldn't complain.

"I'd better get to sleep. Marina gets up early for work and I like to have breakfast with her before she leaves.

"I love you. Save a place at the table for me."

Chapter Eighteen

I got home very late from the airport and Marina and my father were already asleep. Marina was in the guest room, and as much as I would have loved to have awakened her to come into mine, that seemed rather selfish. If Marina ever so much as yawned in front of her class, she would feel guilty for a week, and I didn't want to be responsible for that. I set my alarm for 6:20 so I would be up to wake her in the morning.

"You're back," she said sleepily when I leaned over to kiss her and snuggle in beside her. "What time is it?"

"It's morning."

"I'm sorry I didn't wait up for you last night."

"I got here at a quarter after two."

She stretched and rolled over to kiss me. "In that case, I'm not sorry I didn't wait up."

I kissed her again and held her. Hayward himself had driven me to the airport the day before, and we sat at the bar exchanging stories. It was the appropriate punctuation for an inspiring trip, and during the flight back, I found myself wishing that I could have had more time out there, that I would have thought to move to a more modest inn and just bask a little longer on my own dime. But now that I was home and holding Marina again, I remembered how much I missed her, and especially how much I missed having her in my arms when we first woke up in the morning.

"I don't suppose there's any possible chance of convincing you to take the day off, is there?"

Marina nuzzled a little closer and kissed my neck. "I can't. I have a conference with a parent this morning and there's the play. If you're really lucky, though, I'll allow you to make me a fabulous dinner tonight."

"You're so good to me." I was mildly disappointed, but I knew that the odds of Marina taking the day off were long. She was never casual when it came to her job. I held her quietly in an effort to extract as much of this time as possible before she got up.

"It *would* be nice to just stay like this," she said.

"What's one missed parent conference?"

"I shouldn't."

I kissed her and she let out a little moan that suggested that my chances were better than I'd imagined. At which point the sharp rap came on the door.

"Marina? Are you okay?" my father said. "It's ten to seven."

"I'm fine, Mickey, just off to a slow start."

I groaned. "What the hell is he doing up already?"

"He's been getting up every morning to have breakfast with me."

"I think I'm going to be nauseous."

"Oh stop. It's cute."

"You and I obviously have different definitions of that word."

She stretched again and sat up on one elbow. She kissed me on the cheek and rolled over me to get out of bed.

"I guess the parent conference is on, huh?" I said.

She looked at me plaintively. I realized I'd never seen her get out of bed in a t-shirt before, and I was surprised at how sexy I found it, especially with that expression on her face.

"I really can't. It's Derek's mother. You know, Derek is the one who just started crying in the middle of class a couple of weeks ago."

"Oh yeah. That was pretty weird, huh?"

"He just always seemed so together before. It's important that I talk things over with his mom."

I lay back in the bed. "Okay, Derek's mother wins. What do you want for your fabulous dinner?"

School clothes on one arm, she walked over to the bed, kissed me softly, and then much more deeply. I swear that I floated a little.

"Use your imagination," she said, walking away.

"My imagination is currently working on a different project."

She turned back and smiled at me before going out the door. I stayed in the bed. The pillow was still slightly warm from where she had been lying, and the sheets held the faintest essence of her. Once the shower went on, I decided to get up. I was tempted to join her, but I'd already slowed her down too much. Instead, I went into the kitchen to find my father.

"Oh, you did get home last night," he said. "I didn't hear you."

"It was late."

"Is Marina up yet? I made her coffee, and she likes English muffins for breakfast."

I laughed to myself. I realized how someone might actually describe this behavior as "cute." "Yeah, she's in the shower. Do you want me to signal you when she comes out the bathroom door so you can start the toaster?"

"Nah, it's okay. English muffins only take a minute anyway," he said, missing my sarcasm.

He looked great. He wasn't moving around any better than he had been before I left, but his spirits seemed high. It was difficult to remember that I had been worried about him before I went on the trip. I should have realized that his spending this much time with Marina would rejuvenate him.

"So, did you get your story?" he said.

"Nailed it, I think. I did a lot of useful writing the last couple of days. By the time I got off the plane, I had most of a first draft."

He handed me a cup of coffee.

"Oh, that reminds me," I said, and returned to my room. I brought him his handmade mug.

"What's this?" he said when I gave it to him.

"I got it in a shop in Yountville. Made by a local artist. I thought it might be time to retire the mug your insurance agent gave you."

He ran his hand over the mug, examining the uneven texture and the understated use of metallic glaze.

"Now all I need is designer taste buds," he said, smiling at me.

"Nah, you always had those."

He went to the sink and poured the coffee from his current mug ("Joseph A. Tress: Put Yourselves in Our Hands") into his new one.

"So you got a good story," he said after trying out a sip. "You should be very happy."

"I am. In fact, I think I'm going to take the day off to celebrate. Maybe go for a drive down the shore. Wanna come with me?"

"Come with you where?" Marina said as she walked into the kitchen, kissing both of us on the forehead. As expected, my father immediately turned toward the toaster.

"I'm giving myself a little break and going for a drive down the shore. I was just asking my father if he wanted to come with me."

"Mmm, sounds great. I wish I could join you."

"You had your chance," I said playfully. "Now the offer's off the table."

Marina responded by walking over to my father at the toaster and hugging him around the shoulders. "Mickey, you're much nicer to me than your son."

My father seemed to be blushing as he said, "I could have told you that."

A few minutes later, Marina was out the door. I really didn't want to see her go, and I made her stop to kiss me goodbye several times on her way to her car. The final time, she actually rolled her window up in order to move me away.

"So are you coming?" I said to my father when I got back in the house.

"Where are you going, anyway?"

"South."

"You mean like Miami?"

"I don't think we'd make it back by dinner time. I don't know, I just came off of a really good trip, and I don't feel like checking my e-mail or returning phone calls or catching up. I just feel like taking the day off and going for a little drive."

"Shouldn't you be finishing your story?"

"The story's finished. I want to take a day away from it to get a little perspective. I'll read it through again tomorrow and make any changes I need before I send it off to Aline." I walked over to put on my sneakers. "So are you coming or are you leaving me alone with my iPod?"

My father laughed and shook his head. "You sure are in a good mood. Yeah, I'll come."

Chapter Nineteen

For a short while, Mickey thought Jesse was simply going to talk nonstop for the entire drive. He'd rarely seen his son this animated. Obviously things had gone well on his trip. He seemed to think he'd made some kind of professional break-through. Mickey was happy for him, though he still thought Jesse would be better off with a stable job that paid a regular salary. He could have his writing breakthroughs in his spare time.

"Hey, did Marina tell you that Brad called while I was away?" Jesse said. It was the first time during his monologue that he'd said anything that required a response.

"No, she didn't mention it."

"Turns out that Gruenbach's acquisition of Lynch is going through just as he suspected. It also appears that his future with the corporation is just as he suspected."

"Oh, that's terrible for him and Denise."

"Yeah, I don't know how they're going to get by on Denise's high six-figures alone. That's not the point, anyway, because he's actually putting a consortium together to start a new magazine."

"Does he know enough about the magazine business to do that?"

"He doesn't even know what he doesn't know, but he's got access to the money and some bizarre notion that this is his next big career move."

"So was he calling you to come on board?" Mickey liked the idea of his son and his son-in-law working together.

"No, thank God. Could you imagine that? That's all I'd need is Denise having control of my income. No, he was calling to get my opinion about editors they should chase for their management team. I was actually a little flattered, if you want to know the truth. Not only did he ask, but it sounded like he was taking notes."

Mickey was pleased to hear the pride in Jesse's voice. Being the youngest in the family had to be a challenge for Jesse, especially in a family of overachievers, and it had to make him feel good to be consulted as an expert.

"So if he hires one of these guys, do you get a finder's fee?" Mickey said.

Jesse looked over at him and smiled. "I like the way you think, Dad. Wanna negotiate that for me?"

Mickey drew up his hands. "Not me. Brad's a barracuda."

Jesse reached over and patted him on the leg. "Ah, come on, Dad. You could kick his ass."

Mickey laughed. He wasn't sure he'd ever seen Jesse so at ease.

They were going south on the Turnpike, having just passed the exit for Newark Airport. Mickey still had no idea where they were going, and it was obvious that Jesse didn't either. After their conversation about Brad, Jesse had stopped talking and seemed intent on driving. Maybe he was wondering if they could get to Miami and back by dinnertime after all.

Mickey had planned on telling Jesse the next part of his story with Gina when his son got back from California. When Jesse asked him to go for a drive, it seemed like the perfect opportunity. Of course, he then had to find a way to get a word in edgewise. The chance finally seemed to have arrived.

"People didn't just jump into bed back then," he started. Jesse looked over at him and it appeared that he wasn't entirely sure what Mickey was talking about. But then another glance indicated that he knew where Mickey was going.

Mickey continued. "I didn't sleep with your mother until our wedding night. But Gina, God, right from that first kiss there was something burning up between us."

~~~~~~~~

It had been the way it was every night since that first kiss. Saturday's date led to Sunday's, which led to Tuesday's and then Thursday's. The only night they hadn't seen each other since then was the one Tuesday when Mickey had a business dinner he couldn't avoid. On every night there was the conversation and the playfulness that existed from the moment they'd met, but now there was something else there as well, an almost magnetic physical connection. They were always touching when out in public, holding hands, sneaking kisses, nuzzling. And on Gina's doorstep, their goodnight kisses were longer, more passionate. The night before, concerned about appearances in view of a doorman she'd known since she was in her early teens, Gina had moved them ridiculously behind a stand of trees. Mickey laughed about it, but the comedy of the situation didn't alter his mood.

And then on this night, while they ate pasta and sipped Chianti at a restaurant that they'd visited twice before, Mickey could barely taste his meal or follow the conversation. All he knew was that Gina's leg rested next to his in their booth, that her arm brushed lightly against his, that her head leaned against his shoulder regularly. Mickey wanted to reach his arm around her to cradle her against his chest, and though propriety prevented it, nothing could stop his imagination.

"You're not eating much," she said during a still moment.

Mickey looked at his plate and noticed that it was nearly half full. Gina's looked much the same.

"You aren't either."

"The portions are so big here."

Mickey reached for Gina's hand and brought it to his lips. "We should probably leave soon anyway or we'll miss our movie."

Gina moved their hands to her cheek. "I think it might be nice to go somewhere quieter instead."

Mickey appreciated the suggestion. He had no desire to have his attention diverted by a film.

"We could go to the Waldorf for a drink," he said.

Gina rubbed his hand against her cheek and then kissed it. "Quieter than that," she said in a whisper.

Mickey looked into her eyes, not entirely sure what she was saying. He didn't care where they went, as long as he could continue to touch her.

"I still haven't seen where you live, Mickey," she said softly, almost shyly.

"It's very quiet there," he said. He could feel his mouth going dry.

They said nothing, not a single word, on the cab ride to his apartment. A couple of times, Gina looked at him and seemed about to say something, but then rested her head back on his shoulder and massaged his hand.

When they got inside his apartment, Mickey took Gina's sweater and placed it on a chair. While he'd been fantasizing this moment for the past couple of weeks, he now found himself very nervous.

"Can I get you something?" he said.

Gina smiled a smile that he knew he would remember the rest of his life. It said so many things at once. It said she considered their life together to be an adventure. It said that Mickey meant more to her than she ever could have imagined. It said that she was at least as nervous as he was. And while she was smiling, she walked up to him and reached a hand toward his cheek.

"Just this." She kissed him more deeply than she had ever kissed him before.

If Mickey had swooned from some of Gina's previous kisses, this time he felt positively electrified. He pulled Gina to him, pressing their bodies as close as possible. He kissed her lips, her cheek, her chin, and her neck. Concerned that he might be moving too quickly, he slowed for a moment, looking into her eyes.

"I can't believe how much I want you," she said.

Mickey let go of the reins on his desire. Kissing her passionately, he worked loose the buttons on her blouse, the zipper on the back of her skirt. Somehow, the buttons of his own shirt had been undone, though he hadn't noticed Gina doing this, so intent was he on revealing her. They made their way to the couch, still fervently undressing each other. They lay down, and Mickey hungrily tasted her shoulders, her arms, her stomach. At last, he reached for the back of her bra and found the clasp. Releasing it, he allowed his lips to lower the straps and then to work down the material covering her breasts.

He pulled back to remove the bra, and he looked down at Gina in amazement, realizing that she seemed more beautiful from one moment to the next. A voice inside of him told him to slow down, to savor what was happening between them. Yes, this desire had been building since their very first conversation. No, he had never felt more enflamed in his life. But this was a moment to cherish, to memorize in the minutest detail.

At that moment, he lowered himself to her slowly, kissing her tenderly.

"You are the most remarkable person I've ever met," he said.

She kissed him and pulled herself tightly against him. "We're remarkable together."

From that point forward, everything slowed, as though both understood that they should draw every bit of sensation from this encounter. Mickey softly moved his lips down Gina's torso, wanting to leave no inch of her un-kissed. She kneaded the muscles of his shoulders, threaded her fingers through the hairs on his chest. She turned him over to unbuckle his belt and remove his pants and Mickey felt not exposed, but released.

For many minutes after that, they held each other tight, their naked legs exploring each other, kissing ever more deeply. Eventually, Mickey pulled himself up and slowly, almost tentatively, removed Gina's panties. He looked up at her and she smiled at him again. It was a smile that spoke many of the same words as before, but also confirmed that what they were doing was unimaginably right.

The next several minutes were a blur of sensation for Mickey. Their bodies moved together, and Mickey reveled in the pleasure. There was nothing in his experience to match what he was feeling with Gina right now. The physical excitement combined with the vision of the woman who thrilled his emotions in unprecedented ways overwhelmed him. He wanted to stay in this moment forever and knew, in some very real ways, that he always would.

After their passion crested, they lay together for a long while without speaking. Silences like these had become welcome interludes over the past weeks. Saying nothing and everything at once. At last, Gina turned to kiss him and then looked back up at the ceiling.

"We've just touched eternity," she said.

~~~~~~~~

"It was the same way every time," Mickey said to Jesse. "Every single time."

Jesse wasn't sure that there was anything he could possibly say. He was moved by the depth of emotion in his father's voice as he spoke, but he also knew that nearly any response would seem trivial.

He wondered if his father would say anything more about Gina today, but he knew from experience that the look on his father's face meant that he wouldn't be talking about it again for a while. For the hundredth time, Jesse wished he could know everything about this mystery from his father's past.

Mickey reached over and turned on the stereo, and they continued to drive.

Chapter Twenty

The night after I returned from California, my father did in fact do the dishes. I was still convinced that he would drop the façade the first night that Marina didn't eat with us, but I figured there was no reason to examine this gift horse too carefully. During the time he'd lived with me, we'd become accustomed to turning on the television after dinner. Having spent the day reading and writing, I was ready to rest my mind and he seemed willing to watch just about anything. But on this night, once he finished putting the dishes away, he came into the living room with a pack of playing cards.

"Anyone for a little poker?" he said. Marina sat up on the couch.

I tilted my head toward him. "A little poker?"

"Yeah," he said, looking over at Marina. "What else are we gonna do? Watch television? There's nothing good on until 9:00 anyway, right, Marina?"

I glanced at Marina, who was already rising and walking toward the dining room table.

"I'm a much better poker player than I am a checkers player," she said to him.

"Well, that wouldn't be difficult. I hope you're better at poker than you are at Monopoly, too."

"One bad roll, Mickey," Marina said, pointing her finger at him in mock recrimination. "One bad roll."

"Yeah, losers always have excuses," he said through a grin.

I watched this exchange as though we had in fact turned the television on after dinner. When had my house been moved to a fifties sitcom neighborhood? When it became clear that my father's invitation had not been a suggestion but an announcement of the next item on the agenda – and that Marina had clearly seen the agenda ahead of time – I got up to join them.

My father played with relish, boasting about his winnings and narrating our performances as though ESPN had hired him for the event. I had never been one for gambling, but since we were using plastic chips with no actual monetary value, I played with abandon. I got my father to fold when I had nothing more than a pair of fours in my hand, and when I pulled an inside straight to beat Marina's three-of-a-kind, she actually threw her cards at me. My father considered this to be the highest form of entertainment.

Sometime after nine, we settled back down on the couch in the den. HBO was showing "American Beauty," which fascinated my father, even as he denigrated its values. I know he was sharp enough to identify the irony in the movie, and I couldn't help but wonder if by criticizing it he was trying to send me a message that I wasn't understanding.

A little after ten, Marina leaned over to kiss me on the temple and said, "I really should get to bed." I was so pleased with her for saying this. My suggesting it would have revealed my true intentions. Her suggesting it would be interpreted by my father as being responsible.

After hearing his story about Gina earlier in the day, it was probably time to stop being concerned about what my father might think about my sleeping with Marina under his nose. While one doesn't necessarily want to consider the image of one's parents in bed with each other, the image of the young Mickey Sienna (whom I continued to regard as a character very different from my father in any case) making love to the mysterious Gina was strangely alluring. That afternoon, I'd called Marina from the road to suggest that she plan on spending the night.

"I guess I'm going to have to go out to buy a bunch of board games to keep my father entertained in the evenings," I

said as we brushed our teeth. "What would you suggest, Strat-
ego, Life, Candy Land?"

"It was fun playing cards with him tonight."

"It was; you're right. It's just been a surprising day."

She put her toothbrush away and kissed me. "Think we
can make it a surprising night?"

"I've been thinking about little else since 6:30 this
morning."

I wrapped my arms around Marina and we slowly made
our way from the bathroom to the bed.

Though my time away from her had made me hungri-
er for her than I ever remembered being, there was nothing
rushed or hurried about our lovemaking. I had always taken
tremendous pleasure in undressing her, in luxuriating over the
exploration of each newly exposed patch of skin. I knew all
of her "secret places," spots that generated heightened pleasure, carnal or otherwise, and she decidedly knew all of mine.
While my senses thrummed in anticipation of a release that
had been building for more than a week, I had no desire to
reach that release anytime soon.

I don't know how much of this was inspired by the story
my father had told me that morning or by my repeating it to
Marina that afternoon. There had always been this sense between us that making love was at once casual and eventful. But
on this night, so many things combined. Our having missed
each other while I was away. Our being primed by another's
tale of passion. My still being buzzed by my accomplishments
in California and endlessly grateful to Marina for allowing
me that opportunity. Even the slight naughtiness of doing this
while my father was watching a movie nearby. It charged the
room. It made each kiss seem just a little softer, each caress
tingle just a little more. And when we finally did head toward
that release, it seemed that we were starting from a different
place than we usually did.

We didn't speak for several minutes afterward. Typical-
ly, one of us says something romantic or affectionate almost

immediately, but this seemed both unnecessary and inappropriate. Having our bodies together, feeling the breaths that each of us took, was enough. At last, Marina propped herself up on one arm and ran her fingers softly through the hairs on my chest.

"This one is my favorite," she said, describing a tiny circle near my breastbone.

"Why's that?"

"It goes in the opposite direction from all the other hairs on your chest, and it's a slightly different color. Lighter. It's your renegade hair. Did you know you had one?"

"I can't say that I did."

She kissed my chest and then kissed me on the lips.

"You have a few things like that. There's a tiny mole on your back that is redder than the others are. And of course there is that thing with your toenail."

"I have a 'thing' with a toenail?"

"You don't know about this? You don't know that the toenail next to your big toe on your right foot is round when all of your other toenails are square?"

As if to illustrate, she moved toward my foot and gave my rogue toe a kiss.

"You have a tiny patch of smooth skin just to the left of your right knee," I said.

"I knew that one."

I sat up with her and moved behind her. "Do you know that you have a little bare spot in the hair on the back of your neck?"

"I do?"

I touched it lightly. "You never felt me do this before?"

"Of course I felt you do it. I just didn't know what you were doing."

I kissed the spot and then kissed her neck and shoulders, and then turned her toward me and kissed her deeply on the lips.

"I love that spot," I said.

"Thanks," she said, almost a little dazedly.

She adjusted herself so that she was reclined against my chest and we sat like that for another quiet time.

"I love you, Jess," she said barely above a whisper.

It was the first time in a very long while that a woman had said that to me. It might as well have been a lifetime ago. The last time I heard it, the declaration had meaning, but I completely misunderstood its implication. The last time I heard it, while I thought it suggested the highest level of devotion, I also believed it could be infinite. Given the relationship I had with Marina and the many levels on which we connected, it was notable that we had gone this long into our affair without saying this. It wasn't as though the thought hadn't crossed my mind. But I thought that her reticence to say the words came from the same place as mine: that doing so would imply that we believed we could battle nearly unfathomable odds.

I held her close to me and kissed her neck. I wanted her to know how much it meant to me to hear her say this. I wanted her to know how deeply I cared for her. I loved her. Of course I loved her. By any reasonable definition of the word, I'd been in love with Marina for some time. While I still wasn't sure what I was saying by acknowledging it, it was important to me that she know.

"I love you, too, Marina."

She leaned back and kissed me softly and slowly. Then she pulled back enough to look into my eyes. I wanted what she saw there to make it clear to her that I meant it. I'm not sure what it looked like to her. After a moment, she leaned back on my chest and I hugged her. We stayed like that for several minutes more.

"We really should get to sleep," she said.

"Yeah," I said, and the two of us moved under the sheets. I reached over to turn off the light.

"I love you," I said again as I lay down next to her, not sure why I felt the need to repeat it.

~~~~~~~~

The next morning, after Marina left, I could think about little else. I remembered back to the very first time a woman told me she loved me. Her name was Lisa and we dated for a month during our junior year in high school. When she said the words, I felt the thrill through every nerve ending. I immediately told her I loved her back and then played with the phrase over and over again during the rest of that date. I called a friend about it. I wrote about being in love in my journal. I said it out loud in my room dozens of times, though no one (most specifically Lisa) was there to hear me.

I wondered why I didn't feel any of that sense of giddiness now. Why couldn't I rejoice over the fact that a woman as remarkable as Marina had told me she loved me? Surely it had something to do with the fact that Lisa and I split up two weeks after that night to be followed by similar declarations and gradual declines with Georgia, Karen, and others. But there was something more here. By telling me she loved me, Marina had acknowledged the phantom in the room. We'd had numerous conversations about our mutual belief that few if any relationships had the power to go all the way. But while we were doing this, we'd avoided acknowledging that our feelings for each other were growing deeper. By doing so now, Marina had announced that these two notions needed to be reconciled. If we loved each other and yet believed that all love died, what exactly were we saying?

I found this notion intensely unsettling. Until now, we had been in love with each other, but chose to allow these feelings to go unnamed. Not that I had been in any way conscious of this, but it was almost as though doing so allowed it to exist as something else, something that was uniquely ours. Something that didn't simply go away with time. As a writer, I tried to remain conscious of the possibility that I took words way more seriously than I should, that I made them larger and more concrete than most people did and that this was something to be avoided. I challenged myself with this no-tion, and for a short while, it allowed me some relief. It didn't take very long, though, for me to come back to another very clear thought that had nothing to do with words: things were changing in my relationship with Marina. We were moving into new territory and we would not find it as easy to traverse as the island we'd been residing on.

I had been really happy on that island. I wasn't sure I was prepared to return to civilization.

Chapter Twenty-One

Not having Marina there the night before had been a little odd for Mickey. She'd been around for nearly two weeks straight, and he had gotten accustomed to seeing her across the dinner table, to playing board games with her and teasing her. She really lit the place up and she was going to make someone a great partner some day – even if it wasn't his emotionally stunted son. Last night, it was just him and Jesse. Something about some association meeting. He had to give Jesse credit, making a nice dinner and suggesting a round of chess afterwards. It was very pleasant, but it wasn't the same.

A few times during the night, he thought about asking Jesse about Marina. Things seemed a little different between them since Jesse had gotten back from California. Maybe the absence actually made his son realize that he couldn't possibly do any better than the woman. Or maybe those looks were all about sex. Sometimes it was hard to tell the difference.

For whatever reason, Mickey felt inspired to talk about Gina this morning. It had only been a few days since he had told Jesse about his and Gina's first night together and he hadn't previously been capable of going back there with him so soon afterward, but it seemed like the right thing to do today. When Jesse padded toward the kitchen to get his third cup of coffee, Mickey followed in after him.

"How's the work going?" he asked.

"Back to the grind," Jesse grumbled. "I turned the Hayward story in to Aline yesterday, so now I'm back to doing another dumb-ass home repair piece. I've gotta get out of this end of the business."

"Could you afford to do that?"

"No," Jesse said bluntly. Then he took a sip from his coffee and relaxed. "I don't know, once the Hayward story comes out, I might be able to pull together more feature pieces. But that's months from now. Hopefully Aline will give me another article before then. But there's no way I could get by on that stuff right now."

Mickey didn't really want more coffee, but adding some to his new cup that was still sitting on the kitchen table seemed to be the right thing to do at that moment. "I've got plenty of money, you know. Certainly more than enough to tide us over while you built up your commissions."

Jesse looked at him oddly and Mickey wasn't entirely sure what was going through his son's mind. Was he considering his offer? Was he offended at the suggestion? Was he questioning Mickey's sincerity? For a good fifteen seconds, he didn't say anything, but then he shook his head.

"Thanks Dad, but no. I have to be able to do this on my own."

Mickey nodded. "I figured you'd say that. But if you ever need to fall back, don't think twice about it."

Jesse appeared transfixed, not ready to move, but also not sure what else he should do. Mickey figured if his son didn't have a snappy reply for him, he had somehow managed to touch him in a place he wasn't used to being touched.

"Listen, if you have a little time, I'd like to tell you some more about Gina."

Jesse smiled at that. "Hmm, it's either that or falling asleep at my computer in mid-sentence. Yeah, I think I can spare the time."

He moved toward the kitchen table and sat down. Mickey sat next to him.

"You're a good audience," he said, not sure that the statement was entirely true. "So anyway, we won't pretend that we can't remember where we left off. After that, Gina and I saw each other every chance we could get. Meanwhile, she had this two-week trip to Italy planned for a month down the road. Just going alone to Tuscany for a couple of weeks. It was so like her to be that independent. Anyway, I couldn't bear the idea of being away from her for two weeks. So we did a little moving and shaking and created a little subterfuge – you know unmarried couples didn't just dash off to Europe together back then – and I wound up going with her."

~~~~~~~~

Gina slept on his shoulder for the last two hours of the flight. Before then, they had talked incessantly about their plans for the vacation: the sights they were going to see, the food they were going to eat, the wine they were going to drink. Gina had a girlishness to her during this conversation that compared to their first visit to Schraft's (there had been others since then). Like everything else about Gina, Mickey found it intoxicating.

Landing in Rome, Mickey saw that there were signs that the great city was still recovering from the war. Several of the posters in the airport spoke of rebuilding, and these same efforts appeared in the headlines in the newspapers. It seemed odd to Mickey that the vacation he'd been so anxiously awaiting was taking place in a country he had contributed in his own tiny way toward defeating only a few years earlier. That this country was also the home place of his ancestors made it seem even stranger. But he reminded himself, as he did during the time that he worked on the American war effort in Brooklyn, that it was not the country that he and his fellows were defeating, but rather the oppressive rulers who'd tried to change it so completely.

Gina had chosen an inn in the walled hill town of San Gimignano. Mickey had never seen anything like it: a rolling landscape that gave way to a huge stone edifice, an archway that led to tiny cobbled streets bustling with shops and history. They had to park their car about a quarter of a mile away from the inn. Mickey noted as he carried their bags that it was a blessing that the walk was downhill. He mused that carrying their luggage up would be just one more reason why he wouldn't want to leave. The sights had already charmed him, none more so than the dazzled expression on Gina's face.

As fairy-tale-like as the setting already was, checking in confirmed for Mickey that he and Gina would be embarking on an elaborate game of pretend for the next two weeks. As they walked in the door with the bags, the innkeeper welcomed them as "Mr. and Mrs. Sienna." Gina could speak Italian and Mickey could patch together certain heavily dialected sentences based on words he'd learned growing up, but the innkeeper spoke to them in English.

"How did you know who we were?" Mickey said.

The innkeeper smiled at him. "You are our only Americans this week." Mickey paused at the notion of being conspicuously American, but was still tingling at their being addressed as "Mr. and Mrs. Sienna." When he'd decided to join Gina on this trip, she'd cancelled her reservation at one inn and made the new reservation here. They couldn't announce they were unmarried. Their reservations might not even have been taken. And they preferred the illusion of a marriage to the illusion of separate rooms. Mickey knew all of this, but still this was the first time he had actually heard the words. His heart leapt as he looked over at Gina, who was admiring the surroundings. How many times had he already imagined their being married? And now, at least for the next two weeks, they would be.

The room itself was a little fussy for his tastes, but Gina seemed to like it, and that made it fine with him. He walked to the window to look down on the brimming street. So much activity, so many shopkeepers calling to one another, welcoming patrons, directing staff. All at a volume that Mickey could recognize from the household he grew up in.

When he turned back around, he noticed that Gina had flopped down on the bed and was smiling up at him. Her traveling dress had ridden up above her knee and at that moment the vision – the woman he adored lying invitingly in a bed in a small hotel in Italy – seemed to him to be the sexiest thing he'd ever seen in his life. He moved over to the bed, his hand immediately going to Gina's exposed knee, and leaned over to kiss her with the slow passion that had become the trademark of these past few weeks. He lay next to her.

"We're here," she said. "I can't believe we're actually here."

"Just you and me with the entire rest of our lives an ocean away."

They kissed again, and Mickey found his desire for Gina was at an almost unbearable level. He always wanted Gina, had from the moment he first saw her, but at this very moment, in this secret place with their fantasy marriage, all he could think of was her skin and her lips and her almost painfully beautiful ankles.

Eventually, they made it down to the street to peruse a ceramics shop and eat dinner at a restaurant the innkeeper had recommended. About halfway through the meal, Mickey's body finally began to acknowledge that they had been traveling a very long time.

They walked slowly back to their room, the wine having more of an effect on their steps than Mickey would have expected. Soft music played through the door of a taverna just outside of their hotel, and they stood for a moment to listen to it, Gina resting her head on Mickey's shoulder.

When he was growing up in Brooklyn, Mickey had often talked about sex with friends from his neighborhood, getting their information from older boys and in turn passing it on to younger ones when the time was appropriate. But in none of those conversations, or any others he'd ever had on the subject, had anyone mentioned the sheer satisfaction to be derived from holding the woman you loved in your arms all night. Each time they'd made love at home, Gina nuzzled into his chest and they dozed briefly, but there was always the knowledge that they would need to get up shortly to return Gina to her parents' apartment. On this first night in Tuscany, though, no such condition pertained. The night was all theirs, as would be the twelve that followed it. For several hours, Mickey willed himself to awaken regularly, to rub Gina's arm, to kiss her head. Eventually, he fell into a deep sleep, one that lasted well into the next morning. When at last he awoke, Gina was looking up at him.

"Good morning," she said, reaching up and kissing him on the chin. "We're still in Tuscany. I guess it wasn't a dream."

Mickey pulled her close to him and then moved down to kiss her on the lips.

"It is a dream," he said. "But it's a real one."

She kissed him and stroked his cheek. "Did you sleep well?"

"It was the best sleep I've ever had."

"Must be the Tuscan air," she said with a smile.

~~~~~~~~

A few days later, they drove through the countryside and came upon the town of Chianti, where they stopped for lunch. Though the Italian food in New York was superlative, nothing matched the meals they had been eating on this trip. Gina's lunch was thick ribbons of pasta with butter, porcini, and sage while Mickey dined on wild boar sausages and roasted potatoes. This after an appetizer of salumi that surpassed any of the cured meats he'd ever been able to buy in Brooklyn, airy bread with a crackling crust, and the densest, most fragrant olive oil that Mickey had ever tasted. It was the latter that nearly stopped him cold. He literally came close to swooning. This flavor was the dining equivalent of Gina's smile. Tuscany was awash with great olive oils, but this was something else altogether. After tasting it several times, Mickey called the waiter over. He tried in vain to ask the man about it, but his Italian was not sufficient. At last Gina translated for him.

"He says that a Mr. Uzzano presses it on his property," she said. "He doesn't make very much and that he sells most of it to the restaurants in the area."

"Ask him where else we can find it. We need to go to all of these restaurants."

Gina asked, and the waiter smiled and responded.

"He says that if we'd like, he can arrange for us to visit Mr. Uzzano."

"Would you mind if we did that?"

"If it means that you'll keep this silly grin on your face, I think that would be fine."

Gina turned to talk to the waiter, who nodded and then kissed her hand.

"I think he's happy to do us the favor," she said to Mickey.

An hour later, they stood on the grounds of a castle that had been erected in the seventeenth century. A town had sprouted up no more than a couple of miles away, but Mickey had the sense that this place was separated by much more than that distance. Were it not for the cars parked on the driveway, Mickey could have convinced himself that he had traveled back three hundred years. Over these past few days, he had been moved by the sense of history that filled this land. Back home, nothing seemed more than fifty years old, and it felt like a new building was sprouting up somewhere in the City every day. But here was a world that had stood the test of time, and while age had removed some of its luster, it could do nothing to diminish its magnificence.

Mr. Uzzano himself was a figure from legend. He dressed elegantly and spoke perfect English in aristocratic tones. He seemed to take great delight in displaying his manor and its grounds. The effect was a bit intimidating to Mickey, but he would soon be surprised when they got to the olive grove. There, surrounded by the heady fragrance of the fruit, Mr. Uzzano explained to him how he hired others to pick the olives but that he pressed the oil by himself in the manner of his father, grandfather, and great-grandfather before him. His air of aristocracy disappeared, replaced by the enthusiasm of a man devoted to his craft.

After the tour, Mr. Uzzano invited them into the castle itself. Mickey could barely believe what was going on. Two hours before, they had been strolling down a modest piazza. Now they were walking among hand-woven tapestries, artfully carved furniture, and elegant staircases. Mickey glanced over at Gina, the now-familiar starstruck smile on her face. There was no question in his mind that all of this was possible because of the magic she created.

They sat on an open balcony and sipped wine ("a private bottling done for me by a vintner down the hill") and ate more bread with that remarkable olive oil. When Gina excused herself to use the washroom, both men tracked her exit.

"Your wife is very beautiful," Mr. Uzzano said.

Hearing Gina referred to as his "wife" still gave Mickey a tiny charge. He almost felt guilty for deceiving his host, and thought that someone as worldly as this man would certainly understand. But he said nothing more than, "Thank you."

"And she loves you with all of her heart," the man continued. "This is very easy to see. My wife passed away a few years ago, but she looked at me the same way. You are very fortunate. Cherish this."

Mickey found himself swelling inside.

"I do," he said. "I do."

~~~~~~~~~

Gelato was a revelation. Growing up in Brooklyn, Mickey had of course tasted it before. But for whatever reason, there was nothing served in the old neighborhood that could come close to the richness and depth of flavor that sprung from every cone he tasted on every day of their trip. They had quickly adopted a routine of stopping for gelato at around 4:00 no matter where they were.

As they settled into a pair of wrought iron chairs, Mickey handed his cone to Gina to taste rather than waiting for her to ask, as she invariably did. She offered a little surprised smile before taking a lick and then took another before giving the cone back to him.

"I suppose this means you'll want some of mine as well," she said.

Mickey took a lick from his own cone and gestured with his free hand. "Only if you are in the mood to share."

Gina grinned over the top of her cone. "Mmm, I'm not. It's just too good."

Mickey laughed and leaned back in his chair.

"You make an excellent pretend husband," she said. "Right down to letting me be selfish with my gelato."

"Thank you. I practice my role every night while you are sleeping."

"Really? Well if so, I commend you both on your hard work and your ability to do it while keeping your arms and legs and everything else as close to me as humanly possible."

"Does that bother you?"

Gina lowered her head slightly.

"I'm sorry, did it sound like I was complaining?" she said with a tempting smile.

Mickey found his appetite for Gina to be voracious. Even a suggestion of the two of them in bed together could make him nearly senseless with desire. But his hunger went much deeper than that. On dozens of occasions in the past few days, her expression or a subtle gesture would inspire him to embrace her, to kiss her temple, to envelop her. He wanted desperately for her to feel not only his burgeoning love for her, but also his overflowing affection. He had never felt either to the level he felt now, and he'd never felt the two of them in combination before.

"Since you brought up the subject, you pretend to be a wife very well."

"Thank you. Of course, I don't need to practice at night the way you might. Women start imagining these things at a fairly young age."

"Really? Even someone as progressive as you?"

"Oh yes, absolutely. I 'married' Tommy Strassi when I was four. And I walked down the aisle in my dreams with numerous boys throughout high school."

Mickey laughed, but he was surprised to discover that he didn't particularly want to hear this.

"Oh, so this mock husband thing is just another day at the office for you."

"Something like that," she said, taking a bite of her cone. "Like ice cream."

Mickey took another lick of gelato and noticed that some had dripped onto the table. He of course knew that Gina was teasing, but this line of conversation left him uncomfortable. A few minutes later, they got up to walk through the street.

Gina had been holding his hand, but now she took that arm with her other hand and pulled herself tight to him while they continued to walk.

"It's nothing like that," she said. "I've never felt anything like this in my life. I never knew I could feel anything like this."

Mickey stopped and kissed her. They held each other tightly for several minutes in the middle of the street until a smiling elderly woman passed them, saying something in a high voice that Mickey didn't understand.

"What did she say?" Mickey said, resting his forehead on Gina's.

"She said something like, 'Newlyweds, so beautiful.'"

"I guess we're very convincing."

"It's easy to perform with you."

They started walking again. Mickey couldn't think of another time in his life when he'd felt this satisfied. He remembered that the day before the trip, he briefly considered the possibility that things might not go well between him and Gina while they were away. They hadn't, after all, spent a large uninterrupted period together. They had never seen each other first thing in the morning. What if they got on each other's nerves? What if mannerisms that he found so endearing in Gina seemed less so when repeated over the course of two weeks? Now he realized that such concern had been frivolous. The only thing that happened as a result of all of this time in each other's company was that he wanted more of it. And while he realized that they were in a fantasy situation in a fantasy setting, he knew instinctively that he would always want more of it. For a moment, he imagined the two of them walking down this same street while in their late seventies, and he knew then that he needed to be with Gina forever.

~~~~~~~~

Two days later, they drove to Florence for the day. They spent the morning exploring the sights, realizing quickly that they would need much more time to do this properly. They walked through the Duomo for an hour and a half, stopping every few feet to marvel at the majesty, the artistry, the sheer magnificence of the structure. They scaled a tower to look down in admiration at the city and then walked slowly by the banks of the Arno.

In the pre-gelato afternoon, they moved toward the shopping district. Mickey had never felt any need for a leather jacket, but now that he was here, he felt compelled to buy one. Still, he managed to hold out as they perused purses, footwear, and pottery. A side street brought them to an artist making small freeform wrought iron sculptures. Mickey had never seen anything like them and he wasn't sure he liked them.

"Aren't these incredible?" Gina said as she walked into the little shop.

"What are they supposed to be?"

Gina moved close to one that curled and weaved in multiple directions. She put a hand up as though to touch it, but stopped inches short.

"They're supposed to be what they are. You're not one of those people who think that something is only art if it looks like an apple or a woman in a chair, are you?"

Mickey admitted to himself that he probably was that kind of person, but he didn't want Gina to see him that way. "I was just wondering how you interpreted it."

"I interpret it as beautiful."

She turned to the shop owner who was at that moment working on yet another piece.

"These are magnificent," she said. Mickey continued to look at the one that Gina had nearly touched. As he did so, he began to find beauty in its sweep and form. Was that because it had come so close to Gina?

"Thank you," the artist said in heavily accented English. Gina switched to Italian and the two of them spoke for several minutes. The artist became more animated and expressive as the conversation continued. Mickey was sure that the artist didn't often find customers as appreciative or knowledgeable as Gina. Just another life that she improved by touching it.

Mickey further studied the piece Gina had first admired. As he looked at it, he began to see how two strands of iron wove together, meeting in the middle and then again near the top of the piece. It suddenly seemed very romantic to him. He picked the piece up off of the shelf and brought it to the artist.

"We'll take this one," he said.

Gina looked at him, surprised. "You want to buy it?"

"Of course I want to buy it. You love it, don't you?"

Gina glanced at the sculpture again. "Yes, I do love it. I was thinking of buying it myself but," she whispered, "it's a little expensive."

"I'm buying it for you. For us."

Mickey didn't actually realize the import of what he'd just said until it came out of his mouth and he saw Gina's expression. He realized that the words felt very, very good, and he thought that Gina hugged his arm just a little tighter when they resumed their walk. They continued on, stopping in countless other shops.

"I'm almost afraid to look at anything for fear that you'll go broke buying things for me," Gina said. Still, when they came to a shoe store, she hesitated longingly over a pair of black leather boots before pulling herself away.

The jeweler was a few shops down. While Gina lingered over handmade silver brooches, Mickey's eyes scanned elsewhere. Past the semi-precious stones to ones that suddenly seemed very precious to him. When they walked out of the store a few minutes later, Mickey turned to Gina and said, "You really wanted those boots, didn't you?"

Gina wrinkled her nose. "The leather was so soft. I can just imagine what they would feel like to walk in."

"Why don't you get them?"

She shook her head. "It's an extravagance."

"I'll buy them for you."

"No you won't. You've paid for too much on this trip already." She offered her most teasing smile. "You can't buy me, you know, Mr. Sienna."

"Shudder the thought. And besides, I know you're priceless. But I also know you really wanted those boots."

"I did."

"Go get them."

Gina looked back in the direction of the shoe store.

"I guess I can afford them. Let's go."

Mickey held up a hand.

"Actually, I think I might wait here." He waved toward a bench. "I'm getting a little worn out by all of this shopping."

Gina patted him on the chest. "Ooh, my big strong man can't keep up. I'll have to take that into consideration."

"Go buy the boots."

Mickey moved toward the bench and waved to Gina as she glanced back at him. When she was gone, he slipped into the jewelry store. He knew precisely which diamond he wanted.

~~~~~~~~

Now that he had the ring, the question was how to present it to Gina. Mickey thought it was interesting that he was far more nervous about finding the right setting in which to ask Gina to marry him than he was about the prospect of marriage. Mickey had friends who were married and they all talked about how carefully they deliberated before deciding to pop the question. The very idea seemed ridiculous to Mickey. He couldn't possibly be more certain of how right marrying Gina would be.

He decided upon a picnic on a hilltop outside of San Gimignano. A blanket borrowed from the innkeeper. Some bread, some Parmesan, some more of those delicious cured meats. A bottle of Chianti, of course. From their vantage point, they could see the bustling walled city while the Tuscan hills opened up in front of them. *I could live here*, Mickey thought. *Right on this spot, me and Gina with the rest of the world at just enough of a distance.*

"You're not saying much," Gina said as they ate.

Mickey realized that he had been very quiet. Part of it was the peacefulness of the setting. Most of it was because he was rehearsing his proposal. "It's very nice up here."

"It is beautiful, isn't it?"

"We'll come back some day. An anniversary, maybe." Mickey realized what he had done. As did Gina.

"An anniversary? Are you trying to tell me something?"

For a moment, Mickey wasn't sure what to do. He certainly hadn't planned to blurt something out like that. He'd been thinking about being married to Gina nonstop since he bought the ring, and the words had come out naturally. It was hardly the romantic speech he had been planning. At the same time, it seemed ridiculous to backpedal now to allow him to make things more romantic later. He did the only thing he could think of. He laughed.

"What are you laughing at?" Gina said when he didn't stop.

Mickey wiped at his eyes. "Yes, I'm trying to tell you something. I just can't believe that this is how I'm doing it."

Still laughing, he looked over at Gina. There was so much anticipation on her face. At that moment, Mickey realized that how he asked Gina to marry him was meaningless. Only that he did so and that she said yes. He reached into his pocket for the ring, taking a deep breath to regain at least a little composure. As he held the ring out to Gina, she gasped.

"I bought this for you yesterday. I had this whole speech planned where I was going to tell you all of these things I've told you already." He got up on his knees. At least he could do that part right. "I love you, Gina. I want to be with you forever. Will you marry me?"

Gina was already nodding yes before he finished. She leapt into his arms, knocking him over, and lay on top of him kissing his face. Mickey realized that he hadn't really pictured Gina's reaction in his mind. He wasn't sure if she would be cool and clever in response, or even dismissive of how traditional a proposal and a ring was. He liked having her bowl him over much more.

"I want my ring now," she said when she at last leaned back off of him. Mickey handed her the diamond, a single oval gem, nearly a karat in size.

"It's incredible," she said, slipping the ring on her finger.

"I'm glad you like it."

"I mean all of it. Everything that has happened between us. A few months ago, I was planning to take on the world alone. And now I have you."

"You'll still take on the world."

Gina smiled. "I will. But I won't be doing it alone. You have no idea how lucky I feel right now."

Mickey hugged Gina close to him and closed his eyes. When he opened them, he first saw the glorious Tuscan landscape. Then, pulling back to look at his new fiancée, he beheld a vision that put the other to shame.

~~~~~~~~

Mickey was staring off to the corner of the kitchen.

"You took on the world, Gina, you really did," he said weakly. "I wish we could have taken it on together. I should have been there with you." He looked down at the table. "I hope you got everything out of it you hoped you would."

Jesse had grown accustomed to feeling a little disoriented after one of his father's stories, but this one made him feel as though he were treading on the lunar surface.

His father and Gina had been engaged? He had never even considered the possibility of this.

Chapter Twenty-Two

I'm not sure why I never realized before that emotional calisthenics were so much more taxing than physical ones. I'd been doing psychic aerobics for most of the last week. The invigoration of my trip to Northern California. My father's sexually-charged tale of life with Gina. Marina's telling me she loved me. And then learning that my father and Gina had been engaged. It was time for my cool-down exercises. I didn't want to talk. I didn't want to write. I didn't want to eat. I was spent.

Marina's telling me she loved me hit me like a time-release capsule. As that first morning wore on and then the next few days followed, I became increasingly focused on the implications. It was impossible for me to take this lightly. No matter what else I did, I would never trivialize anything in my relationship with Marina. At the same time, it was even more impossible for me to receive this with arms wide open. I just didn't know what it all meant about my future with her, and she wasn't giving me any clues.

On the other hand, the news about my father's engagement to Gina came on like a shot of scotch (or perhaps Nyquil, if one wanted to maintain the metaphor). What is it about marriage or the intention to marry that so utterly changes the level at which one perceives a relationship? Why do we regard the breakup of a three-year marriage as so much sadder than the split between two people who had been living together for five?

That my father had asked Gina to marry him changed the dimensions of this story. It didn't matter that he didn't marry her (at least I was assuming at that point that he didn't, though who knew what surprises were still in store?). What mattered was that they had been that serious. Certainly there was every chance that time had obscured my father's memories. It was very possible that their feelings for one another weren't as deep as he made them seem to me. It was even more possible that he wasn't telling me about the difficulties they had, the disagreements, the tiffs. But the absolute detail with which he told these stories – he couldn't possibly tell me nearly as much about last night's chess match – suggested that Gina had affected him at such an intense level that their every act together was seared onto his brain.

Or he was making the entire thing up. I hadn't entirely rejected the notion that this story was all some elaborate invention of his, triggered by an age-scarred mind. There was, among other things, that recent incident where he "talked" to his brother to suggest such a possibility. But this seemed less and less conceivable to me as these stories continued.

This meant that my father had once loved a woman named Gina. They had an electrifying relationship. They merged spectacularly and indelibly into each other's lives.

And still it ended.

Your honor, the prosecution rests.

Whatever Gina and my father had together hadn't lasted. It affected him so deeply that on the morning when he told me about their engagement, he pulled back and addressed the ethereal version of her, still looking for answers to his questions. It moved him so deeply that he shed years as he spoke about her.

But the romance hadn't lasted.

I can't imagine that it was his intention in telling the story, but I couldn't help but come away from what I'd heard so far with one heart-stopper of a question: if a relationship as star-kissed as theirs failed, what chance was there for me and Marina?

And so, depleted from my emotional workout, I sat at my desk and did close to nothing. There had been all too many days like this in my past, but I hadn't expected there to be many in the wake of the Hayward article. Aline had called late the day before to tell me how much she loved it and implied that other such assignments would follow. That should have sent me into a flurry of writing activity, even if it was just completing a rudimentary gig while I dreamed up more ambitious ones, but I could not have been flatter. I could barely get my fingers up on the keyboard.

When the phone rang, I was happy to answer it. It was the kind of morning where I'd welcome a telemarketer. Perhaps even a survey taker.

I didn't even mind that it was my brother-in-law Brad.

"Hey, Jess, how's Mickey treating you?"

"It's like an extended vacation."

"Yeah, I can just imagine. Years from now you'll have to tell me what the hell you were thinking bringing him into your house. I don't know what I would have done if Denise had had the same idea."

You would have alerted the New York Times *that a flock of pigs were circling the roof of your building*, I thought. What I said was, "What's up?"

"You mentioned Mark Gray in our last conversation," Brad said, switching inflections to let me know that I was no longer speaking to a family member but rather a magazine scion.

"Yeah, he's great."

"I've done some checking around about him, and lots of people share your opinion. Any idea why he doesn't have an editor-in-chief's position now?"

"Well, I know for a fact that it isn't because he hasn't been offered one. I also know that it isn't because he's wedded to *The City*. I think he's just being really picky. He's young, he's well paid, he has a fabulous reputation, and when he's ready to make his move, there will be plenty of opportunities for him."

It was quiet on the other end of the phone. It sounded like Brad was writing something.

"Do you think he'd be interested in our magazine?" When Brad said "our," he was referring to himself and his investors. He definitely wasn't suggesting that I was a participant in any way.

"You'd have to make him an amazing offer."

"I think there's room in the budget."

"I'm not talking about money." It didn't surprise me that Brad had missed my earlier point. "He can get money from lots of places. He can even get money from *The City* – like I said I'm sure he already gets lots of it. For Mark to get on board with a new magazine, he'd have to believe that you were very ambitious, that you weren't going to fold in nine months, and that you were going to give him the kind of editorial freedom and ability to call his own shots that he couldn't get elsewhere."

"We're not going to fold in nine months," Brad said stiffly.

"Hey, it's not me that you have to convince."

"The part about being ambitious goes without saying. What kind of editorial freedom are we talking about?"

"Well, no one, not even someone with Mark's ego, is going to think that management is going to give him carte blanche. But he's going to want to know what your basic parameters are, and then he's going to want to know that he can do essentially anything he wants as long as he stays within those parameters."

It was hard for me to believe that Brad understood what I was talking about. To him, a magazine's editorial content was what you included to break up the advertising. That such a thing could affect a career decision more than money was not something he could easily comprehend.

"And this guy would be a marquee name, right?"

"I'm guessing the reverberations would be huge."

"Then I think we could probably give him a lot of room to move around in. Along with all of the salary and perks, of course."

"Look, it's worth a shot. He might even be up for this kind of challenge."

Brad was quiet again. He was definitely writing something. "How'd you like to pitch him for us."

"Huh?"

"He's a friend of yours, right?"

"I've known him since I've been writing professionally. I've never been to a barbecue at his house or anything."

"Do you think you could sell him on the magazine?"

Two thoughts came to my mind at the same time. The first was, *I'm not entirely sure that* I'm *sold on the magazine. In fact, I'm not even sure I know what the magazine is.* The other was my father saying, "So if he hires one of these guys, do you get a finder's fee?" It didn't seem right to bring up the latter with my brother-in-law, even though he was making it abundantly clear through his tone of voice that this was a business conversation.

"I think I'd need to be a whole lot better prepped on the direction of the magazine before I could do it."

"But you think you could do it?"

"If you're asking if I think I can deliver you Mark Gray, who the hell knows? Like I said before, he's gotten plenty of offers. If what you're asking is whether I can pitch him aggressively, yeah, sure, once I know what I'm talking about. But why do you need me?"

"You said he's a friend of yours. And I'm guessing you speak his language. Believe it or not, I'm actually aware of the fact that I don't."

I found the admission a little disarming. Perhaps the shakeup surrounding his severance had actually released some humility into his bloodstream.

"I'd be happy to sit down with Mark for you." I said. "But as I told you before, I'm going to have to know a lot more about the magazine than I do right now, or you won't stand a chance with him."

"That's very do-able. How about your having dinner with me and my partners on –" he hesitated for a moment, presumably to consult his calendar "– Wednesday?"

I pretended to look at my calendar, though I already knew that Marina was going to be out with an old high school friend that night. She had invited me to tag along and I passed, and she actually tried to talk me into it before I convinced her that I really didn't want to go.

"Yeah, Wednesday is good."

"I'll set it up with my partners," he said, and I could hear him writing on the other end. "And Jess, thanks for not asking me what's in this for you. I appreciate that you'd do this as a favor. But we'll talk about what's in it for you on Wednesday."

It promised to be an interesting dinner. Of course the subsequent conversation with Mark would require me to be an Olympian-level pitchman. It would be diverting, to say the least. A diversion seemed welcome.

Chapter Twenty-Three

There are a number of things that I never wanted to be in my life. I had no interest in being a doctor or a lawyer or a financial analyst. I didn't want to be a bricklayer or an ice hockey goalie or a cowboy. Of course I didn't want to be a serial killer or a child abuser or a politician. But of all the things I didn't want to be, the thing I wanted to be least was a cliché.

Yet in the couple of weeks that had passed since my return from California, I was becoming more of one with every passing moment. Man finds girl, they have great time together, their relationship deepens, she tells him she loves him – and man starts to retreat emotionally. It's the third or fourth definition of the word "cliché" in Webster's.

Of course it wasn't exactly like that, and of course I had given huge amounts of advance warning, but it didn't make me feel any better. I didn't want Marina's telling me she loved me (and my telling her that I loved her) to disconnect us from what had been the most natural relationship in my life. But the truth was that it was just about all I thought about when we were together. And what I thought about saddened me deeply: that this event had signaled the final act of our affair. We're in love. Love dies. The show's big, weepy ballad was probably less than half an hour away.

As a sign of how confused this all made me, I still hadn't told Marina about my father's having been engaged to Gina. There was no way to do this without talking about how much that information had shaken me up. And doing that would lead to my talking about why it shook me up so much, and that was a conversation I wasn't equipped to have. So I reserved a story I would have run to Marina with just a few weeks before. I pulled back.

What a cliché.

"So he hasn't said anything to you?" she said as we walked through the downtown streets after dinner one night.

"No, nothing."

"Isn't this driving you crazy? It's driving *me* crazy. I wonder what's going on. I'll bet the next story is going to be huge and he's working up the energy to tell you. I wonder what it could be."

We walked quietly for a while. We stopped into a convenience store because Marina remembered that she needed to buy a birthday card for a fellow teacher. While we were in there, we saw a photograph of an actress on the cover of *Rolling Stone*, which led to a lengthy conversation about the actress's best and poorest roles. It was very easy to talk about this and I found myself participating with gusto. There was no unsafe ground here. I could have any opinion I wanted, I could disagree completely with anything Marina said, and she would do nothing more than question my taste. We both loved movies and we both respected each other's opinions, and therefore we could debate endlessly with no downside. The same would have been true if we were discussing the death penalty, or excessive uses of force, or the role of religion. The fact is, the same would have been true if we were talking about the delicacy and perishability of romantic unions. I just had stopped being able to understand that. It didn't matter that we loved each other before we told each other that we did. It was the saying it that triggered this in me. Yes, that was ludicrous, but I had no way of understanding that just then.

The conversation about the actress continued all the way back to the car when I told Marina that my favorite of the actress's movies had been a mother/daughter drama she'd done about five years before.

"Oh, God, remember that one. I'll bet you were bawling like a baby when she decided to move to New York at the end."

"To tell you the truth, what I remember best were the amazingly short skirts she wore in just about every scene."

Marina slapped me on the shoulder. "Yeah, right. That's just like you. You like this movie the most because she showed a lot of leg in it. Did you start crying before she said goodbye to her brother or after?"

"I didn't say I didn't cry during the movie. I just remember the skirts."

"Yeah, and Bogart had great pecs in 'Casablanca.'" She took my face in her hands. "I know you like movies where you can get all worked up. That's one of the many reasons why I love you."

I put my head against her forehead and then pulled her closer, but I didn't say anything. When I pulled back, Marina gave me a brief curious look and then got into the car.

We didn't talk for a few minutes after I started driving. I hadn't intended to avoid telling Marina that I loved her while we were standing outside, but I couldn't pull the trigger. I was as baffled by it as I'm sure she was. But one of the things that I loved about her was that she didn't allow things to hang in the air.

"What was that about back there?" she said when we got to a traffic light.

I turned to her. "What do you mean?"

She tilted her head. "You don't do coy well."

"It didn't mean what you think it meant. It just got stuck in my throat. That's all."

The light changed and I started to drive again. Marina turned to look out at the road.

"And what did you think I thought it meant?"

"I thought you might have thought that it meant that I didn't love you."

"Jess, I wouldn't need for you to not tell me you loved me for me to know that you didn't love me. I know that you love me. I also knew that it was bound to get 'stuck in your throat' sometime around now."

I turned to her briefly. "How did you know that?"

"Because you've been just a tiny bit more reticent about everything lately. I figured at some point you'd own up to it, but now's as good a time as any for me to say this to you."

"What's that?"

"Stop. Just stop. Nothing changed. I know that you think it did, but it didn't. Did you think that I started loving you the first time I told you? Do you think that that's when you started loving me? Of course not. We'd both been feeling it for a long time before then. And everything was fine. We still have the same relationship we had before. We're still taking it day to day. We're still acutely aware of the odds. I could have told you I loved you a month after we started dating, but I thought it would scare you too much. Maybe I should have waited a while longer. I love you. I didn't ask you to marry me and I didn't ask you to revise your entire worldview. But I do love you. Get over it."

I reached over for her hand. At that moment, I wasn't sure if I should feel stupid for feeling the way I had the previous couple of weeks, relieved that Marina had broken the ice, or just glad to be completely honest with her again.

"I love you," I said. "You just amaze me."

"Yes, you're a very lucky man."

I kissed her hand. "I'm fully aware of that."

I would tell her about my father's engagement the next day.

~~~~~~~~

That Saturday, Marina left the house very early to attend a teachers' conference on Long Island. I slept until around 9:30, and when I walked into the kitchen I saw my father sitting on the patio. It was mid-March and the sun angling in through the kitchen windows made it feel as though the temperatures had climbed into the eighties. They hadn't, but it was obviously warm enough for my father to take his coffee outside.

"The first spectacular day of the year," he said as I walked out to join him. He was right about that. It had to be in the low seventies already, and it was cloudless and beaming. I hadn't been out back since the last snowstorm nearly a month before, and it was nice to see that the ground appeared dry and that some buds were showing up on the bushes that rimmed the patio.

"We should do something," I said as I sat down next to him.

"I'm thinking of putting in a garden," he said, eyes cast off to an unshaded corner of the property.

"I was thinking we could have lunch someplace with outdoor seating."

He offered me a brief, unimpressed glance, and then turned his gaze outward again. "This backyard sings out for a garden."

"When did you turn into Walt Whitman? And how come your old backyard never sang out for a garden? You lived there for more than forty years. Do you even know anything about gardening?"

"Last I heard, it was somewhat simpler than nuclear science. Have you heard differently?"

I laughed. I had no idea where this inspiration was coming from.

"And last I heard, gardening involved things like bending down. Not exactly your favorite act. I'm not sure you're physically up to this, Dad."

He sighed deeply while still looking out at the property and then turned to me again. "I am if I get a little help."

It would have been very easy for me to say no. I could have reminded him that I didn't have the time to dedicate to the upkeep that would certainly become my responsibility. I could have mentioned that there were any number of farmer's markets from which to get very fresh produce all summer long. I could have told him that I didn't like to get my hands dirty, which was largely true. But just as some voice spoke to him on this first glittering pre-spring day, something told me that in some way this was the kind of thing I had been thinking of when I asked him to move in with me.

"Not a big one, okay?" I said.

"Just some vegetables and a few herbs. Stuff you like to cook with."

"Do you have any idea whatsoever what you're doing?"

"None at all. That's what nurseries are for. They'll tell us exactly what to do."

A couple of hours later, we were breaking ground. For the first hour, while I dug out the plot, my father did little more than sit on a lawn chair, supervise, and bring me a cold drink. Once the soil was exposed, though, he became an active participant. He raked and fertilized precisely the way the salesman at the nursery had told him to. And when I knelt down to begin planting, he knelt down right beside me.

"Isn't this killing you?" I said.

"With all that nice soft topsoil we just laid down? It's like kneeling on a pillow."

"I can handle this part if it hurts too much."

"I'm fine. I told you that I would do my share."

My father insisted that starting with greenhouse-raised seedlings was "cheating," so we planted seeds. I won the negotiation to keep things as simple as possible to increase our odds of success. We chose Roma and Beefsteak tomatoes, bell peppers (only after I secured his agreement that we wouldn't pick them until they turned red), zucchini (the salesman at the nursery said we'd need to be 'absolute black thumbs' in order to fail with these), basil, cilantro and rosemary. I dug each hole, and my father dropped in the seeds, replaced the soil, and patted softly. Though I saw him wince a couple of times as he moved through the plot, he remained steadfast.

As we drove back from the nursery that morning, I wondered if my father was going to tell me more about Gina. He hadn't said anything since telling me about the trip to Tuscany, and these were the ideal conditions. I also thought for a while about talking to him about what was going on with Marina. She'd eased my mind on the drive back from dinner a few nights back, but I still couldn't help but continue to think about where we were going. In the end, neither woman came up in conversation. Instead, we talked about the family.

"So I'm having lunch with Mark Gray on Tuesday," I told him.

"This is that editor that Brad wants?"

"Yeah. He's the editor that Brad is salivating over."

"You think this magazine of Brad's has a chance?"

I looked over at him, surprised. "You said that like you thought it might not. I thought you thought Brad was a genius."

My father dropped some more seeds in the ground and shrugged. "Brad's a good numbers guy. From what I can tell, he's a good corporate guy. I'm not sure he can be a good magazine guy. There's a difference."

Of course, I knew there was a difference. I was a little surprised to hear my father say that he knew this, though.

"I have to admit, he kinda sold me," I said. "The first part of our dinner was classic Brad: talking about demographics and advertiser appeal and that sort of thing. And the guys who were with him made a suit like Brad seem like a poet. But when I finally got them to tell me what the hell the magazine was, they were pretty good at answering from an editorial point of view. Especially Brad. I was a little impressed."

"You'd better hope he never talks that way in front of your sister. She'll dump him for breach of contract."

I laughed. "Gee Dad, much as I'd like to defend Denise, you've got that one nailed."

He shrugged, as though this admission had cost him a little something. "I love my daughter, but I *know* my daughter. So did you do as I told you to do and ask him what you got out of this?"

"We had a conversation about it," I said. I didn't feel the need to acknowledge that it was Brad who'd brought it up and not me. "Brad made some vague allusions to their 'showing their appreciation.' I sort of interpreted that as meaning that there might be some compensation involved if I perform a miracle and get Mark on board, and if I don't Brad will try not to be openly hostile at family dinners."

"You're right; I should have made this deal for you."

"Hey, there's still time. 12:30 at the Union Square Cafe. I'll keep my cell phone on."

My father didn't say anything but instead concentrated on laying down a row of cilantro seeds.

"You're not going to be upset if all we get on this plot is a bunch of crabgrass, are you?" I said.

He patted the topsoil down with one hand while he turned to look over at me. "Why would that happen? We're doing all the things that the guy at the nursery told us to do."

"We've just never done this before. We don't even have houseplants. We barely have shrubs."

"The occasional flash of optimism wouldn't hurt you, you know."

"I just don't want you to be disappointed."

He gathered himself up, walked over to me and kissed me on the top of the head. "Thank you, Anna, for worrying about me. Get out of the way, I'm going to water."

I dropped the last of the pepper seeds into the ground and patted the topsoil over them. My father's reference to my grandmother was obviously intended as a way to tell me not to "mother" him. I was flattered, to be honest.

He turned the hose on and sprayed water over the entire plot, drenching the topsoil as the guy in the nursery had told us to do. I stood there watching, until he turned the nozzle of the hose in my direction and sprayed my shoes. I wasn't looking and was momentarily stunned by the act, wondering if something had gone wrong. When I realized that nothing had, I took two quick steps out of the way of the water.

"Hey, that's totally not fair," I said. "You know that I'm not going to try to get revenge on an old guy with creaky knees."

He sprayed me directly in the face.

"That's for calling me an old guy," he said before releasing the nozzle and throwing the hose on the ground.

I wiped my face with my hands. The water was a little chilly, but I didn't want to go inside for a towel. He walked to the edge of the garden to survey the quality of his sprinkling. When I walked over toward him, he flinched a bit, probably assuming I was going to take the hose to him.

"It's safe," I said, putting my hands up. He turned back toward the garden, as did I.

"It's not too wet, right?" he said.

"Nah. Looks about the way the nursery guy told us it should look."

He nodded. He seemed surprisingly proud of this accomplishment.

I put a hand on his shoulder. "If nothing grows, though, we'll know it's your fault."

~~~~~~~~

Mark Gray kept me waiting for around twenty minutes that Tuesday. The time was hardly wasted, since I had an article with me to edit, but it did present me with one of those conundrums I've never known the etiquette for. Ordering mineral water and drinking it was of course acceptable while waiting for one's guest. But what about the bread on the table? Were you allowed to eat it before your dining partner arrived? Was it okay as long as you didn't have a half-eaten piece on your bread plate when he came? In all of my years of restaurant meals (many of which involved waiting for editors to show up), that question had never been sufficiently answered for me. I decided to leave the bread alone and concentrate on the manuscript.

If I didn't know him as well as I did, I could easily have formed an impression of Mark as someone who too carefully crafted a pushing-the-outside-of-the-envelope image. Hair slightly long. Clothing crisp but decidedly casual. Just enough stubble on his face to suggest three o'clock instead of five. He'd signed on as Features Editor of *24-Hour City* (known to those

of us on "the inside" as *The City*) at the same time that Jeff
Mingus had been tapped as Editor. Mingus's job was to make
one last effort at reviving a magazine that had had its heyday
in the late sixties and had stumbled out of favor somewhere
around the same time as Ed Koch. Jeff had done an impressive
job of righting the ship, romancing big-time writers and doing
a great song and dance for prospective advertisers. But it was
Mark's work that generated the buzz. With Mingus's support,
he took wild chances, commissioning writers to extend beyond their areas of expertise to write pieces that either failed
spectacularly or electrified with uncommon nuance and texture. The former pieces were quickly forgotten. The latter were
regularly bandied for Pulitzers (with one piece winning the
award two years earlier). Circulation rose by more than fifty
percent, but more importantly, the magazine was hot again.
Ad pages tripled from the point at which Mark stepped in to
the point at which I sat there wondering if I should sneak a
slice of sourdough olive.

In the general media, Mingus got most of the credit. But
within the industry, people knew how much Mark Gray had
to do with it. As a result, there seemed to be a new rumor every few weeks about some magazine dangling a top editorial
gig in front of him. And yet, he was still seated in the same
office in the east twenties that he'd occupied for the past five
years.

"Sorry I'm late," Mark said as he sat down at the table and
reached for a piece of bread. "I was in the middle of a screaming match with a writer that was too good to walk away from."
He took the bottle of mineral water from the middle of the
table, poured himself a glass, and then refilled mine. "It's good
to see you. It's been a while."

"Yeah, I think the last time was the *Tapestry* cocktail party."

"Right, at that Cuban/sushi place. It closed something
like a month later. Talk about a high-risk venture. So what
have you been up to? Your father had just moved in with you
the last time we talked. How's that going?"

"I think it's going okay."

"You're a better man than me. I think I'd last about thirty-seven minutes with my father in my house."

"We've had our moments."

"Yeah, who doesn't. So I was really glad you called me. There's something I want to talk to you about. I was talking to Aline Dixon the other day and she told me about that piece you did on the new Hayward consortium."

"I didn't know you knew Aline."

"Who doesn't know Aline? She's great, and if she likes you she invites you to those tastings they're always having. Anyway, she e-mailed it to me. You really nailed it. I've seen a number of pieces on Hayward over the years. I think we actually did one a while back when he put that experimental thing together at the Brooklyn Academy of Music. But this is the first time I've seen him come across as a human being. You have a future as a novelist."

"Every word of it is true."

"I figured that, actually. But it was really good stuff. Really good stuff. Don't take this the wrong way, but it was light years ahead of your other writing."

"I appreciate the compliment and I'll get over the criticism."

"So after reading it, I thought of you for this piece I want to do."

I'd been waiting for Mark to say something like this for years. I'd pitched him a number of stories at *The City* and other places, but never even gotten close to connecting with him. Of course, his timing could not have possibly been worse. If I were successful at convincing him to move to Brad's startup, he wouldn't even think about commissioning me for anything because of my relationship to Brad. It wouldn't be seemly for the renegade to be charged with bowing to nepotism in his first top editorial gig. This wasn't an issue that had occurred to me earlier, because I'd all but given up hope of ever working for him. I gave a moment's thought to betraying my brother-in-law and then decided that I couldn't go through with it.

"You might want to hear why I asked you to lunch first."

"You're moving to Northern California."

"No, though the thought has entered my mind."

"You've decided to open a restaurant in Newark."

"Right, because I want to work fewer hours."

"You're not really thinking about becoming a novelist, are you?"

"No, no. This isn't about me. It's about you. Someone has asked me to talk to you about taking the top editorial spot at a startup with great financial backing."

His eyes grew wide. "A job? You called to recruit me?"

"You say that like I'm asking you to join a cult."

Mark laughed and sat back in his seat for the first time since he entered the restaurant. "I just signed a new contract with the magazine. A great new contract, I might add."

"So break it. What's a contract?"

"Hmm, maybe I should re-think the commission I was going to offer you. The issue isn't the contract. It's the job. I don't know why people keep trying to hire me. I thought I'd made it very clear that I wasn't moving."

"Yeah, but everyone thinks you're just posturing."

He shook his head. "Figures. If I were actually posturing, no one would want me. I'm not playing. I have the perfect situation for me. I get to do basically anything I want. I work for people who love me. And I don't have to take all the shit that Mingus has to take at budget meetings. It's about as no-lose as these things come."

"So you don't even want to hear my pitch?"

"Do you feel morally obligated to make it even though there is absolutely no chance I'll take you up on it?"

"Not when you put it that way."

"So then let me tell you about this other thing."

While Mark moved back to the front of his chair, I considered the expression on Brad's face when I told him that I not only hadn't pitched for him, but I didn't even get to stand on the mound.

"What do you know about home schooling?" Mark said.

"Just about nothing."

"Excellent. I suppose that means you don't know anything about what AnnaLee Layton is doing with a bunch of kids on a block in Yonkers."

"Nope."

"It's amazing stuff. One kid wins a statewide science award, another gets 2210 on his SATs, and another has an essay published in a local magazine – and she's eight."

"Wow."

"She's pretty impressive. School boards all over the country are trying to get her to tell them what she knows and she says she doesn't have time. She'll let us do a piece, though. Do you want it?"

"I truly know nothing about this subject."

"What's your point?"

"And I'm dating a schoolteacher. Is that something like a conflict of interest?"

"Are you trying to find a way to say no? I can handle rejection, Jess."

"No, it sounds great. I'm just doing the full disclosure thing."

"Fine. So do it. It would be fun to work together on something."

Yes it would, I told myself. This was the last thing I had expected to happen at this lunch.

Brad was not going to be happy. But he'd get over it.

Chapter Twenty-Four

When Mickey thought about it, he realized that he probably hadn't been in the City in a couple of years. He used to love going into town with Dorothy; she had a thing about Rockefeller Center, which somehow always led to a trip to Saks. For a simple woman, she had an incongruous fascination with silk scarves. It was really her only impractical extravagance, and Mickey was more than comfortable about satisfying it.

A couple of months before they found out she was sick, Dorothy stopped showing any interest in traveling into Manhattan. She even turned Mickey down when he suggested it a few times. Mickey still didn't understand what that was about, since there was no indication that she was really sick before going for that procedure. And then after she died, he just never found any reason. Denise lived in the city, but when she wanted to see him, she came out and Mickey would never have thought of inviting himself over. Jesse went in all the time, but Mickey never had any reason to join him. After a while, he just stopped thinking about going there at all.

Jesse's mention that he was having lunch in Union Square got him thinking, though. His old apartment had been a short walk from Union Square, and he would often wander over there when he went out walking. He hadn't been down in that area in easily twenty years. It would probably be unrecognizable, though of course, some things would be the same.

Jesse was watering the garden. It had become a habit of his to do so after breakfast before he got to work. Mickey felt like it was really his responsibility, since he had talked Jesse into planting the garden in the first place, but Jesse insisted it was a good "focusing tool" for him. That kid had so many different techniques that he used to get himself going, it was amazing that he didn't spend the entire day in preparation.

"See anything yet?" Mickey said as he walked up to his son. It had been five days since they put down the seeds.

"Yeah, I was going to come get you when I finished. If you look really closely where we planted the cilantro, you can see a couple of tiny shoots."

Mickey looked over. If he squinted, he could see perhaps an eighth of an inch of green poking out of the ground in two places.

"They're probably weeds," Jesse said. "But at least we didn't sterilize the ground."

Jesse continued watering. It was probably just Mickey's imagination, but it seemed that he eased up on the spray just a little when he got near the "shoots," as though he wanted to handle them delicately. He finished and started walking the hose back to the side of the house.

"My apartment was on Gramercy Park," Mickey said as he walked with Jesse. Jesse threw him a glance that made it clear that he had no idea why Mickey felt it important to mention that then. "I had a key to the park and everything."

"Really? That must have made you a popular guy."

"It was a big deal then, but not as much of one as they made it later. It just meant I could get into a nice place to read the newspaper on Sunday mornings."

Jesse nodded and set about coiling the hose back on its rack.

"I haven't been back in a couple of decades," Mickey said.

"I get over there every now and then. There are some great places to eat in that neighborhood."

"That's what I've heard."

They went back into the house and Jesse refilled his coffee cup.

"Wanna go?" Mickey said.

"Go where?"

"To Gramercy Park. If you felt like taking a walk around there, I wouldn't mind seeing my old haunts."

Jesse wrinkled his nose. "I sort of have a bunch of work to do. I have to get my thoughts together for my first interview with AnnaLee Layton."

Mickey was disappointed. He'd pretty much convinced himself that he was going into the City, and it wouldn't be the same if he went in by himself. Jesse must have noticed this because a few seconds later, he added, "As long as we're back by the middle of the afternoon, I should be fine."

They didn't say very much while they were in the car. Jesse talked some more about this teacher he was doing an article on, and they put on the radio and disagreed over a news story about tax appropriations. Otherwise, Mickey didn't say much. He realized as they came out of the tunnel and headed toward the east side that he was feeling a little nervous. He wasn't sure what was waiting for him there.

Jesse pulled into a parking lot about a block from the park. The neighborhood was made up mostly of brownstones, nothing particularly distinctive. People kept their places up, which was smart considering how much they were paying to live in this area. Mickey felt himself calming as they started walking down the block. He realized it had been a very long time since he'd been in a real Manhattan neighborhood. The streets were different here. Far fewer people, and most of them seemed to have some idea of where they were going. It wasn't as though anything specific was familiar – certainly nothing jumped out at him or called to his memory – but there was a familiarity to the entire thing. Maybe it was because he had been spending so much time in this neighborhood in his mind lately. This felt a little bit like home.

By the time they got to the southwestern corner of the park, Mickey was feeling transported. There were probably only a dozen or so people inside the private park at the moment. A guy about his age reading the *News*. A guy in his early twenties wearing headphones and rocking left and right as he walked. A woman in her mid-thirties sitting on the edge of a bench talking intently into a cell phone. A guy sitting on a bench further down with his laptop open, his closed eyes searching the skies for inspiration. With the exception of the guy reading the paper, none of these types were anything like the people who had frequented the park when he lived there. All the same, Mickey felt a sense of collegiality with them. Maybe the woman with the cell phone sat on that bench holding her boyfriend's hand on Sunday mornings.

"Too bad we can't go in," Jesse said.

Mickey shook his head. "It always seems like a bigger deal on the outside than it does on the inside. Let's keep walking."

As they did, Mickey picked up his pace. His knees weren't hurting as much as they normally did, and he actually felt a little spring in his step. They passed a dry cleaners he used to bring his suits to, and Mickey wondered if the same family still owned it. There was a deli down the block with a sign that could easily have been from Mickey's time. Mickey wondered if the current residents thought the sign was quaint or an eyesore. They got to the corner of 18th and Lex, and Mickey simply stopped and looked around. It didn't matter that there wasn't a single familiar sight. Mickey knew this was the location of one of the most meaningful kisses of his life. It was the kiss he gave Gina, right out there in the open, the morning after the engagement party.

"I'm kinda hungry," he said to Jesse. "Want to get something to eat?"

"There are some great Indian places a few streets up."

Mickey threw his son a smirk. "You're kidding, right."

"I am, yes. There's a nice Italian place a couple of blocks down."

The restaurant was nothing like anything that was in the neighborhood when Mickey lived there. A lot of brass and marble and hard lines. Too flashy for Mickey's tastes, but Jesse said the food was good, and one thing he'd learned was that when it came to food (at least the kinds of food that Mickey liked to eat), Jesse knew what he was talking about.

Mickey looked through the menu quickly and was glad that the waiter was attentive. The walk through the old neighborhood had left him in the mood for talking.

~~~~~~~~

Gina's mother had never embraced him before. She nearly wrenched his back when she did it after he and Gina announced their engagement. He was relatively sure that Mrs. Ceraf would accept the news enthusiastically, but he wasn't at all prepared for how enthusiastically she responded. It actually hurt a little the next day.

Of course Gina could not return home from Italy to tell her parents that she was engaged, as her fiancé was not supposed to have been with her on the trip. They talked at first about elaborating on the illusion by having Mickey "pick Gina up" at the airport and proposing then, but ultimately Mickey suggested that something critical was missing from that scenario. In spite of the very un-traditional woman he was marrying and the decidedly un-traditional way in which he had proposed, he wanted to maintain a critical part of the engagement tradition. He needed to ask Gina's father's permission.

"If he says no, does that mean that I need to give the ring back?" Gina said.

"Do you think he'll say no?"

"Of course not. I think he thinks you're a good catch. But if he did say no, what would you do?"

Mickey pretended to think about the question for a moment and then he shrugged. "Ask someone else to marry me, I guess."

Gina punched him on the arm and then glanced again at the ring on her finger.

"I suppose that would be okay as long as I got to keep this."

"And people call you a socialist. You are going to take that off before you go home, right?"

"For the only time in my life, yes."

Talking to Mr. Ceraf had been as much of a formality as Mickey expected, and three days after Gina returned from Italy, his future mother-in-law nearly broke his back. Two weeks later, the Cerafs hosted a lavish engagement party for Mickey and Gina in their apartment.

It was the first time that the Sienna family and the Ceraf family would be meeting, an occasion that gave Mickey some pause. There were huge cultural differences between the two families. Mickey wasn't at all sure how they would blend. Like with asking for Gina's hand, however, Mickey shouldn't have been concerned. Gina's parents made the entire Sienna clan feel welcome. When Mickey saw his mother trading sewing tips with Gina's aunt, he knew that everything was going to be okay.

There were easily two dozen people at the party that Mickey had never met before. He had been to a number of family functions during the months he had been with Gina, but this occasion introduced an entirely new layer of relatives – each of whom drove home the point that he should be counting his blessings. Mickey thought it was a little funny that anyone thought that he needed to be told how special Gina was, but he accepted it all in the spirit in which it was intended.

"She's our jewel," said Gina's paternal grandmother.

"A spitfire from the day she was born," said one uncle.

"If you know what's good for you, you'll just let her have her way," said a cousin. "The rest of us figured that out a long time ago."

"I'm sure you think you realize how lucky you are, young man," said another uncle. "Let me just tell you right now that you don't know the half of it. Gina's a one-in-a-million girl. I wish my son had even a small percentage of her zest for life."

Mickey smiled and glanced over at his future wife, who was at that moment less than ten feet away from him experiencing some level of teasing from some older cousins.

"I understand what you're saying, sir. I've been pinching myself regularly since the day I met her."

At that moment, Gina's father sidled up next to them.

"What are you filling my future son-in-law's head with, Malcolm?"

"Just making sure he knows what a prize he's getting, Dan."

Mr. Ceraf clapped Mickey on the shoulder and said to his brother, "And what about the prize my daughter is getting? Have you ever seen my Gina so head-over-heels about anything? I'd say that Mickey here either has her hypnotized or he's going to be one heck of a husband."

Mickey felt himself blushing. Mr. Ceraf had been unremittingly complimentary since he'd asked for Gina's hand. Mickey felt a little guilty about concealing the actual timing of the engagement from the man. At the same time, though, he knew that he would do everything in his power to be the kind of husband to Gina that Mr. Ceraf hoped he would be. In the end, he figured, that mattered much more.

Toward the end of the party Mickey made his way over to the bar to get a drink for Gina. Carl was there and raised his glass toward him as Mickey walked in his direction.

"Brother-in-law," Mickey said as he touched his glass with Carl's. "Who would have ever thought we'd wind up being family?"

"Not me," Carl said, shaking his head. "I would have thought you stood a better chance of marrying my mother than my sister."

"Gee, thanks for the compliment."

Carl put his arm around Mickey and walked him toward a relatively quiet corner.

"It's not you, Mick. I just never thought for a second that Gina would get so serious so quickly. Even when the two of you started seeing each other almost every night, I figured it would pass. Gina's never given any indication before of being the marrying kind."

"I guess she just had to meet the right man."

Carl offered a little laugh. "I really just never thought it. I always thought she'd be too caught up in trying to do something big with her life. First woman president, maybe. It's hard to imagine her cooking dinners and taking care of babies. You have to understand that it's not her nature."

Mickey was surprised to hear Carl talking this way. He thought that Carl knew both him and his sister better than that.

"Is that what you're worried about? Do you think I'm going to saddle Gina with a half-dozen kids and a long list of chores?"

"Life is different for a woman after she gets married," Carl said. "I guess you don't understand that any more than Gina seems to. I like you, Mickey and I think I'll like having you as my brother-in-law. But you aren't going to be able to contain Gina. And even if she let you do it, it would be a terrible shame if you did."

"You're just going to have to wait to see, Carl. I have no interest in containing Gina. And we haven't even talked about having kids yet. Believe me, the last thing in the world I would want to do is prevent Gina from being everything she was meant to be. We're going to do it together."

~~~~~~~~

The pasta on his plate had lost its appeal. Mickey looked up at Jesse and felt the tears in his eyes. That was the first time that had happened. These stories were getting harder and harder to tell.

"We were going to conquer the world together first. There would be time for kids later. We were supposed to conquer the world together."

Mickey put down his fork and took a drink of water.

"I'm going to get a little air," he said, standing up. "Get the check, will ya?"

Chapter Twenty-Five

"He nearly cried," I said to Marina that night. "The only time I've ever seen him cry was at my mother's funeral and he was almost in tears this afternoon telling me about something that happened at his engagement party with Gina."

We were sitting in a movie theatre eating a huge bag of popcorn for dinner. Not nutritionally sound, but a great guilty pleasure and a necessary one considering that we were both running late that night.

"He seems to be getting more and more emotional every time he tells you about her. What do you think that's about?"

"I don't know. It's all part of the mystery. It was strange enough seeing him transform before my eyes while he was telling the stories. Now this."

I wasn't being entirely honest with Marina, something that, in spite of my best intentions, was happening with greater frequency these days. There were some big issues that I needed to resolve in my own mind before I could work them out with her.

I was almost certain that my father's getting more emotional was directly related to the way in which his affair with Gina ended. For the first time, I started to feel angry with Gina, blaming her directly for breaking my father's heart. This was paradoxical in any number of ways, but I couldn't help it. Just looking at him struggling to keep the tears in his eyes at lunch made me want to rail against someone.

I'd spent the entire afternoon – time that I'd intended to dedicate to preparing for my interview – preoccupied with how things ended between them. What did she say to him? Was the conversation with Carl Ceraf a clue? Did she leave a letter on the kitchen table for him saying that she needed to do more with her life and that she was heading off to fight for women's rights in Kenya? Or did it all come down to one explosive moment when my father tried to hold on too tight and she burst away from him. There was no question in my mind at this point that she had been the one to break it off.

I also began to wonder if perhaps the entire purpose behind my father's telling me this story wasn't to send me a message at all but simply to unburden himself. Surely the message, if there was one, could only serve to underscore conversations I'd already had with him – in which he had taken an entirely contrary position to my own. Because what was coming across loud and clear from the tale of his life with Gina was the message that not only does even the most intense love fail, but if you give yourself over to this love entirely, it has the power to scar you for the rest of your life.

I had been distractedly eating popcorn for several moments when I brought myself back to the movie theatre and Marina.

"Anyway, the whole trip into the city sort of screwed up my schedule. I didn't get nearly enough background work done on AnnaLee Layton."

"Is that going to be a problem?"

"I'm not seeing her until three tomorrow. I should be okay. I just hate leaving anything to the last minute."

Marina nodded in commiseration. "My lead in the play broke her leg."

"I don't suppose you're speaking metaphorically, huh?"

"I wish I were. Jerry and I spent most of the afternoon rearranging parts and moving stuff around. I think I'm being punished for the hubris of thinking that this year we'd put on a show where the audience was paying attention even when their own kids weren't on the stage."

"I'll take that as an object lesson."

"Meanwhile, I think it's going to put a little bit of a crimp into our weekend. Jerry was pretty insistent about our getting together at some point to work out all the new details."

"Sounds like he has a Bob Fosse complex. Actually, if you could pull it together for Sunday afternoon, that would be great. In a surprise move, Denise and her family announced they were coming over again."

Marina was quiet for a moment and looked away toward the movie screen. "So you wouldn't mind if I set this up for Sunday afternoon?"

"Not at all. It would be perfect actually. Get two things out of the way at the same time."

Marina nodded and reached for the popcorn. It was abundantly clear that I'd said something wrong. Before I could ask what was bothering her, the house lights dimmed and the trailers came on. I offered Marina some popcorn and she took the entire bag out of my hands. That too didn't seem to be a good sign.

The movie was eminently forgettable, which was unfortunate since I'd been looking forward to it. It was one of those concepts that made a great paragraph, translated into an intriguing trailer, and then proceeded emptily out of the projector. It's entirely possible that I wouldn't have enjoyed "Citizen Kane" this evening, though. That little exchange just before the lights went down was nagging at me.

"Listen, do you think you could drop me home tonight," Marina said as we got into the car.

"What's going on?" Since I'd come back from California, we'd spent most nights at my house, and it was clear that I wasn't being invited to join her at hers.

"Nothing, I've just got a bunch of papers to grade and another parent conference in the morning. I should have said something to you earlier."

In which case we would have arranged for both of us to stay at her place.

"Are you all right?" I said.

"Yeah, I'm fine." She looked at me with the kind of expression that said she was working overtime to convince me.

"You don't seem fine."

"I'm fine, Jess. You know, we don't have to do everything together."

I decided to drop it, because I didn't know how else to address it and Marina was being uncharacteristically closed. Considering how long we had been together, this was surprisingly uncharted territory. I drove her home, kissed her in an approximation of the way I always kissed her (what is it about the disequilibrium of one partner in a relationship that can make the other so unsteady?) and then took off for home. It was only when I got most of the way there that I realized what had set Marina off. I hadn't invited her to dinner with Denise. In fact, I not only hadn't invited her, but had made a point of how convenient it was that she had something else to do.

While part of my mind worked at chastisement, the rest wondered at how I had so naturally excluded Marina from a family event. We'd managed to circumvent Christmas because she had flown home to spend the holidays with her parents. Other than that, there hadn't been terribly many times when any part of my family had been around. Matty had come in for a couple of days a few months back, I hadn't seen Darlene since the Summit After the Fire, and Denise showed up with about the same frequency as the equinox. Marina hadn't been to these functions in the past, and I wasn't in the practice of including her.

This was the convenient explanation, if not the actual explanation. If everything had been as it should be, I would have naturally invited Marina. If everything had been as it should be, I would have assumed she would have been there simply because we were always together on Sunday afternoons. In fact, if everything had been as it should be, I would have checked with her to make sure we didn't have any other plans before confirming the date with Denise.

But everything was not as it should be. It couldn't be, because, whether he'd intended this (which was extremely unlikely) or not, my father's story of his romance with Gina was causing me to seek out every potential pitfall in my relationship with Marina. What was going to scuttle us? Was she going to become too needy? Was I going to tire of speaking my heart and resent her for asking me to do so? Was there some unanticipated event waiting around the corner that we were going to react to so differently that it would drive us in opposite directions?

I didn't want to be so close to her that I'd be talking about her decades from now with tears in my eyes. I didn't want a story about how we'd just missed or about how we'd burned brightly for a brief while before the bitterness set in. The fact was that, while I wasn't paying attention (or, more to the point, while I had been blithely believing that my eyes were fixed clearly on what was in front of me), I had gotten to precisely the place that I'd promised myself I wouldn't get with another woman: the point where it would really hurt when it was over. That little gesture that Marina had made just before the movie started was the kind of thing I'd convinced myself I'd never see with her. I'd even started to believe that I could acknowledge being in love with her and still not worry about what happened when things went wrong. It was monumentally naïve.

As I pulled into my driveway, I realized that I was rapidly getting to the point where I was going to have to do something definitive. Whatever the hell that was.

~~~~~~~~

My father insisted on having dinner against the backdrop of the shoots peeking out of our garden.

"I'm pretty sure that when the people who owned this house put in the patio, they were thinking that the patio table would go there," I said as we were setting it up just outside of the plot.

"You lack imagination."

"There's also that little thing about its being April. It's nice now, but it could get pretty cold by four or so when we have dinner."

My father put down the chair he'd been rearranging, walked over to me and put a hand on my chest. "Live a little, Jess."

He was in a good mood, which was helpful, since I hadn't been in one since that difficult episode with Marina. The next night, we'd only had a brief exchange about it.

"Look, I can't believe I was so stupid as to not invite you to dinner with Denise on Sunday," I said when I picked her up.

"It's not a problem."

"Of course it's a problem. And I know that you realize it's a problem because you were upset about it last night."

She glanced at me with a guarded expression as we walked to the car. "I was just overreacting because of the thing with the play. You don't need to invite me to dinner."

"I'd like you to be there."

"That's nice. Really. But it doesn't matter anymore anyway. I have plans with Jerry and he'll start to hyperventilate if I change them."

"I'm not getting the impression that you're really okay about this."

She stopped outside of the passenger door and looked at me across the hood. "Jess, sometimes your impressions are wrong."

She got into the car. When I settled in next to her, she said, "I'm probably not going to come over afterward, though. Jerry and I are likely to run pretty late and it'll just be simpler to stay home."

We moved on from there. The conversation made me feel like I'd just eaten a plate full of styrofoam, but I couldn't think of another way to approach it that would be more satisfying. I drove off to the movie theatre. Two movies in two nights was decidedly not our style, but Marina said that was the only thing she was interested in doing. She stayed over, but it was almost as though she were doing it to avoid having a conversation about not doing it.

On Sunday morning, we had breakfast with my father and read the paper for a while. I needed to make some preparations for dinner, but I didn't want to make them in front of her because I thought it might insult her. Never once before had I needed to be polite with her.

As I began to consider the timing of the meal in my mind, she put down the Arts and Leisure section of the *Times*, kissed me on the forehead and said, "I've gotta go back to the house. There are some things I need to do before I meet with Jerry." She then walked over to my father and kissed him on the forehead and grabbed her car keys. I'm not sure I said anything more than "bye." If my father had noticed any tension between us, he wasn't mentioning it. Probably because he was too focused on her kissing him.

I wasn't sure how I was going to respond to Denise's visit. In some twisted way, I resented her because of the difficult patch I'd encountered with Marina. After all, if she hadn't invited herself over for dinner, I wouldn't have failed to invite Marina to join us. On top of everything else, I wasn't sure what things were going to be like with Brad. He'd accepted the news about Mark Grey gracefully and even congratulated me when I told him about the feature piece that Mark wanted me to do, but I wasn't sure how much of his immediate reaction was simply Wharton-schooled polish. Now that he'd had time to think about it, would he see me as a failure, or even as someone who had sold him out?

If there was going to be any animosity between anyone on this day, though, my father defused it. As soon as Denise, Brad, and Marcus arrived, he brought them out back to the garden. He spoke excitedly about how we had dug and planted it, and then even got down on his knees to explain to Marcus the various growing patterns to the seeds we'd sown.

"He's not really bending over regularly to take care of this stuff, is he?" Denise said to me in a stage whisper.

"Sometimes he does, yeah."

"With joints like his?" She lowered her voice. "Do you have to come out here and carry him back into the house?"

"You'd be surprised."

For dinner, I made a lasagna using my mother's exact recipe. On top of all the other swirling emotions befuddling me at this point was an aching nostalgia for the late Dorothy Sienna. There had been a certain predictability to this since my father started telling me stories about Gina. There would be the hours (sometimes as much as a day) when I was simply caught up in the romance of those episodes. I had developed a very real image of Gina in my mind and an equally real image of my younger father. This couple would dance in my head, replaying certain scenes from their drama. At some point, though, my mother's face would peer out from one of the many photographs I kept of her and I would feel a little like I had betrayed her, and a lot like I would love to have her back. Since the last story, I found that I missed my mother even more. I wanted her to be as corporeal as Gina and Young Mickey had become to me. Making the lasagna was a way to conjure her.

"Delicious, Jess," Denise said when she had her first bite. "This tastes a lot like Mom's."

"It should. I did everything the way she used to do it."

"You mean there are no pumpkin seeds or wild rice or ground buffalo in here?" This was a reference to meals past when, if I chose to make a traditional dish, I would insist on adding a personal tweak.

"No, really. Just the way Mom used to do it."

"Well, you didn't make the pasta from scratch, did you?"

"Of course I made the pasta from scratch. How else would you make it?"

"How would I make it? I'd make it by sticking the leftovers in the oven the day after I had it at Carmela's."

"That's why we never come to your house for dinner," my father said with a smile. I think everyone at the table knew that the reason we never went to Denise's for dinner was because she never invited us, but that wasn't the point. "Who would eat second-rate take-out when you could eat like this?"

"And in a garden setting," I added, pointing to the spottily verdant plot of dirt. Denise chuckled, but she offered a confused expression to my father and I wanted to change the subject as quickly as possible. I couldn't remember the last time I had done something like that to spare her feelings.

Toward the end of the evening, Brad pulled me aside. "How's the piece for *24-Hour City* going?"

"I'm not sure yet. I did my first interview with the teacher a couple of days ago. I'm going back to see her next week. Hopefully, she'll let me get a little closer this time, because she definitely didn't want to open up in our first conversation."

Brad nodded. I probably gave him much more information than he was really asking for.

"I got Ed Crimmins."

"You did?" I was genuinely surprised. Ed had been in the business for more than twenty years, the last half dozen or so as the Editor of *Contemporary Man,* a major monthly.

"It turns out that all of the prep work you made us do on Mark Grey came in handy. Ed was impressed with our plans for the magazine. I also think he was pretty impressed with our proposed compensation package. He's resigning tomorrow morning and he'll be on board at the end of the month."

"That's great news. Quite an accomplishment."

Brad grinned. For a moment, he seemed practically giddy. "Thanks. With a name like Ed Crimmins on the management team, the rest of the financing will fall into place easily. We're going to shoot to have a premiere issue out in October, then do six issues next year, and a full twelve the year after that."

I found that I was genuinely happy for him. This wasn't just about being let off the hook with regard to Mark Grey, but also about seeing Brad in a new way. I had begun to change my impressions of him after the dinner with his backers, and I found now that I was actively rooting for his success.

"Anyway, Ed and I would like to get together with you sometime in the near future to talk about some things."

Ed Crimmins had been one of dozens of editors in New York whom I hadn't been able to impress with my feature pitches.

"Sure, anytime you want."

~~~~~~~~

Of course Denise had herself and her men packed up and out the door by six. So much to conquer, so little time. I walked the three of them out to the car and waited to kiss my sister goodbye while she instructed Marcus on the proper position-ing of his shoulder belt. This to a kid who'd probably done a paper on restraint systems for fun during summer vacation. She turned around and I kissed her on the cheek.

"So when are we going to meet the mysterious Marina?"

"You know, she keeps running out every time she hears you're coming around. I don't know what it is. I say only the nicest things about you."

"Yeah, I believe that one. If she can handle Dad, she can handle anybody."

"Dad? He's like putty in her hands. Make that Silly Putty."

She smirked. "I'm serious. I'm starting to believe that you and Dad are making her up." She got into the car.

"Maybe I'm just waiting for an invitation to your fabulous apartment so I can show her the lofty circles my family travels in."

Denise lifted her chin slightly. "Yeah, we'll have to set that up."

Deflecting everything should be that easy.

Chapter Twenty-Six

Mickey kissed the picture and rose slowly from the bed to put it back in its box. His knees were very tight this morning. That either meant there was rain coming or he really was an old man. Kneeling felt like hellfire, and on top of it all, there was that lightheadedness again when he bent over. He was going to have to get to the doctor soon, even if the man was useless.

As he opened the box and placed the picture on the top of the pile, Mickey thought about Jesse. It was certainly the first time that had ever happened. He hadn't intended to draw the story out as long as he had. He wondered what Jesse thought of it all and he wondered why he didn't simply discuss it with him directly. But something overcame him when he began to talk to his son about Gina. Things that made sense before just didn't seem to make the same sense after. It didn't really matter. He'd be getting to the point soon enough. Maybe even today if he could hold up.

Looking back at the picture, he realized that he still hadn't shown Gina's photograph to Jesse. He called out to him, but got no response, which meant that Jesse must have already gone into his office.

Mickey raised his voice. "Jesse, can you come in here a second?" He heard the office door open.

"Where are you?" Jesse called out.

"I'm in the bedroom. Come in here a second."

Still kneeling in the closet, Mickey turned his head when he heard Jesse coming into the room. Just in time to see the startled expression on his son's face.

"Dad, are you all right?" Jesse said, rushing over to the closet and putting his hands under Mickey's shoulders as though to lift him up.

"I'm fine. Why are you picking me up?"

"Are you okay?"

"I said I was fine. I want to show you something."

Mickey struggled to get to his feet. Jesse reached down again to help him, and Mickey glared him back. He sat on the bed, gestured for Jesse to sit next to him, and held up the picture.

"This is her," he said.

Jesse reached for the picture, but Mickey held on to it. Jesse moved his face a little closer.

"Wow, she really is beautiful. She looks a lot like I imagined her. You described her well."

"Yeah, maybe I should be a writer in my next career."

Jesse made brief eye contact with his father and then looked back down at the photograph. "Was this taken professionally?"

"By the Mayor's office. Right after he appointed her to Young Women for a Better New York."

"I never even heard of that organization."

"That's a story in and of itself."

Jesse reached for the photograph again and Mickey reluctantly let it go. "So you've had this picture in that box?"

"In and out of it. Often. I thought you might be interested in seeing her."

"Yeah, of course, though like I said, she's not all that different from what I was imagining already."

Mickey took the picture out of Jesse's hands and got up to put it back into the box. Again, he felt lightheaded and needed to sit back down on the bed.

Jesse put a hand on his shoulder. "Knees really hurting?"

"Yeah. I think I might spend some time in bed reading today." Mickey put Gina's picture on the occasional table that had served as his nightstand since moving to Jesse's house. "We picked that out together, you know."

"Picked what out?"

"The table."

"That table? The one that was in the living room for my entire life? Did Mom know?"

"She knew it came from my apartment and that it meant enough to me to keep even after we got new furniture."

~~~~~~~~

The doorbell barely awakened Mickey. When it rang a second time, he rolled over to look at his alarm clock. 8:18. Doorbells didn't ring at 8:18 on Saturday mornings. One of the privileges afforded those who worked very hard and got up very early during the week was that they didn't have to do either on Saturdays. When the bell rang a third time, Mickey realized that ignoring it was not going to make it go away. He pulled on a robe and walked to the front door. Gina was standing there smiling at him.

"Time to get going," she said, as she walked into the apartment.

"Get going where?" Mickey wondered if he had forgotten about something they'd planned. He couldn't imagine having done so. He certainly would have remembered something that required his getting up early on a Saturday morning.

"Furniture shopping. It takes at least three months to get furniture delivered, and we're getting married in three months and a week."

"We need furniture?"

Gina gestured around the apartment. "You think we don't need furniture? First of all, you don't have very much, and second of all, what you do have…" She rolled her eyes and then handed him a bag. "Here, I brought you coffee and donuts."

"Furniture stores are open at 8:18 in the morning?"

"No, but they will be open by the time you eat your breakfast, take your shower, shave, and do whatever else you do that takes you so long to get out of the house in the morning." She drew up next to him and kissed him on the neck. "You forget that this is one of the secrets about you I already know from our illicit trip to Italy."

Mickey grinned and wrapped his arms around Gina for a longer kiss. They had been together in this apartment less than eight hours earlier and he longed for the days – not far off now – when they wouldn't need to be separated at night.

"I'll be ready to go in a half hour or you can have final say on all of the furniture."

Gina smiled. "I'll have final say anyway, but if you're ready in a half hour, I'll let you pick out a lamp or two."

Mickey wasn't ready for more than forty-five minutes. He'd never noticed that it took him a long time to get out of the house in the morning. Maybe he was normal and Gina was just especially efficient. That probably wasn't the case. Gina would know about these things, and if she thought he was slow, he probably was. He promised himself to add it to the list of ways to improve himself for his future wife.

"Not that I really care," Gina said, throwing Mickey a grin to let him know that she was kidding, "but do you have any preferences?" They had just entered Bloomingdale's and were walking through the crowded aisles toward the furniture department.

"I like dark brown."

She laughed. "Dark brown? I was wondering if there was a style you preferred."

"I'm sure there are styles I prefer, but I couldn't tell you the names of any of them. I do know, though, that I like dark brown furniture."

Gina seemed to find all of this amusing. "I'll keep that in mind."

Over the next hour and a half, Mickey realized there were places in his relationship with Gina where they were not on equal footing. While she pelted the salesman with questions about manufacturing methods, types of wood, types of finishing, patterns, and fabrics, Mickey stood mute. For a few minutes, this disturbed him, but then he realized that Gina's superior knowledge in this area was a tremendous added benefit to their household. Because he was marrying a woman with discerning taste and a discriminating eye, he would have a nice-looking home. The fact that he made virtually no contribution to the purchases involved was purely secondary.

They had already settled on a bedroom and a dining room and were reviewing living room sets. Gina stood in front of a sofa and love seat with a mahogany coffee table and end tables.

"Do you like this?" she said. "It's dark brown."

Mickey nodded. Of course it was beautiful and of course he could imagine it in his living room. He sat down on the love seat and asked Gina to sit next to him, putting his arm around her and reclining her back.

"Yes, it's absolutely perfect," Mickey said, squeezing Gina's shoulder.

"Mickey," Gina said, pulling herself back up but tossing him an affectionate grin. "I'm sure Mr. O'Donnell here doesn't want to see us cavorting." She put special emphasis on the last word to indicate to Mickey that she was looking forward to doing exactly that with him on their love seat in the near future.

Mickey looked up at the salesman. "I apologize, Mr. O'Donnell." When he glanced out, his eye settled on a small table with carved wood and brass appointments. He stood up and walked over to it. "I really like this."

Gina came over to him. "It's lovely, but what would we do with it?"

"We'd put knick-knacks on it. Things like that sculpture we got in Tuscany and other things that we buy on future vacations."

"It isn't part of the set, though."

Mickey bent down to examine the table at eye level.

"See the way the wood is carved here in intertwining lines? That's you and me."

He looked up at Gina and saw her kneeling next to him, her eyes softening. He glanced over at the salesman.

"It's an occasional table," O'Donnell said, "which means that it's an additional piece. And it is mahogany, so it would certainly blend in with the rest of the set."

Gina looked up at the salesman, ran her fingers over the carving, and then looked over at Mickey. "We'll take it."

After they'd filled out the paperwork and paid the deposit, Mickey and Gina went to the store's restaurant for lunch.

"I can't believe we just bought an entire apartment's worth of furniture in a couple of hours," Mickey said while they waited for their food.

"It's all beautiful, isn't it?"

"Not nearly as beautiful as the other addition to the apartment that will be arriving in three months and a week."

Gina smiled shyly. Mickey loved the fact that he could still get a response like that from her after nearly nine months together. They had scheduled the wedding for the one year anniversary of their first date. The day couldn't arrive soon enough for him.

"We didn't spend too much, did we?" Gina said.

"That deposit was the single biggest check I've ever written, but we didn't break the bank."

"It's all excellent quality. Mr. O'Donnell said the furniture could last a hundred years if we take care of it properly."

Mickey took a sip of water and allowed himself to imagine the new pieces filling their home for decades to come.

"Well, I guess we know what the great-grandchildren can get us for our hundredth anniversary present, then."

Gina beamed and reached out for his hand.

They were going to be separated that afternoon by a meeting that Gina was attending. Gina wasn't entirely sure what it was all about, but it involved some senior staff members in the mayor's office regarding some kind of committee the mayor wanted to put together. Mickey hated losing a Saturday afternoon with Gina, but if it was going to happen, this was a good reason for it.

"So are you nervous about your appointment with the mayor today?"

"I'm not meeting the mayor. Just some of his staff. I've met most of them already."

"But the mayor could stop in, couldn't he?"

"I'm fairly sure the mayor is in Montauk for the weekend. To the best of my knowledge, we weren't invited to go with him."

"Once he gets to know you, he's going to invite you to all kinds of things."

Gina laughed. "Thank you for having so much faith in me, but I doubt that the mayor will ever even know I'm alive."

"Really? You don't think he'll notice when you become Governor?"

Gina laughed more loudly. "This is one of the many, many reasons why I'm marrying you."

Mickey kissed Gina's hand softly. When they finished lunch, they walked slowly down the street toward Gina's apartment building. Mickey wasn't in any rush to let Gina go, even though he knew she had something important to do. When they got to her door, the doorman greeted them and then discreetly turned his head as they kissed goodbye.

"Dinner is at seven tonight?" Mickey said.

"That's when my aunt and uncle are supposed to arrive. Are these events getting a little tiring for you?"

"Do you mean would I prefer to be out with you on a Saturday night dancing cheek to cheek? Of course I would. But I think it's nice that your mother is so excited about our getting married."

"She just wants to show you off and brag a little about the great catch her daughter made."

They kissed again, slowly, in denial that there was anything else in the world that needed to happen other than this very kiss. At last, Gina pulled away.

"I love you," Mickey said. "Save a place at the table for me."

Gina smiled. He'd been saying that to her every time they parted for the past few months. It all started one Wednesday when, after several nights out in a row, Gina informed him that she just wanted to spend a nice quiet evening with a home-cooked meal.

"Come on over around 6:30. Mom will make something fabulous, I'm sure, and then my parents will make a great show of 'leaving us alone' in the den."

"Think we can get rid of Carl as well?"

"We'll just kick him out. I think it might be time to inform him that you already know about the tutu incident. He's going to be devastated when he realizes that he doesn't have anything left to blackmail me with."

When Mickey arrived, Mrs. Ceraf answered the door.

"Mickey, how good to see you," she said, kissing him on the cheek. "But I'm a little surprised. Gina told me she was going to be having dinner at home tonight."

"Well, she is."

Mrs. Ceraf seemed confused.

"Were you on your way somewhere?"

Now it was Mickey's turn to be unsure of what was going on. "I can be."

Just then, Mrs. Ceraf's hand shot up to her mouth and her face flushed.

"Oh, my, you're coming to dinner as well."

At that point, Gina came to the door and kissed Mickey on the cheek.

"Gina, you've embarrassed me," Mrs. Ceraf said.

"What are you talking about?"

"You didn't tell me that Mickey was coming to dinner."

Gina looked at her mother with a mixture of disbelief and consternation.

"Mom, Mickey and I are together every night now. When I said I was staying home, I assumed you knew that I meant *we* were staying home."

Mrs. Ceraf became more flustered. Mickey was certain he saw tears in her eyes.

"Mickey, I'm so sorry," she said. "Let me set another place at the table." She ran off to the dining room and Mickey didn't see her again until dinner. Even then she still seemed contrite. Mickey found the entire thing amusing.

"Is everything all right, Carla?" Dan Ceraf asked when he sat down and saw that his wife was not only out of sorts, but had given herself barely more than a forkful of fish. Mickey realized right away that she had only bought enough for her husband, her two children, and herself. He wanted to offer her some of his, but he wasn't sure how she would react.

"No, everything is not all right, Dan," she said, eyes downcast. "I'm afraid I've given our son-in-law the impression that he isn't a member of our family." She looked up at Mickey. "Mickey, I'm so sorry."

"It was an honest mistake, Mrs. Ceraf," Mickey said.

"No, Mickey," she said. "It was thoughtless of me. You will always have a place at our table." At which point, she started to cry.

Mr. Ceraf put his arm around his wife and turned to Mickey.

"I don't presume to know what this is about, Mickey," he said, "but you're already family. I hope you know that. Once you entered Gina's heart, you became family forever."

Mickey wanted to laugh at the extreme way at which his future in-laws were reacting, but at the same time he was touched. Still, it didn't prevent him from teasing Gina about it every time they parted. It was his playful way of reminding her to keep him in her heart while they weren't together.

Gina turned toward the apartment building and blew Mickey a kiss.

"You have a place at my table forever," she said before going to get ready for her appointment at the mayor's office.

~~~~~~~~

Mickey had been staring at the picture for a couple of minutes without speaking. At last, he said, "I love you. Save a place at the table for me." Jesse had no idea what that meant, but it obviously had significant meaning for his father because he smiled and continued to stare lovingly at the photograph. Finally, he brought the picture to his chest and looked up at Jesse without saying a word. Jesse got up from the bed and kissed his father on the forehead.

"Rest your knees as much as you can today, Dad."

Chapter Twenty-Seven

They say that statisticians can turn any set of numbers around to make their case. They say that political spin doctors can take almost any statement by an opponent and turn it to their candidate's advantage. They say that a cynic can look at just about any situation and find confirmation that the world is an ugly place.

I suppose in the end I was doing much the same thing – manipulating the information available to me to support my stubbornly held beliefs. Of course there were other ways to interpret what my father was telling me with his stories about Gina. But because there was a way to read between the lines and come to my old standby conclusion that passionate love could never last, this is what I chose to do. I don't like what this says about me.

Seeing Gina's picture that morning made everything about their relationship seem so much more solid to me. While I had a 3D image of her in my mind already – one not that different from the one in the picture – seeing the photograph gave it yet another dimension. It was as though Gina had until that point existed in another universe and when my father showed me the picture, she crossed over into ours. While I suppose it was possible to imagine that he had picked up this photograph somewhere and built this entire elaborate hallucination around it, it was almost inconceivable at this point for me to doubt that Gina had been a very real person. She had captivated my father in such a way that decades, a wife, and four children later, she could still inhabit his thoughts. And she could still reduce him to tears or speechlessness because she had gone away from him.

Things had been awkward between Marina and me since the conversation about Sunday dinner with Denise. It wasn't that we had never had tense moments before. Certainly there had been times when we'd skirmished over something or other. It hadn't happened often, and in most cases it had as much to do with tiredness or hunger or a rejected story pitch as it had to do with us. But there had been times. The difference here was that this got at something fundamental, something I'd chosen to ignore, or at least avoid. Both of us knew that there was no way to resolve this conflict without adjusting the very foundation of our relationship. And so it just lingered there while we attempted to grow new skin around it.

Meanwhile, I spent endless amounts of time thinking about it. I knew deep in my heart that the awkwardness between Marina and me was the signal that the downturn had begun. One of the corollaries to my theory about relationships is that not only does love always die, but it never ages gracefully. It is always withered and gnarled at the end. There's never a point at which, like a superstar athlete after one last career year, you can bow out before you can no longer compete.

I wish now that I hadn't gone through this process, but I began to "spin" my relationship with Marina. She was too nurturing – it couldn't last. She was too willing to please me – she'd never keep that up. The things that I derived the most pleasure from were the things that would fade in time and leave me feeling absolutely empty. I found myself making sarcastic comments to her and criticizing her for her compassion and optimism, even though those were two of the traits I found most admirable. Though it wasn't entirely clear to me at the moment, I had begun the process of uncoupling. I was dehumanizing the enemy.

For the first time since the very beginning of our relationship, I had absolutely no idea what Marina was thinking. I wasn't asking her and she wasn't saying. Was she coming to the same conclusions about us, or was she simply hurt about the Sunday dinner thing and confused about the long silences that now chaperoned us? She could still sparkle, especially when talking about her students. She could still cajole and stimulate my father. She could still engage me in brisk debate over one of our many "safe" topics. But when it came to the end of the night, when it was just the two of us alone, she was walking on the same eggshells that I was walking on, but in a different direction. We hadn't made love since the night of the face-off, but she would still hold me tightly as we lay in bed, still tell me she loved me before turning out the light.

A week had passed since that conversation in the movie theatre when we decided to go out to dinner. I specifically suggested an Italian restaurant we'd gone to several times before because I thought it might help to normalize things. But things were anything but normal. In fact, they were agonizingly polite. We smiled pleasantly at one another, we talked about inconsequential matters, we didn't challenge or tease. At one point, I found it all so frustrating, that I left the table to spend several minutes in the bathroom. Of course, when I got back, I simply smiled and asked Marina what she thought about the olive oil.

I was stuck in neutral. I didn't want to say anything that would provoke a confrontation that I knew could be resolved only one way. But I also didn't want to try to make it better because I believed with absolute conviction that it wouldn't stay better for long.

As usual, whenever we were downtown, we took a walk afterward. I thought doing something that we had done so many times before was an indication that normal wasn't as far away as it had seemed. But we were still simply being polite again. Neither wanted to suggest a break in the routine.

"What's going on with the play?" I said as we walked.

She brightened. "I think it's going to go great. The changes we made in the script after Patty got hurt have helped a lot.

I think we probably won't invite a reviewer from *The New York Times*, but the parents should have fun and the kids are really enjoying themselves."

"That's really good. You've put so much into this, it'd be a shame at this point if you weren't happy with it."

"Oh, I would have been fine either way. I get worked up about it when we're rehearsing, but when it comes time for the show, I just want the kids to have fun and for no one to throw up on stage."

We walked quietly for a while, stopping at a craft store window to look at some handmade pottery. I noticed some earrings in the corner of the window and my first thought was that they would look good on Marina. My second thought was that I wasn't sure I should be thinking that way anymore.

"I'd like you to come," Marina said when we started walking again.

"Come where?"

"To the play next Wednesday night."

I'm not sure why it didn't dawn on me that she might ask me to do so, but I was totally unprepared for it. I knew, regardless of what she was saying, that the show was important to her, and I should have assumed that she would want me to see it. But at the same time, this was about crossing a line. Boyfriends didn't go to elementary school plays directed by their girlfriends. More permanent partners did. If I went, I'd be introduced to colleagues who would perceive me as a very significant part of Marina's life. You didn't bring dates to these kinds of things.

This seemed to be coming at the worst possible time. I was at a stage where so many of my thoughts were pointing away from a future with Marina and here she was asking me to perform a gesture that would suggest a very real future. The first thing that came to my mind was that she should know better than to ask, given how awkward things had been between us in the last week. But perhaps that was why she was doing it. Regardless, my immediate reaction was to have no reaction.

"Is that a problem?" she asked. "Do you have something else going on that night?"

"No, no, I don't think so. I just think I might feel a little weird – this guy in a crowd of parents."

"I'd introduce you to some of the other teachers. You wouldn't have to sit by yourself, if that's what you're worried about."

"No, actually I kind of figured you'd introduce me to other people."

She turned toward me and tilted her head. "What's wrong with that?"

"There's nothing wrong with that," I said, not making eye contact.

"Obviously you think something is."

I looked at her for a moment and then glanced off down the street again. "It's not a big deal; it would just be a little weird. I mean, how would you introduce me? 'This is Jesse. We hang out a lot together?'"

"'Hang out a lot together?'"

"You get my point."

She began to walk down the street again. "I think I'm beginning to."

"What does that mean?"

"The thing with saying 'I love you,' or going out with me and an old high school friend, or having Sunday dinner with your family, or now this. You think it all binds you to some unspoken contract. It all says that we've changed the rules of the game."

"Yeah, I guess in some way it does."

She stopped again and turned to face me head on. For that brief moment, I don't think I could have broken eye contact with her with a crowbar.

"You really think that?"

I looked down and then back up at her. "We had this great thing. It was strong, and it was fun, and we didn't get hung up on the implications."

"And you really thought a relationship could stay in that place indefinitely?"

"I really thought that *our* relationship could stay in that place indefinitely. I thought you did too."

"Without ever evolving."

"I didn't want to think about evolving. I know where evolving leads."

"To making something more permanent out of this."

"To disintegration. Come on, Marina. Look at my father and Gina."

Marina turned her back toward me. I thought she was going to start walking again, but she simply stood there.

"You're not going to do this to me," she said after a while.

"What are you talking about?" I said, even though I was fairly sure that I knew.

"You're not going to put me on hold forever. I've got that t-shirt already."

"That's not fair. I'm not Larry, and our relationship is not like yours and Larry's."

She turned back toward me.

"No, you're not Larry, Jess. But in some ways what you're doing is even harder to accept. You're not waiting for the Big Love of Your Life to come along. You're just looking to play out the string. You want to be in love and have someone be in love with you without any of the unfortunate attachments that go along with it."

"I didn't ask to fall in love. I didn't expect to fall in love."

"And it doesn't change anything that you *did* fall in love?"

"Yeah, it does." I looked down at the street again. "It makes it worse."

Marina let out a sound that was a bit like a sob and then seemed to regain her composure quickly.

"I'm obviously in this much deeper than you are," she said. "Let's stop this now before it gets much too painful."

As much as I had been thinking about the inevitability of our breakup, I wasn't at all prepared for it. In my mind, we would just even out again for a while and, as always, leave the big decisions for another day.

"We don't need to stop," I said. "I don't want to stop."

Marina looked at me with more resolve in her eyes than I had ever seen before. "I'm not asking you if you want to stop. I've got to do what's best for me. I'd appreciate it if you drove me home now."

She walked off toward the car and I followed her. My legs felt rubbery. I was still having a difficult time comprehending what had just happened. If I had said, "Sure, what time on Wednesday?" would everything have been completely different? Did romances really rise and fall on such exchanges? I knew that they didn't, of course. Just as I knew that as much as Marina's response stunned me, I wasn't emotionally equipped to do what was necessary to change her mind.

When we got to Marina's house, I didn't turn the car off. I shifted slightly toward her as she removed her seat belt.

"I'd really like to say goodbye to your father," she said, "but I'm not sure I could handle that."

"He'll probably come track you down. He'll probably try to make his move on you now."

Marina smiled and then looked away. "He's a great guy, Jess. And the two of you have really started to have a good thing together."

"You and I have a really good thing together."

"We did, I know. But I guess it's run its course. We both knew that it would happen eventually. You were right."

I nodded. Again the words to stave off this eventuality eluded me. I couldn't summon them, even though my conscious mind begged me to do so. There was that other voice inside of my head. The stronger voice. The one saying that this was the way it was always going to be.

Marina opened the car door and left without saying anything else. I watched her enter the house before I backed out of the driveway.

Chapter Twenty-Eight

Over the next couple of weeks, the garden seemed to blossom in inverse proportion to the barrenness I felt inside. The shoots had taken on form, stalks rising, leaves sprouting, the first tiny buds appearing. Nature obviously didn't discriminate. If the soil was good enough, if the water was plentiful, if the sun provided sustenance, the plants would rise. Even if they were being nurtured by Mickey Sienna of the black thumb and his son Jesse of the black heart.

Since I'd split with Marina I felt a persistent dull ache. It was like the onset of the flu: the jitteriness, the reduced appetite, the slight numbness at the tips of your fingers. That feeling that you're a quarter of a step behind the rest of the world. I called her once. Not with any particular agenda in mind, but with the hope that something would simply emerge, as it did so often when we were together. She was very cool on the phone. Not chilly, just cool. Resolute. As though she was saying, "If you don't have anything meaningful to say to me, then let me get on with letting you go." Since I couldn't think of anything meaningful to say, the conversation ended quickly. I wasn't calling to see if I could get her back. As out of synch as I felt without her, I knew that our starting up again was only going to get us to a place where I would have the same feeling six, nine, eleven months down the line. Making a move like that to forestall the inevitable not only wasn't appealing, but would have been a sad abuse of Marina's spirit.

For any number of reasons, I couldn't get myself to tell my father about our breakup. I knew he was going to take it badly, both in terms of lecturing me, and also in terms of grieving the loss himself. My father had embraced Marina as completely as I had ever seen him embrace a person, and I knew it wasn't going to be easy for him to let her go. I even imagined his seeking her out and continuing his relationship with her around me. I made numerous excuses for why Marina wasn't staying over, taking advantage of his not knowing that the play had been the week before. The pretense reached its absurd pinnacle when I actually spent the night in a motel so he would think that I was staying at Marina's house. I'm not sure what I was waiting for. He wasn't going to forget about her. At some point, I was going to have to tell him. It just never seemed to be the right time.

He must have sensed something, because his demeanor was devolving to an earlier stage in our relationship. Whether it was because he missed the leavening influence that Marina had on him or because he was perturbed at my denying him her company, I wasn't sure. But our exchanges were more monosyllabic these days, and he hadn't said a word about Gina for a long time. This just added to my overall sense of malaise. I had gotten into a very pleasant rhythm with him and hadn't expected to fall out of it. I found myself doing all kinds of things to please him – suggesting games to play in the evening, making his favorite dishes for dinner, attempting to plan excursions. His not playing along made me feel chastened, like I was being punished for bad behavior.

Still, I kept trying.

"Hey Dad, look at this," I said, kneeling by a zucchini plant. We had been weeding and watering, and when I looked up I noticed the smallest tip of a yellow bud peeking out.

My father crept over. As the soil in the garden became packed down, he was having increasing trouble spending time there on his knees. At last, he leaned over to where I was kneeling and examined the tiny bud.

"Hmm," he muttered.

"This is a big moment – the beginnings of our first zucchini flower. Don't you find this a little incredible?"

"We did everything the guy in the nursery told us to do. You didn't expect to get some flowers?"

"I still find it very exciting. I can't believe you aren't excited about this. Hey, have you ever eaten zucchini flowers? They're great in a tempura batter."

"Can't say that I have. I haven't eaten roses or daffodils either. Does that make me a bad person?"

I glanced over at him. Since I was feeling guilty about not being truthful with him, I figured I deserved a little abuse, but he was very quickly reaching his quota. He held eye contact with me for a second or so and then moved away. As he stood, I saw him hesitate and he seemed a little disoriented for a moment.

"What was that?" I said.

"What was what?"

"That thing that just happened. What's wrong?"

He glared at me, as he had done every time I questioned him about his health. "Nothing is wrong."

"I want you to see Dr. Quigley."

"So make an appointment."

"You'll go if I make an appointment?"

He looked at me with even more heat in his eyes. "I said make an appointment."

He walked back to the house and I followed him. He looked fine, but I just wanted to make sure that nothing was going on. When he got into the house, he grabbed his coffee mug and poured himself another cup.

"When do you think your girlfriend is going to be able to have dinner over here again?"

"She's been really busy, Dad. I've never seen her so busy. I'm not sure when things are going to lighten up for her."

He simply stared at me.

"I'll see what I can do, okay?" I said.

He didn't say anything in response. After a minute, I said, "I'll see" again and walked out of the room.

~~~~~~~~

That afternoon, I had lunch scheduled with Brad and Ed Crimmins. It required getting over "the flu" for at least a couple of hours. Even though I had no idea what Brad and Ed wanted to talk about, I knew that I couldn't possibly play in Ed's league if I was distracted.

The piece on AnnaLee Layton had offered the only real respite from my preoccupation over losing Marina. Slowly, AnnaLee opened up during interviews and I think I ultimately wrote a powerful article that would move and perhaps even motivate a number of readers. Mark Gray seemed to like it and, just as Aline Dixon had before him, suggested that he might have another commission for me in the near future. I went from that to a quick piece about cardiovascular exercise that I had gotten a month before, but then after that decided that I needed a little time to think about the direction of my career.

The trip to California and the time I spent with the Hayward people had caused me to reconsider the way I approached writing. I brought something different to the last two feature pieces than I had brought to any previous assignments. At the same time, the other events in my life over the past year had influenced me at least as much. The rise and fall of my love affair with Marina. The changes in my relationship with my father. The story of Gina. All of these things that hadn't been there a year ago were in my head now and it's foolish for any writer to ignore the effect of the life they are living.

I had decided articles about hanging draperies and preventing gingivitis were in my past. They had been the journalistic equivalent of waiting tables for me, and it was time to perform without that kind of day job. The problem was that it was unrealistic to expect the Mark Grays and Aline Dixons of the world to consistently decide I was the ideal writer for an assignment. I was going to have to develop my own pitches, seek out my own stories. And there was the complication. For whatever reason, I was dreadful at the pitch. I almost never had the inspiration for a feature piece that an editor wanted to embrace.

As I drove into the city, I thought about why Brad and Ed had set up this lunch. I figured they would offer me an article or two as a gesture of appreciation for indirectly getting them together. I was sure that Brad would be able to sell Ed on that much, though I doubted that Ed would be particularly willing to entertain this nepotism in anything but a cursory way. Maybe I'd get a few sidebars, perhaps a couple of thousand words on something.

We met at an Indian restaurant in Chelsea near the new magazine's offices. Both the restaurant and the location of the offices were interesting choices, as they were considerably less elegant than Brad's usual. They suggested not only that he knew the difference between working for a corporation and working on his own, but also that he was serious about making the magazine profitable. Again, I was impressed at his dedication.

Traffic through the tunnel was more onerous than usual and I was the last to arrive. I saw Brad and Ed before they saw me. They were laughing over something and speaking to one another as though they'd been associated for years. I wouldn't have expected them to get along so casually, though I was quickly coming to expect that I didn't really know what to expect with my brother-in-law. With this came curiosity about him and my sister. I'd always imagined that they made a decent partnership because they were so monomaniacal. If Brad was in fact much more three-dimensional, what did this say about their marriage? Was it possible that there was more going on between them when they were alone together than I could see from the outside? I still couldn't envision my sister as being warm and cuddly with anyone (this was, after all, a woman who went back to work a week after giving birth to Marcus), but seeing Brad in a new way required me to think of Denise differently as well.

As I walked toward the table, Brad saw me coming and stood up to shake my hand.

"Sorry I'm late," I said. "The tunnel."

"Been there. You know Ed, right?"

I reached over to shake Ed's hand.

"Hey Jesse, good to see you," he said. "It's been a while."

"Yeah, I guess it has. It's pretty exciting seeing the two of you hooked up on this new venture."

"I know I'm excited. Your brother-in-law has some big plans. It's nice to be part of them."

Brad gave a modest shrug and then suggested that we look at the menus before "getting down to business." When we took care of that, Ed reached for a pappadum in the basket that was sitting in the middle of the table and then gestured toward me with it.

"Brad told me about the pieces you'd done recently for *Food and Living* and *The City* so I got copies of both of them."

Since neither had been published yet, this meant getting them from the inside. It always surprised me when I heard about this kind of thing happening. I suppose there had never really been a reason for anyone to do this with me before.

Ed continued. "There was good work in there. You've grown as a writer."

"Thanks."

"It's always nice to see when that happens."

"I appreciate your noticing it."

Brad leaned forward in his chair. "I asked Ed to take a look at the pieces because I didn't want him to be uncomfortable in any way about what I was suggesting we do with you."

I looked over at Ed, who nodded and then took another bite of pappadum. I looked back at Brad.

"We'd like you to give serious consideration to coming on board as a staff writer," Brad said.

I'm sure the surprise showed on my face because Ed stepped in quickly. "You know what we're trying to do with the magazine. We're trying to cover a lot of ground and do it in a way that won't bore the crap out of people. It's going to be fast and furious around the offices, and we need some writers on the staff who have the kind of range that you have and can take on different kinds of pieces at different times while doing a good job with all of them."

I was flattered. I was also stunned. I hadn't imagined for a moment that they would be talking about a staff position for me. Certainly, if Ed was worried about the appearance of nepotism, the last thing he'd want to do is put Brad's brother-in-law on the staff, which meant that he truly believed I had something significant to contribute.

"You'll be good with us," Brad said. "Ed really wants to open things up and do things in a new way. There's going to be a ton of energy in the room all the time between the print edition and the digital edition. I think you'll enjoy it. And I think you'd be great at it."

I smiled and looked down at my lap for a moment. This conversation was incongruous in so many different ways.

"I'm really flattered," I said. "Really, really flattered. And I'm sure the two of you and the team you put together are going to make the magazine a heck of a place to work." I stopped to allow myself just the briefest instant of consideration. "But a staff position isn't right for me."

Brad held up a hand. "Don't react so quickly. Let us tell you more about what we're planning to do. And I know you have the thing with Mickey, but we can find a way to work around that."

"The situation with Dad is definitely part of it," I said, "but it isn't the biggest part. I'm just not a show-up-at-the-office kind of guy." I looked over at Ed. I could tell that he was disappointed, but he didn't seem to be surprised. Once a freelancer, always a freelancer. I looked down at my lap again and then looked up at Ed.

"I have another idea," I said, though it was just beginning to form in my mind. Ed tilted his chin forward to show me that he was listening. "I want to do a ten-part series."

It was Ed's turn to show surprise, along with a little bit of discomfort. I imagined that he was wondering how he was going to reject a big project by his boss' brother-in-law gracefully.

"I want to do a series of articles about going out on a limb. I want to profile people similar to Grant Hayward and AnnaLee Layton who take huge chances and defy the odds in order to do something important with the things they love."

I expected to see Ed already formulating his rejection. I knew the look from the few times I had pitched things to him in the past. But I wasn't seeing it now.

"There's a chance, of course, that you couldn't find ten worthy subjects," he said.

"No there isn't," I said with a confidence I didn't realize I had until that moment that. "Ten people in the entire country who care about something enough to make it happen even when it isn't supposed to? I'll go to England if I have to. I'll go to Nairobi if I have to."

"And the overall message is 'go for it?'" Ed said.

"No. 'Go for it' is trite. The overall message is that there's a reason why the odds are so strongly against things like this happening. That every step of the way there are a million things that could go wrong and probably will. That the only thing that drives these people to overcome the odds is absolute conviction in their inspiration and an unconditional love for what they do."

Neither Ed nor Brad said anything for a moment, at which point the food came. I cursed to myself because the appearance of the waiter broke the connection and gave them the ideal opportunity to formulate a reason not to pursue this. Both of them tasted their dishes. I continued to look from one to the other, considerably less interested in my meal than I usually was.

"In a lot of ways, this is what we want the magazine to be about," Ed said.

Brad nodded and said, "Absolutely. A series like this could not-so-subtly send all kinds of messages about our agenda."

He poised his fork in the air and said to Ed, "What did you order?"

"Same thing I always order. Stupid, I know, but I have a thing for Chicken Vindaloo."

"Vindaloo, I love it. Can I try?"

Ed gestured and Brad reached his fork toward Ed's plate. I couldn't believe the way the two of them had connected. At the same time, I couldn't believe that talk about curries was getting in the way of my pitch.

"I guess it would be a little obvious if one of the subjects of your series was Ed, huh?" Brad said after his next bite.

Ed laughed. I still hadn't tasted my food. I laughed as well.

"Just a little," Ed said and then turned to me. "How much have you done on this?"

"I could lie to you and say that I've been scouting subjects for months, but the truth is, it came to my mind while we were talking."

"But you think you can pull it off."

"Yeah, I know I can pull it off. I know how to find these people. And I know how to talk to them. I kinda think I was made for this story."

Ed looked at Brad, who offered the kind of shrug that said, "Seems worth it to me."

Ed turned back to me. "I'm going to want to know who each of your subjects are before you get started."

"Yeah, of course."

Ed took a sip of water and then said, "Do you think you could have the first piece done in time for the inaugural issue?"

"Absolutely."

"Then get started."

I smiled, glanced over at Brad, who seemed genuinely happy at this turn of events, and then finally tasted my food.

"So, do you know anyone looking for a staff position?" Ed said.

~~~~~~~~

We parted about an hour and a half later. Brad and Ed were more than willing to talk about their plans for the magazine, and I found myself suddenly more than willing to listen to them talk about them. Interestingly, though I had turned down a position on the staff, I felt in many ways as though I had just joined it. This was now my magazine as well. The financial deal we made would allow me to concentrate almost exclusively on this series for the next year. I had very clearly aligned myself with a publication that wouldn't even exist in the public's mind for another nine months. I'm not sure I could think of another time in my life when something like that wouldn't have frightened me silly. For some reason, though, this just felt like the right thing to do.

When the two of them left me on the street to go back to their offices, I started toward the parking lot where I'd put my car. Now that they were out of range, I could allow my excitement to come to the surface. I didn't do anything as ridiculous as shout out loud or leap into the air, but I thought about doing those things. I really wanted to celebrate. I wanted to buy a great bottle of wine and toast the end of my days as a word-server. I got my car and didn't even notice the intensity of traffic going through the tunnel.

It wasn't until I was in New Jersey again that I began to realize that the person who I really wanted to celebrate with was Marina. It was she, after all, who had asked to read everything I'd written the entire time we were together. Even things that couldn't have possibly interested her any more than they did me. It was also she who helped me practice my pitches and offered me encouragement when they didn't go as planned. And then of course there was the part about her simply being the first person I thought about when I thought about celebrating anything.

I seriously considered calling her, if for no other reason than because I thought she would be pleased to hear about this. She knew how important this kind of work was to me and I was sure that she would be happy for me. But then I thought back on that one conversation we'd had since our split. How clear Marina had made it without saying anything of the sort that she wasn't interested in the occasional casual talk. Of course she would be happy for me and she certainly wouldn't do anything while we were on the phone to make me feel it was inappropriate to give her this news. But somewhere along the line, we'd both realize how artificial it was and we were both likely to be feeling empty. For the first time, I began to understand that while our relationship could survive (and even perhaps thrive) on the notion of an indefinite future, it couldn't even exist on the notion of no future. I had been fooling myself all along, believing that we would segue from romance to lifelong friendship.

It was sobering to think about, and it drew me out of my reverie. Of course there were other people I could call to celebrate with. Friends, fellow writers, people I knew in the industry. There was even the old guy at home. But the thought that I couldn't include Marina on the list changed the tenor of things for me.

By the time I got off the highway and started driving toward home, I had begun to recover. I drove past my favorite wine shop and decided to double back to buy something indulgent, settling on a Barolo the owner recommended. I stopped into the specialty market next door and bought chanterelles and heirloom tomatoes and then at the fish market down the road for fresh tuna. Even if it wasn't quite the same thing, Mickey and I were going to enjoy ourselves that night.

The only problem was that my father seemed to have spent the hours I was away practicing surliness. With everything that had happened during lunch, I'd forgotten the tension between us when I left that morning. Unfortunately, while I was busy staking out new territory in my career, he was probably on the phone with Aunt Theresa and maybe even Matty bitching about something that I had done to offend him, though he wasn't bothering to tell me what it was.

I called to him when I got in the house, telling him that I had great news. There was no reaction from him, so I continued into the den. He was there working on the computer, and he barely looked at me when I entered the room.

"I had that lunch today with Brad and the editor he hired, Ed Crimmins. They wanted to offer me a position on their staff."

This caused him to glance up at me. This was the point at which I remembered what it had been like around the house for the past week or so.

"I turned it down," I said, which caused him to turn back to the computer screen with a tiny smirk on his face. "But then we got to the great part. I pitched them on a ten-part feature series and they went for it."

He took his hand off of the mouse and turned toward me. "That's good."

"Very well understated, Dad."

"Is there money in it?"

I slapped my hand to my forehead. His lukewarm response was precisely what I didn't need at that moment. "Money. Damn, I knew there was something we forgot to talk about."

He turned back to the computer and started typing something.

I continued. "Of course there's money. Pretty decent money, actually. Not as good as if I were doing a multi-parter for *Vanity Fair*, but that's next year's agenda, not this year's. You might even have to make some investments for me."

"Congratulations," he said with the faintest trace of emotion.

I was beginning to feel deflated. "I knew you'd be thrilled. Listen, I know you're about to suggest that we celebrate by going to a fabulous restaurant and your treating me to champagne and four-star cooking, but I really don't want you to go through all of that trouble."

"Why isn't Marina taking you out to celebrate?"

I paused. This was definitely not the right time to tell him about my splitting with Marina.

"Same reason that she hasn't been around the other nights lately. The play and stuff."

I knew this wasn't really working anymore (and just in case I didn't know it, his scowl at my last comment made it clear), but it seemed to at least keep the lecture at bay.

"Look, Dad. I have a really nice bottle of wine, some tuna, and a bunch of other stuff. I'm really buzzed about this deal, and I'd appreciate it if you would help me mark the occasion."

"So we'll mark the occasion," he said and then clicked onto another web page.

I spent the late afternoon calling a few friends and fellow writers and beginning to scour the web for subjects for the series. The former allowed me the opportunity to share some of my excitement and receive some applause. The latter gave me the chance to begin to dig in and realize how right this project felt to me. Both brought my spirits close to where they had been when I'd walked into the house a few hours earlier. This was a good thing, because dinner was enervating. I attempted to stimulate conversation, but my father was decidedly not in the mood. I wound up drinking most of the Barolo by myself while we sat silently at the dining room table.

My father's one gesture toward me was his offering to wash the dishes. While he did so, I read a magazine in the living room. When he was finished, he looked in.

"I'm going to see what's on television," he said. "Do you want to come?"

I sighed and put down the magazine.

"Hey, you don't have to come," he said.

I looked at him. There was a sourness to his expression that said the invitation was purely ceremonial, something he did out of habit. I picked up the magazine again. "I think I'm going to stay here."

He shrugged and walked away. I once again thought about calling Marina. The last thing I expected on a day like this was to feel sorry for myself, but that was the way things were playing out. I had no one with whom to celebrate the biggest event of my professional life. I wondered if this was one of the reasons why people stuck it out in relationships even after they knew they were going nowhere. Just in case something really good happened, they would at least have someone to enjoy it with even if only for one night. Certainly in partnerships such as the marriages Darlene and Matty had (I was no longer sure about anything when it came to Denise and Brad) there was room for that much. I'm sure my sister-in-law Laura did a great job of celebrating Matty's latest promotion even if she did go to bed right after the sitcoms ended the next night.

Ultimately, I realized that the combination of unexpected melancholy and three-quarters of a bottle of wine would lead me to a conversation with Marina I'd feel squeamish about for a decade or so hence. I told myself that I would call her tomorrow, if for no other reason than I thought she would actually want to know about it. I read for a while longer and then decided to call it an early night. I passed my father in the den on the way to my room and told him I was going to bed. He just nodded his head in my direction.

About ten minutes later, I was just getting into bed when he came into my room.

"I can't decide what it is," he said. "Do you think my mind is too feeble? Do you think I'm stupid? Or do you think I don't care? Which one is it?"

"I'm gonna need just the tiniest of clues about what we're talking about."

"Do you really think I've been buying that garbage about Marina being too busy to come over?"

I got out of bed and threw on a t-shirt. I wasn't going to have this conversation with my father while wearing only boxer shorts. I was hoping the time it took to get the shirt would be enough for me to think of something to say, but that turned out not to be the case.

"I don't think you're stupid," I said.

"Which leaves one of the other two choices."

"It doesn't leave any of the choices. I just didn't know what to say to you. I knew you liked her and I knew you weren't going to take it well."

He gave me an expression I hadn't seen since I was ten. I prepared for him to ground me. "Well what the hell happened?"

"*Things* happened, Dad. Things. We got to this point where we couldn't keep going the way we had been going and it all fell apart."

"Did you break up with her or did she break up with you?"

"What difference does it make?"

"I want to know just how much you contributed to this unbelievable mistake."

I threw up my hands. "Gee, thanks for your support. And do you want to know something, Dad? *You* actually made a fairly significant contribution to 'this unbelievable mistake.'"

"What's that supposed to mean?"

"All that stuff about Gina, the great love of your life. Just further evidence that love always flames out."

He looked at me as though I had just told him the sky was orange.

"You are such a moron," he said bitterly.

"Why am I a moron? I got your little allegory, Dad. Gina was a special woman. Marina was a special woman. Their names even rhyme so there must be some cosmic significance to it all. But you keep forgetting that I know how your story ends. There's that little thing about my mother that sorta gives it away. Unless the point of all of this was to tell me that you've been living a secret life for the last fifty-something years."

He looked at me with absolute contempt in his eyes. "You have no idea how my story ended."

With this, he walked out of the room.

I should have gone after him to further explain my reason for breaking up with Marina. I should have gone after him to force him to tell me the rest of his damn story, enlighten me as to why it was taking him so long to do so, and, even more to the point, reveal his message for the ages. I should have even just gone after him to allow him to vent over losing Marina himself.

I should have done just about anything other than get back in bed to stew for a couple of hours.

Just as I should have done just about anything other than walk into the kitchen the next morning to say, "I'm going to the library, I'll see you whenever."

Chapter Twenty-Nine

I found my father on the floor near his computer when I got back to the house that afternoon. The doctor later told me that at that point he'd been unconscious for less than an hour. The doctor put him on life support, determined that he'd had a stroke, and told me he wasn't sure when or if he would come out of the coma. I called Dr. Quigley, my father's regular doctor, to tell him that he wouldn't be coming in for his appointment the next day.

I let Darlene, Denise, and Matty know. Darlene and Matty told me they would be there in a couple of days. Denise surprised me by coming to the hospital that very night. She came to the ICU where my Aunt Teresa and I sat by my father's side. She took one look at him lying in the bed unconscious and began to cry. I couldn't recall ever seeing her cry before, not even at my mother's funeral.

When she calmed a bit, she turned to me. "What are they saying?"

"They don't know what's going to happen. There was a lot of damage and there isn't a lot they can do for him. They're planning to move him to a private room tomorrow morning."

She reached out for my father's hand and put her head on his chest for a moment. Then she sat back and made a visible effort to pull herself together. She looked over at me and patted me on the leg.

"Brad told me about the magazine assignment," she said with a weak smile. "Congratulations."

"Thanks. I was out researching it, which is why I wasn't home when this happened."

Denise tilted her head to one side and said, "You aren't blaming yourself for this, are you?"

I shook my head. "No. Not for this, anyway."

"Don't. Ever. You have no idea how good you've been for him."

I'm not sure that she'd ever said anything like that to me before, and it brought tears to my eyes. I squeezed her hand and then we both turned back toward my father.

The three of us sat with him until it was nearly eleven. I told my aunt that I would drive her back to her apartment. As Denise and I split up in the lobby, she asked me what time I was planning to get there the next morning.

"I'll take care of the watch," I said to her. "Come whenever you can, but do the other stuff that you have to do. I'll let you know if anything happens."

She nodded. "It's still kind of weird to me that you've become Dad's guardian. Who would have thought, huh?"

Over the next couple of weeks, my three siblings came and went. My father was making no progress, but he wasn't getting worse, either. It was becoming clear that he could stay in this between-place for a long time and it didn't make sense for any of them to turn their lives upside down to wait. On most days, it was just Aunt Theresa and me. I brought my laptop along and would write or read through research for a while, but then would find myself drawn back to my father's bedside, needing to look at him.

Aunt Theresa and I would take turns going down to the hospital cafeteria for meals. As the vigil stretched out, it became obvious that we could have stepped out of the room together, but it was just as well. I'm not sure I'd exchanged more than a couple of thousand words with my aunt my entire adult life, including the many visits she'd made to the house after my father moved in. Even before I knew why it was, I had always had this feeling that there was something missing from her.

The only person I'd ever seen who could get her to lighten up was my mother. Though my father adored her, it was obvious that he tiptoed near her when my mother wasn't around. I had never found a topic that she and I could discuss for more than forty-five seconds. None of this seemed to bother her while we sat in the hospital room. She seemed content to meditate at my father's side, and we simply didn't say much.

Often, when my aunt would take her breaks, I'd go to sit with my father to talk to him. I'd always heard that patients in comas can hear everything said in their rooms, and I thought he might like this, though I was too self-conscious to do it in front of Theresa. I'd talk to him about a variety of things: about how bad the food was in the cafeteria, about how the stock market was doing, about things in the news or the prog-ress I was making in my research. For a long time, I avoided talking to him about Marina because after all this time and even though I knew he couldn't respond, I still didn't know what to say.

I hadn't called Marina to tell her about my father's hos-pitalization because, as much as I thought she might want to know, I didn't want it to seem like an appeal for sympathy. I certainly hadn't stopped thinking about her, though. Just as I hadn't stopped thinking about Gina. The last thing that my father said to me before his stroke was, "You have no idea how my story ended." The thought that I might never find out was nearly as upsetting as the thought that I might never talk to my father again about anything.

After avoiding the subject for a long time, I began to talk to him about Gina. I thought there might actually be some therapeutic value to this. I'd seen him transport himself while he talked about her, and I thought perhaps if I could take him back to his time with her, I could actually in some mystical way pull him out of his coma. I began to speculate out loud about ways in which they might have split up. There was a piece of me that even imagined hitting on the right answer and having my father open his eyes to say, "You're right, but you're still a moron."

I'd just finished one of these sessions during Aunt Theresa's dinner break when she came in, smiled at me, and patted me on the hand. This was the signal that it was my turn to go down to the cafeteria. As I ate the same turkey sandwich on a euphemistically-named hard roll that I'd eaten at least a dozen times over the past few weeks, it finally occurred to me that Aunt Theresa would know something about Gina. In my mind, the man in the stories was so completely different from my father that it never registered that his real sister – who had lived through this with him – was spending more than a dozen hours a day with me.

When I got back to the room my aunt was, as usual, holding my father's hand. And, as usual, she smiled at me when I entered and gestured me with her eyes over to the other chair. This time, though, I turned the chair to face her, which seemed to confuse her.

"Aunt Theresa, do you know who Gina is?"

There was a momentary look of alarm on her face before the confusion returned.

"Dad's been telling me about a woman he used to be engaged to named Gina, and I just realized that you would know something about her."

She looked over to my father, and then turned in her seat to face me. "Why would he tell you about that?"

"That's one of the things we haven't gotten to. It seemed important to him that I know about her, but he would always get so caught up in the stories that he never got very far."

"I haven't heard her name – I haven't thought about her – in probably fifty years."

"But you did know her."

"Of course I knew her. Your father and I talked about everything, and when he was with Gina, he didn't talk about very much else."

"Then you would know how they broke up. I kept waiting for him to tell me that part of the story, but he still hasn't gotten to it."

She seemed even more confused by this.

"Your father and Gina never broke up. They were together until the day she died."

Suddenly, I felt disoriented. Of course I had considered the possibility that she had died, but I dismissed it early on because of the way he "spoke" to her after so many of the stories, and the way he talked about her when he showed me her picture. There had been no question in my mind that Gina was either still walking around somewhere, or if not, had died long after she was no longer a part of my father's life.

"She died?"

"It was terrible," Theresa said. "It was only a few weeks before they were supposed to get married. God, I haven't thought about this in so long, I hope I have it right. Gina had been assigned to this commission by the mayor. It took her all over the city, including some pretty rough neighborhoods. Your father – even the deputy mayor – told Gina that she shouldn't go to these places alone, but I'm sure your father told you that she wasn't someone who liked to be told what to do. She didn't want to believe that there was anything she couldn't handle on her own. So she went to this terrible part of the Bronx and got in the middle of a fight between a husband and a wife. Your father was at Gina's parents' apartment waiting supper for her when the policeman came to the door."

My aunt turned back toward my father and patted his chest. I wanted to do the same thing, but I found I couldn't move.

"Your father was just overcome with grief. He had gone from considering himself the luckiest man alive to being completely destroyed in an instant. For a couple of years, I didn't think he was ever going to get over it. As you probably know, I had a few problems of my own back then, but even I was worried about him. Slowly, he got back to work, but he never even thought about becoming involved with another woman. He just closed himself off. At some point, though, he met your mother at a neighborhood fair. She was the friend of a friend or something like that. It took a long time, but slowly things happened between them.

"It was nothing like what there was between your father and Gina. I've never seen any couple who sparked the way Mickey and Gina did. But your mother was a very good woman. She was a saint as far as I was concerned. It wasn't long before they were in love. I think your father knew that she would take care of him and settle his heart a little."

She paused and leaned over to kiss my father on the cheek.

"I guess she never settled it completely, though," she said, turning back to me. "To think after all these years, he was telling you about this."

Once again, she patted him on the chest and then moved back in her chair. She looked over at me, as though to confirm that she had said everything she wanted to say on the subject. Then she reached for a magazine.

Chapter Thirty

I slept fitfully for a few hours that night. I couldn't settle down after hearing the news that my Aunt Theresa had given me. The love affair between my father and Gina had never ended. She hadn't left him, or tired of him, or grown bitter with him. For all I knew, their love was still on its upward trajectory. For all I knew, that trajectory would never have taken a significant turn downward.

So many thoughts jostled in my mind. Of course, there was a very good chance that my father and Gina would have faltered as their relationship continued. Certainly, there was no chance that they wouldn't encounter adversity or a complication in their dreams or a situation that put them on opposite sides of a critical issue in their relationship. That this hadn't happened in the year that they were together just suggested that they were more fortunate than most. And in fact, they might have been spoiled by that good fortune and completely unprepared to deal with difficulty.

On the other hand, maybe they hadn't encountered the obstacle that was going to prove too steep because they were so well connected and cared so deeply for each other that they managed to keep all of the obstacles scalable. Maybe they really did understand that if you cherished and honored your relationship enough, you could maintain the vibrancy and vitality.

That I was even willing to entertain this notion was a testament to how effectively my father had made his world come real to me. I felt that I knew Mickey and Gina, that I had

spent countless hours with them. That I myself had been impressed with the ways in which they touched each other.

Of course a by-product of that vividness was that I felt
the "news" of Gina's death in a deeply personal way. I took the
blow of the loss of this woman much more intensely than I
had earlier felt anger at her when I believed she had hurt my
father. My heart went out to her parents, long in the grave
themselves, and to her brother, who quite possibly still lived
somewhere in New York City and still thought back every
now and then on the sparkling sister whom he idolized.

But I felt the loss most deeply for my father. I saw two
men in my mind's eye. One was the bedazzled man in his
mid-twenties who couldn't believe his good fortune to have
fallen in love with a woman like Gina. The other was the
bowed man in his mid-eighties whose voice got smoother
and whose face grew nearly boyish when he talked about this
woman who had graced his life. I sympathized with both of
them in different ways. For the young man who had love torn
from him and could barely understand how his life could be
so utterly derailed. And for the old man who could still be
charmed by the past while being so indelibly marked by it.

I understood, finally, why my father seemed so completely transformed in Marina's presence. He knew that she was
a woman who cared deeply and wanted to have an impact,
though certainly he'd met other impressive women. He knew
that I was in love with her and that she made me lighter and
looser, though I know that he'd seen his children in love before. But he also saw the way we blended together, the way
we moved so fluidly with one another. And I'm sure he saw in
that something he hadn't seen very often. Quite possibly not
in nearly sixty years.

I now understood his reasons for telling the story. That
much was easy. It was the only way he would be able to get
the message through to me that I shouldn't be cavalier about
what I had with Marina. That no matter how cynical I had
become about love and relationships, that it would be an

overwhelming mistake to underestimate the power of this romance. Certainly a series of lectures wouldn't have done the job. The only way he could help me to see was to bring me as completely as he possibly could into his own experience, to make the young Mickey and Gina come alive for me as much as possible. I even understood now why it was so hard for him to tell the story and why he could only give it to me in little pieces. It must have been agonizing for him to relive that past when he knew what was waiting at the end.

Yet I'd managed to screw up my relationship with Marina anyway. As I lay in bed, I thought about calling her and asking if I could see her. I even turned toward the phone a couple of times before I thought better of waking her up in the middle of the night. When my phone rang at 3:37, my first thought was that we were so psychically linked that she was in fact calling me.

But the call was from the hospital. My father had died a few minutes earlier. I guess he could in fact hear us talking in his room after all.

I got dressed and went immediately to the hospital, though obviously there was no rush necessary. I wanted to see my father's body before they took it away. He seemed absolutely artificial to me lying there in the bed where he'd died. Though he had not moved in a couple of weeks, there seemed to be so much less of him now. On the drive over, I thought about what I was going to say to him, but once I was there, the idea of saying anything seemed foolish. I spent a few minutes in the room and then left to let the hospital do what they needed to do. I went down to the cafeteria to sit with a cup of coffee. I thought that my father would have liked the coffee because it was so weak and then amended the thought. No, he didn't like it that way anymore. I had at least given him that much.

The next several hours spun past quickly. I called Darlene, Matty, Denise, and Aunt Theresa. I made arrangements with a funeral home, picked out a casket, and signed several pieces of paper. It was nearly ten by the time I stopped and thought about everything that lay in front of me. It was then that I realized I still hadn't called Marina. She would be at school by this point, and I certainly didn't want to have her pulled out of class, so I left a message on her machine at home.

During the first night of the wake, dozens of people showed up, many of whom I hadn't seen in years or had never seen before in my life. Distant relatives, neighbors from the old house, members of a Senior Citizens' group my parents had belonged to while my mother was still alive. Matty and his family got in during the early afternoon, and Darlene and hers arrived just before the wake began. Though the room was dimly lit and the setting somber, it seemed bustling to me. People caught up with one another, knelt by my father's casket, stopped over to say something pleasant about the Mickey they knew and then ask after each of us.

When there wasn't someone paying their respects, the four of us, joined at various times by spouses and children, sat in the front row of chairs and talked about my father. My siblings reminisced. They talked about what a good man my father had been, and about how secure he'd made them feel. They talked about how he would now be "joining Mom" and how they would have eternity together. They talked about the legacy he left for them.

I didn't say much during any of this. Not that my silence was in itself out of character. But I couldn't help but believe that the man they were talking about was in some very meaningful way different from the man that I knew. He always had been. But at the end of his life, he had become something very different to me again. I once thought jealously that having my father move in with me would give me the opportunity to share him with my siblings in a way that I'd been denied my entire life. I childishly believed that I could have a "piece of him" that was mine and that I could wave this in front of them as something only I had. But my father had given me something so precious, so invaluable, that the notion of trivializing it by trying to show it off to the others in my family was inconceivable to me. I knew then that I would never share the story of Gina with Darlene, Matty, and Denise. It wasn't meant for them, and it wouldn't do for them what it did for me.

"He loved being with you," Matty said to me when I was barely paying attention to the conversation. I turned to him to see Darlene nodding in agreement.

"He called me several times to tell me that he couldn't believe the rest of us wanted to put him in 'a home.'" Darlene said.

"It wasn't going to be 'a home,'" Denise said.

Matty laughed and patted her on the leg.

"I definitely got that one wrong, huh?" he said to me. "About a month after he moved in with you, he stopped trying to make me feel guilty for not coming to see him more often and started trying to make me jealous over the way you were feeding him and the things you were doing with him."

I laughed, but I was feeling a little choked up. My father and I had never had that conversation. While I knew that things had come around between us, I continued to wonder whether he regretted moving in with me. And then when things got tense between us again at the end, I was certain that he would have preferred to be just about anywhere else. That he was presenting things very differently to my three siblings was a very powerful thing to learn.

I decided to go for a walk because I needed a few minutes by myself. As I got to the back of the room, Marina walked in.

I didn't startle. I didn't take a moment to appraise the situation. I didn't feel even the tiniest bit of hesitation. I simply walked into her arms. She held me wordlessly, and for a moment, I thought that I was going to break down, even though I hadn't all day. The longer we were together, though, the steadier I felt. It was as if she were feeding me, making me stronger. I knew I had missed this sensation. I even knew how much I missed this sensation. But until this very moment, I hadn't allowed myself to acknowledge just how much, because I wasn't sure that I would ever feel it again.

After a while, we pulled back, though we continued to hold hands. Marina looked into the room toward the casket.

"It's hard to believe he's gone," she said. Her eyes were misty, and I wasn't sure whether it was for him or for me.

"It hasn't completely registered with me yet. I had a feeling he wasn't going to come out of the coma, but I still kept thinking that he might."

"Are you okay?"

"Yeah, I will be. I'm gonna miss him. But at least I won't have to keep the eggs under lock and key anymore."

She smiled and I desperately wanted to kiss her. I think she might have even welcomed it, but there were things I wanted to say to her first. I took her over to an unoccupied corner of the room and we sat across from one another.

"I finally heard the end of the Gina story," I said.

"He told you?"

"Actually, I heard the very end from my aunt. The story didn't turn out at all the way I thought it was going to. It was very sad. I finally figured out what the point was to the whole thing."

Marina squeezed my hand. "And what was the point?"

"That if you're lucky enough to be gifted with a one-in-a-million love affair you treat it like the crown jewels."

She sniffled and held my hand a little tighter. "You mean you stick it in a vault and post guards all around it?"

I smiled and kissed her hand. "Not exactly where I was going with that. Look, I seem to have trouble picking up on the subtleties, even when the subtleties aren't particularly subtle, but I think I finally understand that there may be a select handful of people in the world who actually get to keep things going. Love doesn't always die. Sometimes it transcends everything."

"You're starting to sound like a bad pop song."

"And under different circumstances, I might be ashamed of that. But sometimes you have to risk sounding like a lounge singer to get your message across."

She smiled. "What would that message be?"

"That you and I have the chance to transcend everything. That the reason why what we had between us felt different was because it *was* different. But I kept thinking about it in old ways. My father was right when he called me a moron."

"You should have heard what I called you."

I reached out for her arm, just to put myself closer to her. "And you were right, too. But the point is that these relationships might be one-in-a-million, but they aren't so rare that a father and his son couldn't both have one."

She put her hand over my outstretched arm. "I know."

I reached over and kissed her then. It was the kind of kiss that asked her to forgive me (which I was guessing she already had), to understand me (which I believe no one did better than she) and to stay with me forever (which was something I was willing to reiterate every single day). When we stopped kissing, we touched our foreheads together as we had a thousand times before. Then she kissed me on the nose, and we stood up together to walk to the front of the room.

When we got to the first row of chairs, I introduced her to my family. Even Marcus reached out for her hand. Afterward, I sat down and Marina went to kneel before the casket. Her head was bowed as she talked to my father.

I couldn't hear what she was saying, but I had a pretty good idea.

About the author

Lou Aronica is the author of the *USA Today* bestseller *The Forever Year* and the national bestseller *Blue*. He also collaborated on the *New York Times* nonfiction bestsellers *The Element* and *Finding Your Element* (with Ken Robinson) and the national bestseller *The Culture Code* (with Clotaire Rapaille). Aronica is a long-term book publishing veteran. He is President and Publisher of the independent publishing house The Story Plant. You can reach him at laronica@fictionstudio.com.